THE EXPERT WITNESS

JULIA STONE

CASTLE PRIORY PRESS

First published in Great Britain in 2025 by Castle Priory Press, Brightlingsea

978-1-915970-34-3

Copyright © Julia Stone, 2025
Cover Design: Stella Barnes and Jane Langan

The moral right of the author has been asserted.

All characters and events in this publication, other than those in the public domain, are fictitious and any resemblance to real persons, living or dead, is purely coincidental.

All rights reserved. No part of this publication may be reproduced, stored in a retrieval system, or transmitted, in any form, or by any means, without the prior permission in writing of the publisher, nor be otherwise circulated in any form of binding or cover other than that in which it is published and without a similar condition including this condition being imposed on the subsequent purchaser.

CONTENTS

1988 – one afternoon in June	1
1. The Expert Witness	5
2. Undergraduate Lecture	7
3. Feedback	13
4. Leaving	17
5. Endings and Beginnings	21
The Minefield of Memory - Amanda Dunstan	27
6. Book Promotion	29
1988 – the following weeks	36
7. Editing History	37
8. Mother and Father	42
The Minefield of Memory - Amanda Dunstan	47
9. Aphantasia	49
1988 – a few months later	52
10. Suffocation	53
11. Trap	61
12. McCollins	67
The Minefield of Memory - Amanda Dunstan	74
13. Aftermath	75
14. A Friend	78
The Minefield of Memory - Amanda Dunstan	83
15. Kit	85
16. And Then There Were Three	92
17. Misremembered	96
18. Kathleen's Story	103
The Minefield of Memory - Amanda Dunstan	106
19. Photos	108
The Minefield of Memory - Amanda Dunstan	117
20. Book Shop	119
21. Memorial event	126
22. Flashbacks	132
The Minefield of Memory - Amanda Dunstan	140
23. Memorabilia	142
24. Bad News	148

25. Fragile Ego — 155
26. Insurance — 163
27. Outing — 169
    The Minefield of Memory - Amanda Dunstan — 173
28. Threat — 174
29. Meeting — 180
30. Alibi — 188
31. Disturbance — 192
32. Disclosure — 197
33. Checking — 203
    The Minefield of Memory - Amanda Dunstan — 208
34. Plan — 210
35. Accident — 215
36. Hospital — 220
37. Explanation — 229
38. Recent History — 234
    The Minefield of Memory - Amanda Dunstan — 239
39. Distant History — 241
40. Home — 249
41. Six Months Later — 255
    1988 – That afternoon in June — 259

Acknowledgments — 265
About the Author — 267

*'Innocence has a single voice that can only say over and over again,
"I didn't do it."
Guilt has a thousand voices, all of them lies'.*
Leonard F. Peltier

'Memory is a fragile thing.'
Dr Elizabeth Loftus

*'Memories are like stories.
They are the tales we tell ourselves about our life and experience,
added to and edited in each recall and retelling.'*
Dr Amanda Dunstan

1988
ONE AFTERNOON IN JUNE

It's the hiccupping bawling of the child that makes her stop outside her friend's bedsit, her hand raised ready to knock to announce her visit. Not a grizzly, whiny, woe-is-me cry that you might expect on a clammy uncomfortable day like today, but one of those desperate crying sessions that sounds as if it's been going on for some time, unanswered.

She reverses her steps to the bay window to peer through a crack in the curtains – closed to keep the sun out – hoping to see what's going on. If the baby's kicking off and her friend's in a foul mood she'll just get the bus back to her own rooms at the college. She's got an essay she could finish. Maybe stop and buy an ice cream from the corner shop on the way. Pop into the library to see if they've got that book she reserved.

The room is gloomy, the only sources of light a lava lamp and the muted black and white TV. Her friend is lying on the floor, her eyes closed, although she can't possibly be asleep with all the racket the child is making. The bottom half of her body is out of sight behind the threadbare sofa, but the arm that's in view is bent above her head, the hand resting on the carpet palm up. The finger tips are dirty, as if dipped in mud and red paint and there's more smeared on her forehead.

Blood. It's blood.

There's a horizontal slash of red below her eye and her cheekbone looks misshapen, swollen as if a wasp sting has reacted badly.

The child is next to her, his podgy belly spilling over his sagging nappy. He's plucking at the fabric of his mum's t-shirt trying to get her attention.

'There's nothing here!' A male voice she doesn't recognise. Loud, frustrated. 'There's nothing here!'

Spying from outside the room she shuffles slightly, adjusting her view through the curtains until she can see the source of the words. There's a man squatting on the floor with his back towards her. Saucepans, dried pasta, tinned baked beans, all heaped around his feet where he has pulled out the contents of the kitchen cupboards. A rice packet has spilt its contents over the lino and she is momentarily distracted by the mess, appalled by the waste, her Mother's voice in her head. A saucepan lid rolls across the floor before hitting something out of sight with a clatter and she freezes as the man stands, kicking the discarded objects to one side. He pulls out the drawers one by one: cutlery, a bottle opener, rubber bands, coins, torn scraps of paper – everything tumbling to the floor as he turns each drawer over to inspect the underside before discarding it to join the pile on the floor.

She doesn't understand what is going on, but her first instinct is to run away. While she wouldn't admit it to anyone else, she knows she's a coward; the type who crosses the street to avoid a group of teenagers just in case something kicks off; the person who looks the other way when an argument starts on the bus. The one who keeps their head down to avoid trouble. All three of the wise monkeys rolled into one.

Her friend groans. Mumbles something that sounds like 'for fuck's sake'. She's conscious at least.

The man comes into full view. About five foot ten, the sort of build that a motherly type would want to fatten up. His clothing is dishevelled, jeans torn at the knee. He runs his hand through long dark hair that needs a wash, then he squats beside the prone woman blocking the view of her. He leans forward, raising his arms in a gesture which looks threatening as she watches from outside the room and she automatically flinches.

He is speaking now, but so quietly she can't make out what he's saying above the sobs of the child. She imagines the threatening hiss of his words.

Standing, he raises his voice. 'Well?'

'I'll get it. Give me time. I'll get it.' Her friend speaks loudly, each word emphasised: a strange combination of force and fear, scared but angry.

The man paces back and forth, the few steps that he can in the small room. Clutching her ribs with one hand, her friend hauls herself to a sitting position, using her elbow to fend off the child who is attempting to climb onto her lap.

Positioned outside the window she strains to hear what the man is saying but only catches the odd phrase: '...fecking stupid', '...you owe me', '...won't trust you again.' He stops pacing and looms over her friend. 'You're in deep shit, you'd better have a plan!'

'Well, take the kid then!' Her friend is shoving the child towards the man and the wailing gets louder as the toddler clutches at his mum. 'Take the bloody kid!'

The man shakes his head, frowning, contemptuous. He picks something up from the table and stamps across the room, stopping at the door to announce, 'I'll be back. Don't go anywhere.'

Heart pounding, the watching woman steps out of sight into the alleyway alongside the building. She mustn't be found spying but she needs to be sure he's gone. Hand clasped to her mouth, as if that will stop him hearing her breathe, she watches from the shadows as he strides out of the house. She pulls back further into the dark as he glances in her direction before he turns to run down the road. She tracks his back until he turns a corner, disappearing out of sight.

She's safe.

She doesn't know what to do.

But one thing she does know: no one must find out she was there.

Chapter 1
The Expert Witness
Thirty-Five Years Later

'I do solemnly, sincerely and truly declare and affirm that the evidence I shall give shall be the truth the whole truth and nothing but the truth.'

I read the oath aloud ensuring I speak slowly and clearly, knowing that the judge and jury are already forming opinions about me. At this moment they are judging my credibility, based on nothing more than how I look, my body language and my voice. Conscious of this I stand tall, pull my shoulders back and focus on the testimony I will shortly provide in my role as an expert witness.

In my mid-fifties, I am one of those invisible middle-aged women who usually pass unseen for being perfectly ordinary: genetics keep me to average body weight; I have no outstanding features; there is deliberately nothing noteworthy in my style of dress or jewellery; my shoulder length hair is a conventional shade of brown, no highlights or ombre. This is all in my favour; there is nothing to undermine my status as the expert. Bland is good.

'Please state your name and occupation.'

'I am Doctor Amanda Dunstan. I am a senior lecturer and researcher at Chelmslake University. My specialist field is memory as it applies to witness testimony, an area I have studied for nearly thirty years.' I address the judge, then look to the jury to assess their initial reaction.

Many are nodding and some smile slightly as they catch my eye. Which brings me to the second point in my favour: my face naturally assumes a kindly appearance with no effort from me, the polar opposite of a 'resting bitch face'. People tend to like me on first sight, assuming my slightly upturned lips are a welcoming smile, conveying sincere feelings of warmth towards them and all who walk the earth. It's the reassuring expression you would want to see on a vicar, a social worker or the person at your hospital bedside. My mother used to say it made me look 'a bit dim', but outside the bounds of family it's served me well. It's only when people get to know me that they realise I'm not as warm and welcoming as I appear and this mask of kindliness hides a deeply sceptical nature.

In my view, this case should not have come to court. Too much rests on the statements of two witnesses. But my role is not to judge. I'm not here to argue for or against, merely to explain how memory works and when it can fail us.

The jurors appear to be alert and listening, heads on one side, some taking notes. But over the years I've learnt that doesn't automatically mean they will be fair and unbiased in their judgement. Jurors can place far too much weight on witness testimony; after all, what could be more compelling than someone standing in front of you in court pointing at the accused saying, 'I saw him, he did it,' and reciting what they saw and heard. However, there should be another word in that sentence: it should read 'what they *believe* they saw and heard'.

I'm looking forward to helping them understand more about memory and where things can go wrong. Translating complex research into practical day-to-day application is my superpower, after all.

Chapter Two
Undergraduate Lecture

'How can you prove where you were last night?'

I love this question. It's the hook I use to draw the students in during their first lecture with me at the start of term.

I like to be there in the lecture hall before they arrive, to watch as that year's undergraduates trickle in and find their seats, observing the ones who chat to their friends and those who chose to hide behind their phone screens, their bags or their hair. No judgements, just observation. I like to see if I can spot where the challengers might lie, identify the competitive students, the ones who wanted to look big in front of their mates or demonstrate how much they know, while often proving the opposite.

The lecture hall is quite imposing; one of the old style oak panelled rooms with tiered wooden seating, a central aisle leading down to the podium where I sit. It's not a favourite among the other academics, who kick up a fuss if they are allocated a lesson here by the departmental co-ordinators. So, by default I've ended up in Lecture Hall 103 for the majority of my teaching. Obviously, I made out I was doing everyone a favour, but I actually like it. The upright bench seating doesn't facilitate slouching and no student has to sit with their back to me, so I can see everyone and gauge attention and understanding. It reminds me of an old fashioned court room.

The last few students are filtering in. I watch silent, unmoving, waiting for longer than the few attentive ones expect. From experience I know that this generation are unlikely to fall silent without a nudge from me so, choosing my moment, I flick a switch on my console. The auditorium lights come up to full brightness, pinning the students as if under a searchlight, while I disappear into shadow. Quite theatrical I know, but my intention is to make an impact from the outset.

Loud and firm, I project my voice from the darkness. 'How can you prove where you were last night?' I pause to let the question sink in before I continue. 'A stranger has identified you as the person they saw commit a crime last night. How can you **prove** that you weren't there?'

Still unseen, I look from one face to another, assessing their reactions – the thoughtful, the curious, the gigglers, the cynical. Even at this early stage, I could put money on the ones who would do well and those likely to fail.

'Or the night before that. Could you prove where you were then?'

At this point I've got their full attention and I click the light switch once again, giving them their first opportunity to see me properly.

'Good morning. I am Doctor Amanda Dunstan, your tutor for this module on witness testimony and we will share each other's company for the coming weeks.'

A few more words of introduction from me; the college requirements for health and safety rattled through at the speed of a telesales person covering terms and conditions; handouts passed around; and the course can begin.

In that introductory lecture I want them to understand what it would be like to be wrongly accused; to begin to feel the desperation when it's your word against another's. I always use a real-world scenario, in this instance loosely based on a case I'd once handled in my role as an expert witness for the defence. I refer to the accused man as 'Jason'. He'd been mistakenly identified in an assault case and I still remember how frightened he'd been when I first met him. He'd been a similar age to most of these students, in his late teens/early twenties, but sitting in his crumpled tracksuit beside his suited lawyer, he'd seemed so much younger. His eyes were red from crying and when he wiped his nose with the back of his hand like a toddler, his vulnerability called to me even though I'm not the maternal type. I'd passed him tissues from my handbag.

'Keep the packet.' I suspected he might need them.

'Thank you,' he said and the look in his eyes conveyed the weight of hope he was placing in me.

I want my students to feel that. To know how much this matters.

'I'm going to show you a short video based on Jason's experience. It shows the events leading up to his arrest.'

I used to rely on a slide pack, but although I'd been quite happy with my PowerPoint version, I'd been encouraged to hand the project to the drama students who would create a video for me as part of their course work. The Head of Faculty informed me it was in the interests of *'interdepartmental synergies to broaden the undergraduate experience'* or some such twaddle. To be fair, they'd done a much better job than I'd anticipated and I sent them a thank you email to support their assessment for the module.

I click a button and the video opens with a group of young people in a typical crowded British pub. The camera zooms in on a particular man. Aged about twenty, he's wearing a black t-shirt with a band logo, black jeans, a dark leather jacket slung over one shoulder.

I pause the video. 'That's Jason. It's his case we're going to discuss.'

The film shows the group chatting and laughing, a collection of empty glasses and crisp packets on the table suggesting they may have been there a while. A clock on the wall reads eight o'clock and there's some banter about avoiding the pork scratchings before they all agree to go for a curry. Jason tells his friends to go on without him: he's spotted a woman he recognises from a party the week before. He wants to speak to her, so he'll catch up with them at the restaurant a bit later.

That's where things started to go wrong for Jason. Each time I watch the drama student enacting the steps Jason took that fateful evening, part of me wants to rescue him from the consequences I know are coming. As the young actor chats to the disinterested woman on the video, I recall the real-life testimony the woman had given, describing how she felt hassled by him; pressurised as he tried to interest her in buying a guitar from him after she'd mentioned she was starting to learn. Not taking 'no' for an answer, like the market trader's son he was, trying to haggle and telling her how much he needed cash.

In the video the woman tells him he'd better go; she's waiting for her boyfriend. As he leaves the pub the clock shows twenty past eight.

The video cuts to the next scene: Jason strolling through a dark alley behind some shops, which the film students have made more sinister with dirty puddles, scatterings of broken glass and overturned bins. As he emerges from the alley a police car drives past, then stops. In the back seat there's an older woman and she is pointing at Jason and saying something to the driver.

The police get out of the vehicle and confront Jason. The woman has accused him of assaulting her, knocking her to the ground and trying to steal her bag. They tell Jason that the incident happened in that alley about ten minutes ago. There have been a number of similar attacks in the last few weeks. Not only has Jason just emerged from the alley where the assault happened, but he broadly fits the description she gave the police: white male, average height, slim, wearing a dark colour t-shirt, white trainers and jeans.

I turn off the video before the drama students' credits fill the screen, wanting to keep the class focused rather than looking out for the names of their friends or debating the dubious acting skills of 'The older woman', who was actually Mary, one of the staff from our university canteen, co-opted for the part.

'So, given what we've seen, how does Jason prove it wasn't him?'

A hand goes up. 'He could get the police to speak to his friends, they'd confirm he'd been with them.'

'Okay, but they'd left him in the pub over twenty minutes before – plenty of time to commit the offence. Let's have some other thoughts.'

'How about the bar staff?' someone suggests.

'Or CCTV?'

I record the suggestions on the whiteboard, inviting discussion as to whether these might be helpful given what they'd just observed in the video. I point out that in reality the bar staff were too busy to register who was where in the bar and when they left.

'The woman he spoke to about selling his guitar. She could vouch for him.'

An observant student notices the differences between the eyewitness' description of her assailant and Jason – the height, the colour of his t-shirt and jeans, and no mention of a jacket. And I explain how I'd built on these discrepancies when I gave my expert witness testimony during 'Jason's' real-life trial, explaining that one of the failings of memory is that we subconsciously change our recollection to fit what we see in front of us, in order to help things make sense. The present version overlays the memory.

As the discussion peters out, I summarise, 'The victim in the backseat of the police car said it was definitely Jason that assaulted her. She had no doubts at all. But eyewitnesses are not always right, no matter how certain they say they are.'

'What happened to him?' a woman in the front row asks.

'Ultimately, he was cleared. But it took a year. And in the meantime he lost his job as a security guard and, because he had no income, he also lost the flat he rented with a friend. But – worst of all – he lost his confidence.'

To wrap up the session I give them the shocking statistics from The Innocence Project in the US.

'Using DNA evidence, they've cleared hundreds of people who were wrongfully convicted, but many had already spent decades in prison.' I wait for that to hit home before adding, 'Nearly seventy percent of these innocent people had been wrongly identified by an eyewitness.'

I recommend the students watch documentaries of cases where people were convicted on inaccurate witness identification. 'Watch these,' I say, handing out the list. 'Watch them and you'll understand why this module deserves your fullest attention.'

Chapter Three
Feedback

In retrospect, I should have been more on the ball; noticed the signs that I was being targeted by the senior echelons of the university. The first obvious hint that something was going on came in the guise of the email inviting me to attend my annual appraisal review with my manager, Debbie, the Faculty Head. There was something about the tone, none of the usual saccharine bonhomie – 'Hi, Hope all's well! Can I get a date in your diary so we can chat through the annual review? Thanks, Debs'. Rather, an odd formality in the wording, 'Dear Amanda', references to 'necessary paperwork', a request for me to 'self-assess against our new Values Framework', the latter document helpfully attached. She closed with 'best regards', which I somehow doubted.

Debbie is fifteen years younger than me, in her early-forties and laser-focused on her career trajectory now her children have grown up. But to my mind she has little credibility, having spent more time managing staff than actually teaching students. On top of that she's relatively new to the university and a stickler for forms, spreadsheets and 'S.M.A.R.T. goals'. Fortunately, it wasn't a two-way appraisal or I'd probably have been packing up my belongings and leaving that same day.

As I expected, Debbie follows the textbook feedback formula that all new managers are taught, sandwiching the meat of her criticism between two thin layers of white bread praise. I nod as she tells me about the innovative nature of my lectures and congratulates me on the positive feedback from my students, all the while waiting to find out the volume and exact nature of my sins.

Debbie flicks through her paperwork to ensure she has

the full information, no doubt anticipating that this will not be easy. 'You don't suffer fools gladly,' she says, smiling a fake don't-shoot-the-messenger smile.

'Do you?' I ask.

'Well, no, but –'

It goes on from there. Apparently unnamed 'others' have described me as too cynical when changes are proposed, dismissive to the point of being blunt, not a team player...

'Can you give me some examples?' I ask pleasantly.

The list is quite long. It seems Debbie has canvassed my colleagues in a '360 feedback exercise'. My sins include: not attending meetings and social events aimed at building *'cross college rapport and synergy'*; rejecting the proposed changes to my course titles when the new suggestions were deemed to *'work as sound bites and have more appeal to the target generation'*; and, not engaging with the departmental social media accounts. The latter comment could only have come from Marketing and their card is now marked.

I show no outward reaction, keeping my gaze and voice steady as I say, 'Shall we focus on the facts. Have there been any complaints from the students?'

'No, indeed. On the contrary they all say –'

I interrupt to continue with my summing up, 'My courses are full and I am on budget, yes?'

She's like the proverbial deer in headlights, although given the twitchiness maybe more rabbit-like. 'I...I don't have the figures, but no one's commented otherwise.'

'Hmm. So, the only negative comments come from *colleagues.*'

'Well, I wouldn't say negative as such. Really, it's constructive criticism.'

The comeuppance of all this is the allocation of a management coach who is to work with me on 'addressing development needs and building on strengths'. Debbie passes me a shiny business card: *Shona Kayode, Management Psychologist and Business Coach.*

'Give her a call. It's a great opportunity. An investment in you and your development,' Debbie says.

'Are my senior colleagues also having this *opportunity*?' While the smile remains on my face, I can't keep the sarcasm from my voice.

'Not as yet.' Debbie averts her eyes, focusing on shuffling her paperwork. 'We don't have the budgets for everyone. Just a few chosen people.' She's at least had the decency to look embarrassed.

When I get home and tell my husband, Phillip is incensed on my behalf.

'What is wrong with these people?' He places the opened packet of chocolate digestives within reach before handing me a mug of tea; he's a man who recognises when a sugar hit is required.

'Apparently it's me not them. I don't live up to their new 'Values Framework'.'

He snorts a laugh. Not a corporate man, he has never had to work under the weight of modern management jargon. 'Translate that into layman's English for me.'

'They had some management consultant in to define a 'success culture for the university of the coming decade.' I make bunny ear speech marks to highlight my sarcasm. 'They even have a handy mnemonic for what they came up with – '1 TEAM'!'

'Please don't!' He covers his mouth with his hand, swallowing hard which causes a bout of coughing, his eyes watering. 'You nearly made me spit my tea out.'

'The 1 stands for £1 million. That's the planned increase in our target budget – don't ask me the time scale, could be five years, could be ten, they haven't specified and I'm not sure they know.' I hold up my hand to count off the letters on my fingers. 'The T stands for … hmm, let me think…teamwork! E for efficiency. A for advancement. M for –'

'Merde,' Phillip interjects. 'Complete and utter bullshit. And I hope you told them so.'

'That might be part of the problem…'

He leans forward to chink his mug of tea against mine. 'That's my girl.'

Chapter Four
Leaving

I avoid Shona Kayode's calls and emails for as long as I can, then cancel the first couple of coaching meetings at short notice, claiming student issues have arisen. Obviously, I check Shona's website, find her CV on LinkedIn, read her references and coaching blog. And I have to admit that Shona seems a very professional and capable young woman. Maybe that's what scares me? Another younger woman on her way up. Another illustration that I'm doing nothing but treading water.

Eventually I agree to meet her and find that Shona is as impressive face-to-face as she is online. I like her openness, her lack of bullshit. The first coaching session is booked for two hours and I'd anticipated making excuses and leaving after the first hour, but the time flies by. At the end of the meeting Shona asks me to complete a personality questionnaire before we next meet. She spots my cynical smile.

'Now you're playing to type,' she says, smiling. 'I'm inviting you to hold your judgement until you get the results. I think you'll find it interesting and I'd like to know your views. And – before you ask – this isn't some Cosmo quiz. It's been designed and validated by professional psychologists like yourself – I'll send you the research.'

The questionnaire itself was a pain to complete – lots of repetitive questions with forced options, my own preference not always amongst them. My literal brain struggled with *'I will often help strangers if I see they need assistance'*, questioning how frequently this happens, who are these strangers and why did they need help. And I was unhappy rating myself against the statement *'I prefer to play a lead role in a team',* when in reality I prefer to be left to work on my own.

To my surprise Shona's summary report describes me well. My analytical mind questions whether it's like a visit to a medium, where one can only recall the elements that fit what we want to hear. But having gone through the document marking up the parts that I recognised in myself, the yellow highlighter tells me it's surprisingly accurate. It could have been written by Phillip, someone who's known me for years, who understands my idiosyncrasies and appreciates how to get the best from me.

'What did you think?' Shona asks.

'The test, a nightmare. The report, spot on.' I pause, uncertain how much to share with her. 'This meeting is confidential?'

'Completely. Unless you tell me you're about to do harm to yourself or others.'

I catch myself before I make a tasteless joke about my feelings towards the management team. 'To be honest, your report made me think.'

'Hmm?'

'Seeing it written down like that helped me understand why I don't fit in here... Why it's started to feel like I'm in the right job but the wrong place.'

'In what way?'

'The most important thing for me has always been the students and our educational standards. The quality of our teaching should come first, but as a university we've become far more focused on profit. The fees have stayed the same, but we've shortened the modules – eight weeks instead of ten. Like the supermarkets charging the same price for a packet of biscuits even though there's now less in the packet. It doesn't sit well with me... it feels unethical somehow. The college has changed over the years... and I guess I haven't.'

We spend the next hour discussing the implications of the personality report. At the end of the coaching session Shona says, 'We have four more sessions in the budget. What do you want to achieve in that time? How can I best help you?'

It's a relief Shona isn't asking me to change; no need to fake interest in *development needs*. I take a deep breath, realising the gravity of the decision I've made as we've been talking. 'I want you to help me think about how I leave the college... help me work out what I can do next.'

It seems ironic that the deciding factor that illustrates the end of my thirty-year university career comes down to four letters: INTJ – the code for my profile on the personality questionnaire apparently. I look it up online and find further descriptions and mentally tick every one. A jigsaw piece that doesn't fit the picture on the box, I realise I no longer fit. My academic work, my success with the students, this is no longer enough to earn the respect of senior colleagues. To maintain my professional pride in all I've ever worked for, all I've achieved so far, I must acknowledge it is time to go.

I hand in my resignation after that meeting with Shona. My manager, Debbie, doesn't look surprised and there isn't even a mumbling of dissent.

As I work out my notice period, I feel surprisingly light. I skip departmental meetings without needing to provide an excuse, I delete the Chancellor's weekly update emails unread, I ignore the 'pulse taking satisfaction survey'. Finally, I can just focus on my teaching and the students.

Before I leave they pass round the envelope for staff donations towards a leaving gift for me and rally enough cash to buy me a present of sorts: a fancy branded pen – showing both lack of creativity and lack of effort. It is presented to me in front of a small gathering of my colleagues in a corner of the main office, the potted plants pushed to one side to make space for me to stand. Someone uses the photocopier during my (ex) manager's (thankfully) short speech.

Back at home that evening I show Phillip the pen.

'At least it isn't one of the university ones,' I say as he tests it by scribbling on the back of last week's Sunday magazine. 'Who writes anything by hand these days?'

'If you practice with this I might actually be able to read the hieroglyphics you've written on the shopping list next time I go to Waitrose,' he says. He opens the kitchen drawer where we keep odds and ends: the half used biros, elastic bands, scraps of paper, those little white wire things for doing up bags, a few wooden pegs, some random plastic lids (the containers they belong to lost, like socks in the laundry). He smiles and raises his eyebrows in an unspoken question and when I nod, he unceremoniously drops the fancy pen in with the other odds and ends.

I was more cheered by the card from that year's cohort of students. One of them had clearly looked up synonyms for memory and made sure they'd used every one in their various 'good luck' messages. I'll miss that side of the work. The students were the only thing that made it all worthwhile.

Chapter Five
Endings and Beginnings

Looking back several years later, the timing of my retirement from the university was fortuitous, as soon after, Phillip's hacking cough got worse. After rounds of tests the diagnosis was final. Our time together to be cut short, a message that we had to relish every moment. Not used to deep emotions, I found I was hijacked by feelings of vulnerability, the pain of watching him fade and there being nothing I could do to save him.

I was forty when I originally met Phillip, a couple of failed relationships under my belt. Phillip had been married before, but had been a widower for nearly ten years by then. His first wife, Andrea, sounded like a lovely woman, combining childrearing with her work at a charity and building a warm home life. They'd had a solid marriage for twenty-five years and raised two boys, Andrew and Danny, now strapping men, and solid proof of their excellent parenting and genes. Sadly for Phillip, Andrea died of cancer in her forties. He rarely spoke to me about her unless I asked a specific question, but it was clear she would always be dear to him and I understood why. From all he'd said about her, I think I would have liked her.

To be honest, I don't think I'd ever imagined being married. It was never high on my agenda.

After a first obsessional girly crush that ended abruptly in my early twenties, I became convinced I'd lost my soulmate and would always mourn The One That Got Away. In that self-obsessed dramatic way of young women through the ages, I even tried to write emotional poems about her, but lacking the vocabulary of love and without a shred of creative talent, the end results were closer to limericks than a Shakespearean sonnet. *Her hair was blonde and if I had a wand, I'd magic her back because her presence I lack,* that kind of thing.

When Phillip and I met it wasn't love at first sight for either of us, more a growing awareness that we were having intelligent conversations as well as having fun together. He was someone I imagined I could share breakfast with every day without hating the way he chewed his cereal, the order he put the milk in the tea (always second) or quibbling about the way he stacked the dirty dishes. Basically, he *got* me. One of the few people who would laugh at my sarcasm and not start an argument about whether it was right or wrong for me to judge so cynically.

It was a bit like those matchmaking adverts you see on TV these days, where older couples unite over unlikely joint hobbies like dough making or roller skating. Initially we bonded over a rarely shared (and, as we used to joke, understandably secret) interest in railway memorabilia and model trains. It had been a quiet, practical hobby of mine growing up. An excuse to take myself away from the family and immerse myself in building my own world of train tracks, mountains and tunnels. An environment where I understood – and controlled – how things worked. Phillip on the other hand had loved the old signage, the posters and advertising and helped me to appreciate the beauty of Gill Sans lettering. Our first proper date had been afternoon tea in a converted railway carriage at a museum café.

In that period after his diagnosis I focused on doing everything to make him happy, wringing the joy from every second of the time we had left together. To cheer us both up I engineered some trips down memory lane, revisiting various railway museums, train stations and collections that we'd frequented in the past. Instead of driving we'd make an adventure of it: our journey to the London Transport

Museum taking three hours instead of one when we took the hopper, a two carriage branch line which connected to the mainline train route, then several tube trains, which eventually delivered us to within ten minutes' walk of the museum. For others, probably a tedious journey, but for us a pleasant day out.

Another day we went to an exhibition of vintage railway posters, Phillip investing in one depicting the coastline of Southend-on-Sea in the 1950s, a reproduction of a painting that made the beach front and surroundings look amazingly cosmopolitan. We were almost tempted to take a detour along the Thames estuary to visit the place, until Phillip called up Google maps to compare the *now* with the *then* and we realised maybe we'd missed that moment by a few decades.

At each destination we visited, we relived earlier trips. Phillip was one of those people with surprising recall of trivial experiences. 'It was raining last time we came here and you slipped on the steps. Be careful.' 'The Ploughman's was great last time, huge portions. Do you remember you asked for a doggy bag for the cheese you couldn't eat?' (I could recall neither, but both would have been in character.)

In contrast I might say tentatively, 'The Olive Branch? Have they changed the name of the café since we last came here? Wasn't it called something like The Lilac Tree?'

And Phillip would give me a hug, tucking me under his arm to kiss the top of my head. He'd point to the two well-established olive trees, one either side of the entrance, chuckling. 'They don't look like lilacs to me.'

Since he's been gone, a glimpse of 'Secrets of the Underground' while flicking through TV channels can leave me feeling tearful. Not a typical reaction, even in those who find the presenters patronising or loathe the programme.

Phillip would have loved it.

We'd been married almost fifteen years when he died. When we first met, we'd both overlooked the significant age gap between us, two introverts looking for someone to share hobbies and a home, rather than a partner for cruises and clubbing. But even so, I'd never imagined being a widow in middle-age. Phillip's son, Andrew, now lives in Scotland and the youngest, Danny, is on some contract that means he's working in the States. They send me a card at Christmas, keeping me up to date with their news and Andrew was very supportive when Phillip died, helping me with practicalities and speaking at the funeral.

After sorting all the administration around Phillip's death, I was lost for a few months.

But I asked myself, what would Phillip think of me sitting around the house doing nothing?

Alongside my occasional expert witness work, I ended up taking on a temporary role at a sixth form college covering someone on maternity leave. It was something to do, to fill my time more than anything else: there's only so many sudokus and crosswords one can complete in a day without going a little crazy.

Then came Covid. During the lockdown period all the college lectures were conducted online and, overnight, we tutors were expected to add Teams and Zoom to our kitbag of expertise.

Unlike Phillip, I'm no luddite. Technology holds no fears for me. In our house, it had always been my role to work on anything deemed 'tech': dealing with the alarm system when it showed an error code; completing Phillip's tax return online; writing out step by step instructions for the Smart TV and ensuring the channels were updated when needed. So I'd embraced Zoom – initially. It wasn't the fault of the application, but the sixth formers at the college made it hard. Too many students had technical problems or elected to have their cameras off. It was like talking to myself; sitting at home in my office staring at my slide material, anyone who did bother to show up, unseen and on mute. It seemed to underline how alone I was in this huge house, with Phillip gone.

My heart wasn't in it and it showed, my creativity and passion sapped. When the job holder returned from maternity leave, the sixth form college didn't extend my contract or offer me another role.

I wasn't the same since losing Phillip. I just wasn't the same woman. The full-stop signalled by the menopause, the yoyo of the intermittent lockdowns, the vast flat plains of time to fill since retirement from my academic career and the loss of identity that entailed. Each had knocked me flat, like waves destroying the sandcastle as they crash one after another on the beach.

While I still loved my occasional work as an expert witness, I only took on cases that sounded cut and dried, where I could definitely make a difference. The reason I'd got into this in the first place: righting wrongs. As I'd ticked on the personality questionnaire,*'I will often help strangers if I see they need assistance'*. It felt good to use my expertise in a constructive way, helping people who needed my professional knowledge. But there weren't that many court cases and I still had too many hours in the day to fill.

To my surprise, it was Phillip's old friend Don who suggested I use my professional expertise in another way. 'Write a book,' he said, 'You're an expert on memory. Make it accessible, readily understandable to the layman. Just like you do for the students.'

This was just what I needed. A way to prove my expertise was valued, to make my old colleagues at the university recognise they were wrong to let me go without a fight. To force them to acknowledge that they'd placed too much weight on my unwillingness to kowtow to internal politics and petty rules. To recognise that I'd deserved those promotions I never got, always passed over for someone less qualified, less experienced, but ultimately more amenable.

So I set out to write my book.

Excerpt from chapter titled 'How Common Is Common Sense When Assessing Eyewitness Testimony?'

Reproduced from The Minefield of Memory by Amanda Dunstan

Sadly, people's beliefs about memory are often at odds with reality and the decades of research evidence. Many think that our memories are like a video recording; falsely believing that we take in information and store it exactly as it happened and later, when we recall it, the memory plays back exactly the same each time.

In fact, memory is open to corruption at every stage of the process. For example:

- *We may misinterpret what we experience (like mishearing a song lyric) or not observe the full event, even though we were physically present (like when we start daydreaming during a conversation or film).*

- *After speaking with others we may change our own opinion and adopt another's version of events, assuming their recall to be better than ours.*

- *We can also overlay one memory with another, melding the two to create one new memory that never actually happened.*

To avoid these problems in a court of law, a judge can read out a statement to help the jurors understand the way memory works and the impact this may have on witness evidence. In the UK this is known as a Turnbull Statement and explains the myths held about memory and the factors that can impact the way we form memories. However, this is only compulsory if the case rests substantially on witnesses' evidence and often judges will give their own warnings, even when they have had no training in the science of memory.

Another alternative is to call on an expert witness. This would be a scientist who has researched and studied memory who can give their advice to the court. But sadly this doesn't always happen. The most frequent reason given for not calling on the input of an expert witness is that memory is 'common sense'.

As I hope this book, 'The Minefield of Memory', will show you, it is far more complicated than that.

Chapter Six
Book Promotion

I have to admit, I'm pleased with the finished book. And I'm not the only one. My agent seems thrilled with its reception, the publisher keen to get me out on the road with talks and promotions. And we all love the cover – an elephant walking away into fog – and the title, *The Minefield of Memory*, both proposed by my editor.

The book launches to potential readers with pre-publication reviews in the press. The Times deems it 'accessible without being patronising'. The Guardian runs a half page article weaving a recent miscarriage of justice with some of my case studies, with the header 'Eyewitness testimony – a flaw in the justice system'. And the Mail target their readership with, 'New book reveals why your memory of events isn't always right!'

My agent encourages me to build on this momentum. 'Get out there. Let people hear you talk about it – show your passion. And contact The Crime Writers Association and see if you can get a speaking slot at their next conference. They'll love you!'

It feels good to have people on my side since Phillip is no longer around. Strange, but good.

Taking advantage of early reviews, I seek out other promotion opportunities. While very used to speaking in public, my first radio interview causes a relapse in my IBS and my stomach feels very uneasy. Memories of those sixth form students on Zoom perhaps? An invisible radio audience, their reactions unseen.

When I get to the studio, I'm still ill at ease and my brain starts focusing on all that is wrong. For a start, the chair they've given me in the studio is too high, my feet hanging uncomfortably off the floor like a schoolchild, but I don't say anything or try to adjust it. As a guest at the radio station, I don't want to get off to a bad start by appearing like a prima donna, but there are many improvements they could make to their hosting of visitors. For one, directions to the car park that don't include a ten-minute detour round the one-way system.

The intern has given me white coffee when I asked for black, but whereas the old me would have (politely) pointed this out, I drink it without comment. I straighten my jacket and hook the heel of my shoe on the foot bar to stabilise me, my today-polished shoes catching the light from the console with a tiny flash of green. I'm a guest of Rebecca, 'Call me Bex', Wilson, the host of this local radio chat show.

Rebecca glances at me out of the corner of her eye. 'Okay?' she asks, her voice so syrupy with reassurance that I almost expect her to lean over and pat my leg or promise me a sticker for being a good girl. 'We'll be starting soon.'

I study her as she clicks some switches on the panel in front of her, adjusts the huge black microphone, shuffles papers around. She is younger than I expected and sports a nose piercing, a sleeve of tattoos and unnaturally bright red hair. But having worked with students for so many years I've learnt not to judge on appearances. She clearly knows her stuff. A copy of my book lays on the desk in front of her, various pages tabbed in readiness for the interview, and I'm impressed by her preparation.

'Ready?' Rebecca asks, gathering her long dark hair in her hand and pulling it into a scrunchy. 'Good morning, listeners. This is your host, Bex Wilson, and I am thrilled to welcome the criminal psychologist, Dr Amanda Dunstan, to the studio. She's here to talk with us about her new book, *The Minefield of Memory*.'

I lean forward towards the mic, even though I've been told to sit back and relax.

'Thank you. It's a pleasure to be here.' My voice sounds loud, but it was probably my imagination. Rebecca clearly knows what she's doing.

'Let me start with a brief introduction for our listeners.' Rebecca consults her notes.

'Dr Dunstan is an expert on memory in the context of criminal cases. Over her thirty years as a university lecturer, many students have benefited from that depth of knowledge. She's also played a role as an expert witness in a number of court cases. But today she is sharing that knowledge with us.' She raises her head to look at me, the cue that a question is coming.

'Amanda, *The Minefield of Memory* is your first book. What prompted you to write this book now?'

I've seen the questions in advance, had time to prepare a sanitised answer that doesn't include the death of my husband, frustration with Zoom meetings and being passed over for promotion too many times.

'It seemed a good time to refocus my career. I've been collating the research findings for years and wanted to put all that data to good use; to present it in a more interesting way that everyone could understand. And correct a few misconceptions too.'

'Misconceptions?'

'Far from what many people think, memory is *not* like a video recording of life. We don't remember every experience we've had. In fact, far from it. Our brains would be far too cluttered if we did.'

'Having read your book I can now appreciate that! You open with an interesting statement: *Memories are like stories. They are the tales we tell ourselves about our life and experience, added to and edited in each recall and retelling.* Can you say more about that?'

'We think our memories are what actually happened. But memory doesn't work like that. Our memories can be very close to the original experience, or they can be completely fabricated, unknowingly borrowed from somewhere or someone else. Each time we recall something, we subtly change the story without realising, editing it so it fits in with how we see ourselves and makes sense in the context of the rest of our lives.'

'That is *amazing*.' Rebecca speaks with the exact intonation of the barista that took the order for my morning coffee; one of those young people whose stock responses are 'no problem' or 'for sure' when informed the customer would like an Americano.

Rebecca continues, 'In your book you say it's common to experience memories that we later find out could *not possibly* be true. When I read that I had to laugh, because that happened to me! I have a vivid childhood memory of my dad driving me to hospital when I broke my arm. But my mum recently told me he was away from home, working on an oil rig at the time. It was the man next door who took us to A&E. Can you explain why this false memory happens?'

'To put it simply, our brains like things to make sense. So if there is a gap in our memory – without consciously thinking about it – we frequently fill in with information that seems likely, for example, combining events that happened at different times. Maybe your dad was the one who usually drove you places, or you saw him as the one who came to the rescue when you needed help.'

'Gosh, yes. Mum wasn't a confident driver.'

'As you can see from the cases in my book, *without realising* we can also completely fabricate a memory. For example, falsely remembering something we've read about or seen on TV as if it happened in our life. Or believing an experience that happened to a friend or family member happened to us. Experimental researchers have convinced people that they were lost in a shopping centre as a child, or had been arrested. And these people will describe the imagined events in fine detail as if they really happened – where they were, the colour of their clothes, how frightened they felt.'

'Fascinating.' Rebecca holds up her hand, palm towards me signalling a pause. 'For those listeners who have just joined us, today I'm talking with our expert on memory, Dr Amanda Dunstan. Our phone lines are open. Call us if you have a question for Dr Dunstan or would like to share your own experiences.' She moves to the next phase of the interview as we wait for callers. 'Your particular interest is unreliable memories in the context of criminal trials. You give a neat example of how easy it is to corrupt memory in your chapter *Leading the Witness*. Could you read that for the listeners?'

I open my copy of the book, the spine cracked at the page. Key parts of the text are marked in yellow highlighter, to remind me where to lay emphasis as I speak. I start to read the familiar words.

When I finish the excerpt, I shut the book and look up at Rebecca.

'That's chilling,' she says. 'You make it easy to see how wrongful convictions could occur if there is only eyewitness evidence.'

'Even more so when you think how difficult it can be to prove your alibi if you were at home alone.' My mind flits back to those initial lectures I used to give my new students.

Rebecca does a three second countdown on her fingers as she says, 'We're now going to hear from John calling from the town centre.'

John's anecdote is about his memory of working in a pub when he heard a radio announcement that Elvis was dead. 'I remember how shocked I was. I can smell the stale beer and see myself mopping the counter down, the radio on in the background. They played his records all day and it was all people talked about that lunch time... But I did a pub quiz recently, turns out he died in 1977. I was twelve at the time...'

Rebecca is encouraging as she draws out similar stories from Teesha (recalling being taken to London by parents to lay flowers after Princess Diana's death; the whole family were actually abroad that summer); and AJ (a memory of attending a protest march at university, when her friends say no such march took place). Rebecca's reassuringly good at her job and goes up in my estimation. She calls upon me for parallel examples from research studies and I explain my survey work on misremembered events.

'Maybe the listeners would like to pose the question on social media,' I say. 'Ask your friends if they've experienced anything similar. It might show you how common it is to have this sort of mistaken memory of historic events.'

Rebecca mouths 'great idea' and gives her habitual thumbs up again.

'And our next caller also has a question.'

There's some clattering and buzzing, slight feedback on the line as if there's a radio on in the background.

Rebecca moves a button on the console. 'Kay from Stanton, you're on air. Can we have your question for Dr Amanda Dunston?'

The caller's voice sounds distorted and it's hard to make out what she's saying – something about 'editing history'. Rebecca shakes her head frowning, leaving me to build on what I've managed to make out.

'You're so right, Kay. Without us realising, our memories are all edited versions of history. Do you have a personal example to share, or a question for me?'

There's a couple of seconds of silence, then the murmur of a whisper which is hard to catch, then a bang and a click as the call cuts off. Rebecca shrugs. 'Sorry, we seem to have lost Kay. Do call us back! Meanwhile, let's move to Hassan from Dunstable.' Hassan launches into his anecdote about a family wedding which he swore his great aunt attended 'but she's not in any of the photos…'

But I'm only half listening, my brain still going over what I heard the caller say. It was hard to make out, but I'm pretty sure the whisper that followed the comment on 'editing history', was three little words: *'But I know.'*

1988
THE FOLLOWING WEEKS

Guilt – 'a feeling of worry or unhappiness because you have done something wrong, particularly to another person, or against your moral principles.'

Over the following weeks she is two people.

On the surface she carries on as normal. Takes her lunch to the same table in the canteen to sit with her 'friends', even though there's now an empty seat. Nodding along to small talk, laughing when others laugh as they discuss plans for the summer holidays. (She is going home, of course, her mother having found her a job in a bookshop to keep her busy for the two months.) They discuss the coming academic year, ideas for dissertation projects, where they will live now they have to cede their campus rooms to first and second year students. No one asks her where she will be living, which is lucky as she no longer knows.

She is two people.

On the inside she is Lady Macbeth repeatedly trying to scrub away her guilt. Going over and over the events of that evening. Validating her decisions as the only ones possible. Convincing herself she did the right thing.

She doesn't realise at the time, but – just as we all do – she is subtly changing the memory with each silent retelling.

It's the only way she can live with herself.

Chapter Seven
Editing History

I'm not by nature a worrier, but on the drive home from the radio interview my brain inserts a sinister tone into my recall of that ambiguous whisper, and I find it keeps bobbing to the forefront of my mind. *'But I know.'* What did the woman know?

My recent history is too dull to warrant dramatic calls to radio stations, so I sincerely doubt it is anything directly to do with me. Although... as I wait for the traffic lights to change tapping my fingers on the steering wheel, there is a flicker of something in my mind. A feeling of something I once should have done, or not done, or handled differently. Like a brief movement in peripheral vision which is gone when you turn to look at it. Whatever it was about, it's accompanied by a vague feeling of unease, but nothing specific comes to mind. That sometimes happens when I try to recall someone's name; I find it's best not to dwell on it but trust that it will pop into my mind later if it's important.

As I put the car into gear I ponder other interpretations. *'Editing history'... 'but I know'.* It's likely the comment was linked to the topic we'd just been discussing in the interview. Maybe a criminal case where the caller had some evidence she could offer? I do a quick mental run through of court cases I've been involved in.

I'm intrigued. Her comment implies she knows 'the truth' about something, but what exactly might that be? Was the caller a conspiracy theorist, believing she's uncovered some government secret? Was it a message aimed at someone else who might be listening to the show, maybe an ex-partner who'd had an affair and denied it?

I'll have to be content with not knowing. But my thoughts

bring me in a circle to a question I've always found intriguing. When looking back over your own life, how can you ever know for sure that things happened the way you remember?

The earliest incident I recall from my own childhood was of Felix-Felix. At six years old, I'd politely written a begging letter to Father Christmas citing the many ways I'd been a good girl and all the reasons this track record deserved a kitten. I'd already chosen its name – Felix – which Father had told me meant lucky. But Christmas morning hadn't been so lucky as Father Christmas had seen fit to reward all my efforts with a doll. A chubby cheeked plastic baby with pouty demanding lips. In my disappointment I'd turned the present sack inside out, throwing other gifts to one side searching for the missing kitten, the offensive doll discarded. There had been a good few minutes of inconsolable tears before I was instructed to pull myself together because Santa was watching and taking notes.

I had no mental images of this emotional scene to draw on, no recall of the room, the specifics of the decorations, my parents' responses. I only knew this version because it had been rolled out as a family story for many years – one of the 'remember when Amanda …' series – my extreme reaction turned into a joke for everyone to share.

My mother had named the doll Felix-Felix, 'because a doll is twice as good as a cat', and life went on. I took to carrying Felix-Felix everywhere, tucked under my arm in order to keep my hands free to play with other more interesting things. This wasn't out of love for Felix-Felix but to stop my older brother, Dereck, getting hold of her and using it as a means to bully me. He'd already coloured in the tip of her nose and drawn whiskers on her rosy cheeks with biro, claiming he thought I would like it because it made her more catlike. And he had once thrown Felix-Felix through the kitchen window 'to see if she had nine lives'.

The unlucky doll met an untimely end the following Christmas when I was seven, when it was burnt into a lump of twisted plastic on the open coal fire in the lounge. But there were differing explanations as to how it happened. As a witness to the event, I *knew* it was Dereck's doing. Felix-Felix was already down to three lives at that point due to his destructive behaviour and he'd deliberately held her over the open fire until her nylon hair caught fire, dropping her before he burnt his fingers.

But Dereck's story differed substantially: he claimed I'd told him that I was going to hang my Christmas stocking over the fireplace, against explicit instructions from Mother. He claims he told me not to; he knew it was dangerous; he claimed he'd even offered to help me later on when he'd finished tidying his room. Of course, Mother had believed him as she always did. The story that went down in family history was that Felix-Felix had fallen from her clamped position in my armpit as I raised my arm to wedge my Christmas stocking under the candlestick on the mantlepiece.

Even now I still wonder which version was really true. Did Dereck set fire to the doll as I believe? Or did I drop her by mistake, the whole thing an accident? Or had I edited my memory of events in order to blame my brother, when really it was me that threw the doll I'd never liked on the fire to be rid of her? There was no way to know.

Back in the present I check my watch – thirty minutes until I reach home – pulling on to the local roads, glad to now be on the final strait. Driving on automatic pilot my mind wanders again, back to my days teaching at the university and how much I used to enjoy designing ways to demonstrate psychological theories to the students. One lecture that always sparked debate was designed to prove how much our recollections can be edited by others' inputs.

'Any classic film buffs in the lecture hall today?' I used to ask.

I'd usually get a chorus of no's and a few groans for answer, but occasionally one of the older students would raise a hand as if discretely bidding at an auction.

'So, I doubt any of you will have come across the film Rashomon? How about Reservoir Dogs? The Usual Suspects? Kill Bill? Vantage Point?'

A few of the students would nod in acknowledgement. Others jotting down the titles. All at loss as to where this was going.

'Before we go any further…'

On cue, there would be the sound of a door banging at the back of the room. A student in a hoodie would rush down the central aisle of the lecture hall towards the front where I was standing. I'd leap back out of their path as the stranger grabbed my bag from the chair beside the desk, before they disappeared through the exit door at the front of the hall. The whole incident took seconds, ensuring that even the most social media savvy student didn't have time to hit record on their phone.

The class would react with shock, voices raised in a babble of confusion about what had just happened.

'Everyone calm down.' I would shout to silence their reactions. 'Without conferring or looking at your phones, record your estimate of the time the incident happened. Then write a short statement about what you just witnessed with as much detail as you can recall.'

Afterwards I would ask for their versions of events. Of course, at this point there was a mess of differing perceptions. Some thought the thief had been a woman, led by the height and slight build of the perpetrator. Many said that she/he came from the side entrance from where the loud bang of a door had been heard, but those at the back said the perpetrator had been seated in the room all along. Some reported that she/he was holding a weapon in their left hand, a knife maybe, those nearer the front with a better view said it was a rolled up magazine. A student who had sat nearby was sure it was a man and confirmed that he'd been taking notes with his right hand. Variously he stole my handbag/rucksack/mobile phone, depending on where the student sat, what they had observed in previous lectures and the perpetrator's sleight of hand.

Once they'd quietened down again, I explained the phenomena known as The Rashomon Effect, named after a 1950's Japanese film where four witnesses give completely different accounts of a murder.

'It's seen in a lot of popular films and reflects the way in which we all interpret events though our own filters,' I would explain.

But the learning didn't end there. After collecting in their initial written descriptions of the event, I would put the students into groups to share their views and discuss what they had seen.

A week later in their next lecture, I would ask them to write an account of the event once again. By now, the stories had merged. Without even realising, the students had adopted parts of each other's stories, adding in details they hadn't seen and couldn't possibly have known. 'This is what happens when witnesses talk to each other. The technical term for it is social contagion of memory. The stories start to align as people unconsciously adopt parts of others' versions of events.'

Case proven.

Chapter Eight
Mother and Father

I ring the doorbell of my parents' house with a familiar sinking feeling, my stomach already contracting at the imagined smells and textures of overcooked lamb, undercooked roast potatoes and soggy greens. Worse than school dinners had ever been. It is the last Sunday of the month which means I'm at 'Mummy and Daddy's' for the traditional lunch. I've tried to rebel over the years – about both the lunch and the 'mummy and daddy' bit – but while my husband, Phillip, had been allowed to refer to them as Beth and Ernest, I always got the deep breath and the silence whenever I'd tried. They are now in their eighties and can still do that magic thing all their generation mastered when parenting: one look and I'm straight back to childhood compliance.

But they don't know what I call them in secret.

Mother's voice is muffled through the front door, no longer as loud as it had once been. Back in the day she'd have been heard above a passing train. My father is no doubt in the conservatory, buried under the Sunday papers. I should have brushed up on the news in the right-wing press, as he will no doubt want to debate the latest ethical, moral or economic failures of government over lunch.

There's a scraping sound as my mother manoeuvres, her wheelchair bumping off the wall where they'd 'had a man in' to attach plastic sheeting over the anaglypta wallpaper to protect it from her five-point turns. Beth is as bad in the wheelchair as she was driving. The door opens and she critically appraises my appearance, scanning me from head to toe before offering her best hostess smile, so I assume I've passed. For my part, I'm surprised how sprightly my mother looks. Her colour-coordinated trousers and blouse, her polished shoes (Father's doing no doubt), bob-cut hair neatly clipped back from her face. She looks as if she's test-driving the chair for someone else and will spring up any moment to hand it back.

'I won't get up, darling,' my mother jokes. I dutifully smile and bend to kiss the proffered cheek as expected, catching the smell of talcum powder with eye watering notes of Deep Heat. Her back must be playing up again.

Mother had broken her left ankle and damaged her right knee when she'd slipped into one of the trenches at her last archaeological dig. Despite the fact she retired more than a decade ago, she continues to volunteer. Although, they now keep her busy backstage. Or try to. She'd been asked to focus on cataloguing the historical finds in the safety of the tent, but couldn't resist nosing around, no doubt offering her opinion on the direction and depth of the exploratory trench. Archaeology was her reason for being and it was hard to take that away from her, but I seriously doubt that their insurance covered eighty-year-olds getting involved in digging on an active site.

'How is the leg healing?' I ask.

'Slower than Daddy would like but faster than I should expect at my age.' She reverses the chair as I shut the front door. My father had attached a Heath Robinson contraption to the latch so Mother can reach it from the wheelchair. As it clanks against the closed door, I immediately feel trapped.

I'd decided to aim for 'benign tolerance' in order to keep the peace this lunchtime. I plan to refrain from countering my father's trite observations, which will no doubt be scattered liberally through the conversation, seasoned with Latin quotes and classical references, ('Those who are too smart to engage in politics are punished by being governed by those who are dumber'). I will show an interest in the plans for their next bird watching trip; appear to absorb any personal criticism rather than get defensive; and mind my Ps and Qs just as they taught me.

It doesn't go well.

It's like a pincer movement. My mother starts as soon as we finish lunch. She neatly aligns her knife and folk on the plate then dabs gently at her lips with the napkin. 'I read your interview. The one in last week's Sunday paper.'

I raise my eyebrows, smiling encouragingly. 'And?'

'Was that the most interesting example you could pick from your book?' She directs her attention to folding her napkin, avoiding eye contact with me as she aligns the edges, even though she will throw it in the washing basket later. 'Of course, I've not read the whole text, but the example you gave seemed a little… simplistic.' She glances up with a benign expression which conveys a curious mix of warmth and concern overlaying something darker. I'm braced for the dagger. 'Convoluted but simplistic… Of course, a good editor could've sorted that out for you, but as we know from Daddy's books, they don't like to make too many changes to academic texts. And yours was *based* on research I gather?' Her tone implies doubt.

'*Accessible*. That was the word they used in the reviews, wasn't it?' It's my father's turn.

I nod, flattered he's read them and actually remembers something they'd said. 'I wanted to help people understand that memory doesn't work the way novels and films suggest.'

'Lowest common denominator. Soundbite writing,' he says, snatching away my naïve moment of belief that praise might be in the offing. 'No one's taught to think these days. I remember when I published my first research paper…'

I tune out, getting up to clear the table, taking the plates to the kitchen as an excuse not to take part in another trip down memory lane where the students had IQs over 120, academic discipline was highly valued and the grass always emerald green.

I should be used to it by now. When we were growing up, I was always critically compared to Dereck. From their perspective his halo always sparkled, whereas mine had been used as a hula hoop and discarded in a field somewhere. But they weren't aware of his lies.

The first time I spotted it was when he was regaling them with the story of how he'd single-handedly won the inter-school cricket match, forgetting I had been there to witness the fielder catching the ball before Dereck had even completed one run. His deceit was blatant, adding layers of detail to win their admiration and I looked from him to my parents searching for signs of doubt. But they fell for every line their golden boy spun. After that I was on alert for his lies and exaggerations. The list grew: stories of how he won the debating certificate; how he got the highest ever grade in his science exam; been lauded in assembly for his performance as fire marshal during the recent drills. All lies.

I started to watch him closely over Sunday lunch when he usually delighted us with these highlights of his week. The only tell-tale sign I could spot that gave away that he was fibbing was a slight twitch around his mouth. He was good. But as they say, practice makes perfect.

Coming back to the present, I can still hear my father droning on in the lounge as I stack the dishwasher, the rise and fall of his voice suggesting a practised monologue. While out of sight in the kitchen, I set an alarm on my phone.

We're finishing coffee when it goes off. 'Excuse me,' I say, peering at the screen, cutting the alarm then holding the mobile to my ear as if it's someone phoning me. 'I must take this call.' I'm conscious of sounding like a character in a TV cop show and a look passes between my parents, flashes of disapproval sparking. Speaking into the phone I conduct an imaginary conversation, 'Yes, of course... hmm...tomorrow?...email me the details...yes... thanks...I'll see you shortly. Bye.'

'Important call?' my father says, his lips tightening in a sign of disapproval. He pushes his chair back from the table to fold his arms across his stomach.

'A meeting with my agent to discuss a booking,' I lie.

'Today? On a Sunday?' He glowers at me, his thick eyebrows frowned into a mono brow, almost daring me to look away first. 'What is it? A last-minute cancellation and you're the stand in?'

As usual, I ignore his rudeness hoping to keep the peace. 'It's a college. They've been trying to find a date I can make for weeks, my diary's so crammed. My agent told them to grab me while they had a chance. In fact, I need to leave now... to prepare.'

Neither of my parents make any effort to encourage me to stay.

'I would see you out, darling,' my mother says, 'but my arms are a bit tired and I think I need a nap.'

As I bend to kiss her goodbye, she offers me her other cheek to kiss, a subconscious reversal of my arrival. I notice her nails are painted a pale pink and, in a schoolgirl-like reflex, I hide mine from view.

My hand is on the door latch when my mother calls from the lounge to throw her last dart. 'Oh, darling. Do remember your posture next time you're recorded. You looked a bit slumped on your TED talk. Remember, shoulders back, chin up. Think *gravitas*, darling. Dereck sent us a link to your cousin Diana's recording. You should watch it if you want to see how it's done. A fascinating talk on bird diversity in Columbia. We're all so proud of her.'

Excerpt from chapter titled 'Lies about Liars'

Reproduced from The Minefield of Memory by Amanda Dunstan

Detectives believe that they can detect when someone is lying, but research shows that they are no better at spotting the fakers than any of us. You may have heard that body language can give away those who are trying to deceive: some suggest that someone looking up is creating an image of the story they are spinning; a person looking down to the left is talking themselves through their lie; folded arms suggest they are putting up a barrier; a hand to the mouth or touching their nose suggests a fib...

Well, maybe...

A practised liar can hide these 'tells', the key is to observe the individual when they are chatting informally or answering more general or factual questions, like 'what's your date of birth?'. Do you see different behaviours when they are answering more targeted questions designed to draw them out, for example, 'how do you account for your multiple phone calls to the victim?'

Criminal investigators used to accuse a person of lying during an interrogation, repeating this accusation again and again over many hours. This practice is one of many that can lead to false confessions and has since been abandoned in the UK.

Constantly challenging a person's story can cause them to doubt their own memory, particularly when investigators provide feasible alternative versions of events. Under pressure the accused can start to wonder if they might have blanked out what really *happened and, in time, come to believe other versions that are offered to them.*

Another commonly used practice was to invite the suspect themselves to describe how the crime <u>might</u> have been committed, a hypothetical version of events. By imagining a chain of events in this fashion a person can begin to believe that this is what really happened. And so, an innocent person can become convinced of their own guilt.

[Chapter continues]

Chapter Nine
Aphantasia

That night after my visit to the family home, I dream that I'm doing a TED talk and Mother is prompting me from the wings, while father heckles me from the audience. I think there was something about birds flying in and out of the auditorium too. Hardly surprising. Counter to Freud's belief that dreams represent unconscious desires, I hold to a more scientific view, believing that dreams are a byproduct of the brain processing the events of the day. No more than electrical impulses triggering random memories, thoughts, and images as the brain metaphorically flips through its files to slot things neatly in place. Not a very romantic viewpoint but, to my way of thinking, pleasingly logical.

In my dreams I live a vivid interior life, full of imagery, colour and imaginings but in day-to-day life I've always had a very poor visual memory, unable to conjure up mental images of people or places no matter how well I know them. In my waking hours I can't voluntarily picture anything at all. At best, my brain might serve up a random image from the past when I'm immersed in something else: the garden of a house I'd thought of buying might flash into my mind while I'm doing the washing up; being in goal in a game of hockey when I was at school appears in my mind's eye while I'm reversing my car off the drive; my grandma knitting in her rocking chair popping into my head as I do the vacuuming. Anything might suddenly appear and be gone before I have time to study it. But if I try consciously to imagine these things nothing comes.

I'd been in my late forties when I discovered there is a name for this characteristic – aphantasia. Literally the inability to create mental imagery.

Like other aphantasics, my memories are largely stored as words rather than imagery. I think of it as akin to diary pages – a verbal account of events. While others can create an image to accompany their memory, maybe even seeing sights, smelling aromas and hearing sounds in their mind's eye, aphantasics just don't. Of course, I was intrigued when I first discovered this – what impact could it have on eyewitness testimony if that witness was aphantasic, like three percent of the population?

It turned out to be a rich vein of research.

Like my husband Phillip, some people have amazing memories for personal details. They can recall what they wore to particular events, what they chose from the menu the last time they were at a specific restaurant, the feeling of the first time they stepped off a plane in a foreign country. Thinking of a familiar song on the radio sparks a memory of when they heard it before and they can see, smell and feel the sensations they had at that time. They store rich sensory data in their memories and when they recall events it's as if they are actually experiencing them again. Clearly these people should make excellent witnesses. However, because they are so good at creating images in their mind's eye, my research suggests that they can also over-embellish the story they recall, adding details that didn't occur or claiming to have seen objects that weren't there.

At the other end of the scale, you have people like me who cannot picture the events, the people or the surroundings. They just *know* they were there and their memories are a series of facts or anecdotes, any specifics only recalled because they consciously made an effort to commit that detail to memory in words ('The man had dark hair and was wearing a grey sweatshirt'), or they've been told by someone else over the years ('When you were five you had a red bike'), or they've been prompted to recall by being given a reminder ('Remember that holiday in Spain when we had a ride in a hot air balloon?'), or jogged into recall when shown a photograph.

Theoretically, the aphantasics should make comparatively poor witnesses, but they often have a good recall of the sequence of events, when and where things occurred. In my research, their sketches of the layout of a crime scene were just as accurate as others, albeit more schematic and lacking detail.

My experiments underlined that while aphantasics can experience rich emotions in real time as events occur, the feelings soon fade and when they recall the experience afterwards, it is typically in a detached and unemotional way. Other researchers have found similar results and even coined a rather unflattering term for this phenomena: Severely Deficient Autobiographical Memory.

Maybe a good thing for me, I surmise, given the family I come from.

1988
A FEW MONTHS LATER

The third year at college starts. The events she'd witnessed that early summer afternoon still pop back into her mind unbidden. One day, she's walking back from a lecture when she hears the sound of a baby crying as she passes an open window. It drags her memory back to that afternoon.

Had her friend's baby actually been crying as much as she'd thought? She'd seen him on the floor next to his mum, holding onto her arm, as she recalls it now. But it was more of a whimper than a cry, as if he'd given up trying to get attention or forgotten what he'd wanted. Hot and bored rather than frightened.

And the man. The more she thought about it she realised, he was more despairing than angry. Fed up about her friend's scattiness and unreliability.

And what was it her friend had said? *'I'll get it'* or was it *'I'll do it'*? As if to underline her commitment to something? As if there was some kind of promise she'd failed to keep? It was just an argument between them. Something private.

A good thing she didn't intervene.

But…

The blood. There was definitely blood.

Her friend hadn't shown up at college the next day.

And she didn't come back for the start of their third year.

They haven't heard from her since.

Chapter Ten
Suffocation

The light on the landline phone in the hall is signalling another message. No doubt from Phillip's old friend Don.

'Please leave a message after the beep,' Phillip's answerphone voice responds when I don't pick up. Most callers don't bother, put off by this voice from the dead. Don is not the only one who tells me it's unnerving to hear Phillip after all these years. He once offered to record a new message for me or show me how to do it, but I already know how and I pretended not to hear him. It's on my to-do list; I'll change it when I'm ready.

I'd missed a call from him already that morning. And last night I'd been standing by the phone in the hallway when he'd phoned, each caller's identity announced by a mechanical voice so I know who I'm ignoring.

Don. What can I say about Don, other than that he'd been Phillip's friend and had known Phillip long before I came on the scene? I'd once asked Phillip how they had originally become friends as they seemed so different in personality. Apparently it was down to the alphabet – their surnames both began with B and they were allocated to the same class in infant school. A friendship made by chance, as they often are.

They'd been there for each other through the whole of their school days; then early careers – Phillip in archiving, Don in surveying. Then came their first marriages...

I never met Don's first wife, but according to Phillip, she had been an intelligent and capable woman who juggled a career in accounting with running the household and managing Don. Eventually she realised she wanted a more equal partnership, divorcing him to marry one of her colleagues in the firm where she worked. On the rebound, Don married their cleaner, Gita, a talented Lithuanian woman. He supported her through art college part-time where she studied photography. As her work took off she gained a reputation, a career and collectors and the impetus to leave poor Don. The last anyone heard she was travelling the world exhibiting her work. He hasn't married again. As yet.

Since Phillip's death, Don has taken on the mantle of my unappointed guardian angel. Whether this is with the hope of something more romantic between us, I haven't as yet confirmed, but suffice to say I keep him at arms' length. He means well, but…

The answer phone light is still beeping at me, insisting on my attention. I show it who's boss by deleting the message without playing it.

It's a sunny afternoon and I decide to work off some of the negative emotion my parents always engender, with a spot of gardening. I'm head and shoulders deep in the privet hedge, stretching to reach something I've spotted glinting in the soil, when I hear Don's familiar voice behind me.

If it is what I hope it is pushing its way up from the earth, I don't want to retrieve it while Don is hovering. Unable to turn without catching my hair in the twigs or taking an eye out, I execute an ungainly reverse.

'…wondered where you were. I phoned last night and twice this morning and when you didn't pick up I was worried.' Don addresses my rear end without waiting for me to emerge. 'I was even more concerned when I just saw your car on the driveway. I thought you might be ill.'

'There is no need to worry. I've been looking after myself for the past forty years without parental guidance and managed well enough so far.' Free from the hedgerow, I stand up and run my hand through my hair, irritated to find I've lost another hair-elastic to a garden bush. 'I've never been run over by a rogue trolley in Waitrose car park. Never been bitten by a rabid dog. Never even caught Covid. I'm pretty robust.'

'I can't help but be concerned when I don't hear from you for days,' Don says.

He is overlooking the fact he never hears from me: he is the one who calls me. Or finds any excuse to pop round. I remove a leaf from my shoulder and brush dry dirt from my top. 'Well, here I am!' I throw my arms wide in a theatrical *ta-da* gesture. Don is yet another person who misreads my benign expression for warmth and friendliness.

'Have you got time for a cup of tea?' he asks. I know he means well. He worries that I'm lonely, when it's he who is the extrovert, the one desperate for company.

In my kitchen he plugs in the kettle and I contemplate him. He and Phillip were the same height and build, but that's where the physical similarities end. Phillip had always looked well groomed, usually clad in a shirt and jumper, his shoes polished; his appearance neat and tidy, like his thinking. Don is always slightly dishevelled, like an older version of Hugh Grant in *Bridget Jones' Diary*; constantly running his hands through his floppy hair to push it back off his face: his glasses lopsided or held together with sticky tape because he's lost the screw and not had time to get a new pair, the lenses always looking like they need a good wipe.

He is humming under his breath (thankfully not whistling today), aligning the washing up bottle with the hand-cream on the side of the kitchen sink while he waits for the kettle to boil. I leave him in control while I go and wash my own hands in the bathroom.

'You've moved the mugs,' he shouts through, an accusing tone in his voice. He is relaxed in our house, treating it like a second home having been here so often over the years. Maybe too relaxed. I turn the hot tap on full blast, watching as the mirror steams up and I disappear.

By the time I return to the kitchen, he's placed the mug of tea neatly on a coaster on the already ring-stained wooden table. I take a sip and push the coaster to one side, placing the mug directly on the tabletop. A mini rebellion intended to signal that this my house and I'll do what I want.

'I suppose it makes more sense to have the mugs on that shelf near the kettle,' Don says.

'So what's today's agenda?' I ask, wary that hours could be lost if we take too many detours.

'Ah, yes. I wanted to tell you about the memorial plans the Committee have discussed.'

There is still some dirt down my fingernail and I excavate it, not looking at him. 'The Committee? The memorial?' I ask flatly.

It's now coming up to five years since Phillip's death and The Bridgeton Railway Museum want to honour him with some sort of memorial, in recognition of his chairmanship. After Phillip had retired he'd become more involved at the local museum, firstly as a volunteer and eventually as a trustee. (Or as one volunteer had described Phillip in his eulogy at the funeral, 'He was a business head at the tiller always keeping us in the right lane', unaware he was mixing his metaphors like ingredients in a Heston Blumenthal recipe.) When Phillip died, they'd asked me to join the committee in Phillip's place – not as Chair, mind – just another member who gets roped in when they needed someone to fund raise. I'd said no, with a smile of course.

According to Don the memorial would involve the renaming of a building and a plaque in Phillip's honour.

'They're approaching the Mayor, to see if she'll come and say a few words,' Don says.

'Why the Mayor? Why not someone from the train company or the local council? Although I don't think any of them have done much for the Museum in the past.'

'We... they... thought it would get more publicity. And

obviously they…we… want you to cut the ribbon.' He pauses and looks up at me like a puppy that's peed on the lounge carpet. 'You will, won't you?'

What would Phillip want, I wonder. If the Museum had done this while he was alive I'm sure he'd have laughed about it, but secretly he would have been pleased. We'd have shared a bottle of wine and role-played the ceremony, hamming it up, wringing out every last drop of absurdity: him suggesting I wear a fascinator with a toy train attached; me proposing I buy him Thomas the Tank engine slippers to wear on the big day. We'd practise a curtsy and bow and discuss the most dramatic methods to cut the ribbon – maybe a ceremonial sword? And we'd laugh and laugh, knowing full well we would be on our best behaviour on the day, because after all, we're British and brought up to be polite. But we'd have to try not to catch each other's eye in case we started giggling.

Don interrupts my daydream. 'You will do it? You will cut the ribbon?'

I put my hands over my face, not wanting him to see that I'm fighting back tears, swallowing hard, hijacked by a sudden surge of grief. I miss Phillip. I wish it was him who was here with me now.

I hear Don's chair pushing back against the floor tiles. I smell his aftershave as he leans close, then through my shirt I feel the warmth of his hand tentatively resting on my back. He's trying to help I know, but I wriggle away from his touch, shaking my head to clear it. *Get a grip.*

I sniff and sit upright, reach for the tepid remains of the tea and take a sip.

'This ribbon thing. I'll think about it,' I say. 'Now, is there anything else? I need to get back to the garden. Rain's forecast tomorrow.'

It turns out there is.

The reason he'd phoned me the previous night was to ask for my help: would I meet his neighbour's son and give the lad some advice? The situation is a sad one. A lad who risks losing his job over an eyewitness' misidentification. The young man has been suspended from work while everything is under investigation.

'They don't have much money,' Don says, 'The mother has M.S. and hasn't worked for years and Tommy's been supporting her and his younger brothers. He relies on that job. Maybe if you could just speak to them, take a look at his case and give them some advice?'

I reassure him I will do all I can and if it seems they need an expert witness, I'll take the case on for free. There are too many miscarriages of justice in the world and I just can't stand by and watch another one happen if he is truly innocent.

'Now, I'd better get back to work.' I nod towards the garden.

Don picks up the cups and takes them to the sink, adding them to the pile of washing-up on the draining board. 'Let me organise a gardener for you. It's a big space and too much on top of everything else. You work too hard.'

I smother my thoughts, telling myself he's just trying to be kind. 'It's fine. Good exercise.' I inject a smile into the words, standing to signal my intent to show him out.

Watching him reverse his car off the driveway I politely lift a hand to wave goodbye. He takes this as encouragement, stopping at the end of the drive and lowering his window.

'I'll see you soon,' he says cheerily.

'I'm sure,' I say.

Back in the garden I return to the privet. It's completely out of control, no longer a hedge, more an amorphous mass entwined with ivy, hard to tell where ivy ends and privet starts. Gardening was Phillip's sphere. He'd be mortified at the bindweed twining round his roses, its tendrils reaching out across the old vegetable patch taking over everything in its path. I try to recall Phillip's instructions: 'Don't try to pull it out in case you leave the roots behind.' I had knelt down beside him to watch his soil stained fingers unravel a length of the weed, more gentle than you'd imagine such a big man could be. 'To do the job properly, take a growing tip and place it in a plastic bag of weed killer and secure it in place. That way you know the job's done properly and it won't come back.'

'Like getting rid of a criminal gang,' I'd said. 'Pointless taking out the fringe elements without eliminating the roots.'

I vow to buy weed killer next time I pass Roy's.

With memories of Phillip and his love for the garden, I feel guilty about the state I've let things get in. I kneel down and tug at the wall of goosegrass blanketing the blackberries, smothering out both light and life. Its tiny hooked hairs catch on my clothes and skin, bringing me up in red welts. It makes me furious just looking at this plant trying to take over, suffocating everything around it. I don't stop until there is a huge mound of the stuff on the lawn.

It's only then, as the sun is disappearing behind clouds, that I remember what I'd returned to the garden to do and I head for the privet to dig up this personal treasure. There's a momentary panic when I can't recall where exactly I'd seen the glint of glass. Crawling the length of the old hedge on my hands and knees, I hope the neighbours aren't looking from their upstairs window: they already have me badged as odd and antisocial. Unable to spot it, I fetch a headtorch, shining it into the shadows, feeling a surge of relief when I spot a small flash of reflected light.

It's then that I realise I want to hold onto that feeling of hope. I don't want to discover it's just the light catching dew held in the bowl of a leaf, or a discarded ring pull. I want to postpone the moment; to hold onto the belief that it will be Phillip's lost glasses, a treasure waiting to be discovered another day – like a gift from beyond the grave, a small memento of him. He lost so many pairs. He used to balance them on top of his head or rest them on anything convenient to peer at something of interest, swearing he saw better without them, but refusing to make an appointment with the optician. I'd find them on top of cupboards after he'd stood on a chair to clean the dust; broken where they'd fallen between the cushions on the armchair and been crushed when he sat down; once even in the fridge – 'Not early signs of dementia,' he'd said. 'I needed to take them off to read the date on the chicken.'

I miss you sweetheart, I say quietly.

I mark the spot with a large pebble.

Returning to the house rubbing at the goose grass rash on my arms, I contemplate how thin my skin is becoming.

Chapter Eleven
Trap

I don't read the daily papers, that was always Phillip's thing. He used to read out the header of articles he thought might interest me, watching for my nod of approval, waiting as I put down my novel and closed my eyes to concentrate as he spoke, unaware that I was focusing on the comforting rhythm of his voice as much as the details of the news.

I'd cancelled the order soon after he died.

There was a BBC app on my phone and I sometimes checked the headlines while I drank my coffee, purely for distraction from dark thoughts. Although usually the news was so grim, it made them darker. And I'd never strayed too far into the territory of social media, merely taking an exploratory step on the advice of my agent: 'You can build your fan base and interact with your readers.' I set up an account as requested, but social media seemed to be misnamed, primarily attracting the antisocial, so that didn't last long. Maybe if I'd been more aware of the wider world, I might have picked up on the rumblings of discontent and done something sooner, but that morning I was completely wrong-footed.

For the previous month I'd been enjoying the acclaim my book was achieving, relishing the opportunity to share my knowledge with people at the talks I gave, thoroughly enjoying the role of being the expert again. The publicity team had done a great job and it looked as if a number of exciting opportunities were in the pipeline. There was talk of a slot on breakfast TV; the idea of pitching for an ongoing role on a new behavioural science-based series on the BBC. And the Crime Writers Association seemed keen for me to be a keynote speaker at their annual conference. While being a successful author had never featured in my earlier career plans, it seemed a great way to combine all of my skills and I was really happy with the course things were taking.

I wake early that morning in a great mood. The weather is glorious and I decide to make the best of such a beautiful day: walk to the local shops rather than drive out to the supermarket. Maybe stop for a coffee before heading for home.

It turns out to be market day and I browse the stalls, taking my time with nothing to rush back for. The fruit and vegetables look fresher in sunlight than under the artificial glare of supermarket LED track lights: the tomatoes deeper red, the richness of the colour suggesting the flavours my generation recall from childhood; the cucumbers surprisingly misshapen but not hermetically sealed in plastic; pears in a range of sizes. The stallholder is a woman about my age, her cheeks tanned by her outdoor role and her eyes rimmed by smile lines. She offers me an apple to taste as I dither over my choice; it smells as good as it tastes and the surge of pleasure in my chest surprises me. We chat for a while – about the weather and parking and the plans for a new supermarket out on the ring road – and strangely I don't champ at the bit to get on, or feel the rising frustration I once would. As she weighs and bags my purchases, providing a banana box for the fruit that won't fit in my hessian bag, I thank her for her kindness.

'See you next week,' she says as I leave. Her smile looks genuine.

I stop for a coffee, choosing to sit outside at one of their pavement tables rather than rush off with a takeaway cup. I stash my shopping around my feet and perch my handbag on my lap, wondering whether to warn the woman at the next table that hanging her rucksack on the back of her chair is an invitation to thieves. Opposite me, a young couple are bickering in a hissed exchange. I'm not close enough to hear what they're saying but the body language is interesting to watch: rolled eyes and dramatic exhaling from her, shrugs and fidgeting from him.

I'm distracted for a moment when the waitress brings my cappuccino. The barista has scattered chocolate powder in a heart shape on the top and there's a free biscotti resting on the paper napkin. Small unexpected pleasures. I spoon the froth into my mouth, the sun warm on my face, the rich smell of Italian cooking wafting from the restaurant.

The young couple get up to leave. They are now holding hands, their hissy-fit dispute forgotten as they head across the square. They stop at a stall selling vinyl records where they both flick through the boxes, holding up album covers to show each other. Even from this distance I recognise Aladdin Sane. Maybe memories of things their parents used to play when they were kids?

This is a strange experience. Something I've never done on my own before: just sitting and watching passersby without someone – Phillip – to talk to. It makes me feel more connected, like I'm part of something bigger, reminding me of how, as a child, I used to lift up the slabs in our garden path to watch the ants; each one scurrying about with its own part to play.

As I set off for home, I vow that I will return to the market next week.

Walking back is slightly less of a pleasure as I'm fairly laden and have to keep juggling my shopping to keep things balanced. The hessian bags slung over each shoulder keep slipping down and the banana box in my arms seems to grow heavier as I try to balance the open tray of eggs on top. Maybe I'll go by car next week. Or limit my purchases. Or bring more suitable bags. Only forty yards or so to go, I think as I turn the corner into my road.

Ahead of me, gathered halfway down the street not far from my house, there's a small knot of people. About eight or ten, a couple of them perched on my neighbour's wall. What a cheek! The Patels won't like that. What can they be doing?

It's only as I take another few steps I see most of them are actually clustered outside my house. Uncertain what's going on, I slow my pace. The energy of the group doesn't suggest an accident: the people on the wall aren't hurt in some way; there's no crashed car at the kerb side. There's no panic or fear emanating from the group. Rather, they seem to be loitering, fidgeting as they wait for something. I narrow my eyes, trying to focus, to see whether I recognise anyone and as I look more closely, I spot microphones and cameras – it can only be journalists.

Before I can analyse the situation further, a man with unruly curly hair looks up from his camera and takes a step in my direction and – seeming to move as one body – the others do the same. Now they've seen me it's too late to reverse my steps and duck back around the corner, so I pull my shoulders back and head towards them, curious as to what this is all about.

I've barely opened my mouth to say a polite 'good morning' when they close in around me. It feels as if microphones and camera lenses are being thrust in my face, the cacophony of speech meaning individual voices are lost in the babble, the confusion making me want to cover my ears and close my eyes to shut it all out.

'Could you…Please…Excuse me…' Without a free hand I try to push my way through the throng using my elbows, intent on reaching my front step so I can unburden myself of my shopping and find out what this is all about. 'Please… Just… can you…' My throat feels tight, my heart pounding and I recognise the signs of panic; I've never been good with crowds. A camera flashes in my eyes and momentarily blinded by the flash and unable to shield my face, I duck my head in an attempt to hide. 'Can you just give me a moment to–'

I vaguely register a deep voice behind me – '...hear your side of the story?' – but my focus is on getting to the safety of my front door. I've reached my garden but the catch of the gate is shut and to open the clasp I need to free up a hand. I balance the box of groceries on the gate but as it swings open the weight tips to one end and my frantic attempts to catch it end up overturning the whole thing.

The noise seems to stop, as if the volume's been turned down, and all I can hear is a pounding in my ears. As I stare down at the pile of my groceries in a heap on my path the thudding in my chest transforms from fear to a low-level anger. *What right do these people have to hound me like this?*

'And now the eggs are smashed.'

'What was that she said?' someone at the back of the group shouts. I must've spoken aloud.

'Something about eggs.'

A louder voice: 'This is your chance to give your view. Tell us what you feel about this controversy.'

I spin around to face the speaker, a man with the tell-tale signs of previous childhood acne drifting over his cheeks, part hidden by a straggly beard. 'What controversy?' I snap, scowling at him. 'I really don't know what you're talking about.'

'Do you think it's right that McCollins should be let out?' The man edges inside the gate, inadvertently crushing the grapes under his trainers as he holds a microphone towards me. I raise my arm to push the mic to one side and take a step backwards. He is in my personal space.

'McCollins? I know nothing about a McCollins.' I shove past him, stepping over the fallen food, just wanting to get to the safety of my home. My hands shaking, I fumble with the keys, dropping them as I try to get the door open. As I bend to pick them up the man is now right behind me, looming over me, trapping me between him and my front door. He bends to wave the microphone nearer to my face. 'What? You can't deny–'

Something snaps inside me: it's like stretching an elastic band to the point where it breaks. There's no conscious decision, but one minute I'm trying to remain professional, the next I've picked up an orange that had rolled near my front step and thrown it hard at the journalists. And once I've started I can't stop: lobbing fallen fruit at the assembled crowd as I hysterically scream at them to leave me alone. Meanwhile, cameras click, videos record and laughter and taunts crowd in on me from all sides.

The peak of my anger abates just as quickly as it arose. I'm aware of the panting of my breathing, my heart thudding in my chest, the ringing of tinnitus in my ears as my pulse races, but the accompanying energy has dissipated. I stand slumped, head hanging as tears of frustration well up.

I don't understand what is going on.

'Excuse me.' It's a woman's voice nearby, pitched to be heard above the babble. 'Can you all please leave?' It is a voice I don't recognise. 'You can see Dr Dunstan needs space. This is private property. I would like you all to leave now... Yes, now. Thank you.'

Frozen to the spot and not knowing what to do, I just stare at the mess on the garden path, part of me aware that the lock of the gate has clicked and the journalists are leaving, their mumbled comments and conversations moving further away.

The woman's voice again, closer. 'It's okay. They've gone.' A hand touches my arm. I'm sapped of all energy; a puppet with the strings cut. 'Let me help you,' she says.

Chapter Twelve
McCollins

I let the woman take my elbow and lead me to the front door, let her pick up my keys from the flower bed where they've been kicked during my tantrum. I watch numbly as she unlocks the door and steps back for me to enter. It's as if all my emotions have evaporated and I'm left washed out, an unfeeling husk. The front door swings open but I don't move.

'Are you okay?' the woman asks.

I shake my head. 'No. Not really,' I mumble.

'It's the shock. They shouldn't be allowed to do that. Turn up on people's doorsteps like that.'

'Doorstepping.'

'Yes. It should be illegal.'

A slight movement of my head signals acknowledgement.

'Look, I don't like to leave you like this. Can I get you some water or a cup of tea or something?' she says.

When I don't react, the woman gently takes my elbow again and steers me through the door, stepping over the post on the mat and into my hallway. On the hall table the red light of the landline phone is flashing '8'.

'I missed some calls.' My voice is flat. A statement of fact.

'It will be them.' Her head jerks towards the front door. She means the journalists. 'Don't listen to the messages now. Let's get you a drink. Where would you like to sit?'

I shuffle towards the kitchen, the woman close at my side, her hand extended as if I may faint or make a bolt for it and she might need to grab hold of me.

In the familiar space of my kitchen I feel myself coming back, a tingling awareness like blood returning to a numb hand. 'Thank you,' I say. 'You've been very kind.'

'It's nothing. You've got more colour now. Would you like me to leave or can I keep you company for a while, until you feel more settled?'

'Stay,' I say, waving towards one of the kitchen stools for the woman to sit, motivated by the need to be polite and hospitable as much as my desire for company. I slowly assemble mugs and milk and fill the kettle, reassured by the familiarity of the routine, making tea without checking this is what the woman wants, not feeling ready to make polite small talk. It's only when I pass her the mug that I really look at her. About my age, her white hair is styled in an urchin cut, her petite face framed by dark rimmed glasses, several small silver studs in each ear from the lobe up to the cartilage. She sits very still and there's a controlled calmness about her that is reassuring.

'Do I know you?' I ask. There's something familiar about her that I can't place.

'You may recognise me. I came to your talk at the library. I asked a lot of questions.'

'I don't recall. I'm not good with faces.'

'It's names that defeat me,' the woman says.

'That too.'

'I helped you with your banner. At the library,' she says.

I'd ordered a six-foot promotional roller banner at the suggestion of the publicity team. Unpacking it at the library I'd discovered it lacked any written instructions and, while not complicated, appeared to require at least three sets of hands. A woman in the front row had come to assist and – more able to convert the diagram into action – had put it up in no time as I watched, redundant.

'In that case I'm doubly in your debt.'

We sit in silence for a while, waiting for the tea to cool. The woman seems intuitively to understand my need for company but not mindless chat. She instinctively knows that just being there is enough, without feeling the need to fill the space. Possibly an introvert, like me.

'The journalists. What did they want?' I ask, eventually. 'Do you know?'

'From what they said it's about the McCollins case. They want your views on it.'

'McCollins?' I frown, shake my head. 'I don't recall working on a case for a McCollins.'

'It's all over the news. Have you not seen anything?' I study the woman as she opens her satchel handbag and searches inside. Something about her seems familiar – her profile? The way she moves, slow and catlike? Whatever it is, it feels comforting. She pulls out a copy of that day's newspaper, opens it to point at a heading in a sidebar – EXCLUSIVE: *Multiple Murderer McCollins Claims Innocence – Full story pages 3 and 4.*

'Oh him. Yes. I've heard of him.' Given more context I recall the name. 'He killed a bouncer ten or twenty years ago. But what's that got to do with me? I never worked on his case.'

'I'm really sorry but you do need to see this,' the woman says, unfolding the newspaper to show me the article. The text surrounds a large black and white image of a man who I immediately recognise from TV news coverage around the time of his arrest. It's McCollins, posting for the camera, sporting one of those grins that my grandma would have called 'cocksure' but I'd term smug.

'Why are they giving him publicity now?' I ask.

'Take another look.'

I shake out the paper and tilt it towards the light from the window, studying the photo. He is clutching a copy of *The Minefield of Memory* in his hands. My book in the hands of this murderer.

'But what's my book got to do with it?'

'He's read it apparently. He's saying it helps refute the evidence used against him.' She pauses. 'He's calling for his conviction to be overturned… His recent case rested on eyewitnesses and one of them wants to recant their testimony.'

'That's why they were here? The press.'

She nods. 'And I expect all the missed calls on your answerphone are from them too.'

'I heard it ring as I went out.' I'd assumed it was Don phoning to suggest he come over to help in the garden, or take me out for the day, or tell me more plans for the memorial service, or inform me that the sun is shining… I hadn't wanted him to interrupt what I'd thought was going to be a lovely day. 'If only I'd answered I wouldn't have been so…' Realisation hits me. 'Oh my God, what have I done? You don't think they'll use any of …?' I leave the question unfinished, unsure how to describe my over-the-top reactions.

'I don't know, but maybe you can come up with a considered response now you know what it's all about. Do a press release or something.'

I take a deep breath. 'Yes. Thank you. I'll do that. Right away.'

'I'll leave you to it, but before I go, would you like me to clear up the mess outside, then you don't have to be in the spotlight again so soon? Just in case any of the press are still around?'

'Thank you. Would you? You're very kind.'

'I hate to see people bullied like that. I couldn't have just walked past and not done something to try to help.' She studied my face as she spoke, an intense look on her face. 'I'm sure you'd do the same.'

I shrug. 'I'd like to think so.'

Ten minutes later she's retrieved a squash, a few salvageable potatoes and some carrots and swept the rest of the ruined fruit into the food recycling bin.

'A bit the worse for wear but still edible,' she says, placing the battered vegetables on the kitchen counter. 'Soup maybe?'

'I've just realised. I don't even know your name.'

'Kathleen.' She tears a corner off her newspaper which is still laying open on the table and scribbles something before passing it to me. 'My name and number, just in case. Call me if the marauding hordes return, or you want to lie low for a bit. I can pop out and get you some shopping or something.'

At the front door Kathleen peers out cautiously before turning to give me a thumbs up. 'The coast is clear. Take care of yourself. Bye.'

She is halfway down the path when I call after her. 'Kathleen! Would you like to meet for dinner some time? So I can thank you properly.'

'Yes. Yes please. I'd like that.'

I wave the scrap of paper with her number on. 'I'll call you.'

As soon as Kathleen has left, I set to researching the current McCollins case. The photo and article Kathleen had shown me were from that day's newspaper so I start there, calling up the online copy of the paper. I find I'm shaking my head, incredulous at what I'm reading: McCollins is referring to my book as his 'get out of jail free card!'

A journalist from the Mail has conducted an exclusive interview with McCollins and managed to fill a double spread with photos and quotes. It seems Mac McCollins was a career criminal. After a period of petty crime he'd escalated to assault and had several GBH convictions. But all that was a warm-up for his first murder conviction at the age of thirty – the savage beating of a bouncer who had thrown him out of a nightclub.

He'd served his time for this earlier murder, on the

surface a model prisoner, studying in the prison library whenever he could. On his release he had lain low for a few years, but now he is back in prison for the bloody murder of Teena Brown, a woman he'd been living with. There was some suspicion that he was guilty of another cold case death that had occurred when he was in his teens: same MO, but no concrete evidence had been found. He was good at covering his tracks.

According to the article, he has a number of female 'pen pals': a common occurrence – there's even a psychological term for it, Hybristophilia, and a body of research on the mysterious attraction that murderers hold for these women. The journalist, however, refers to them as 'prison groupies'. Apparently McCollins has received a huge volume of love letters and gifts from his fan club. A copy of *The Minefield of Memory* had been sent to him by one of the eyewitnesses who'd testified at his trial. She'd told him she was ready to recant her testimony after reading my book, having had a sudden realisation that it was too dark for her to be sure who she'd seen leaving the house. She now believes she identified the shadowy figure as Mac McCollins only because she'd recognised him from previous photos in the press, rather than from actually seeing him on the night of the murder.

If all this was true and the only evidence against him was what was stated in the newspaper article, the case seemed to be based on three things: the history of a volatile relationship and coercive control; a psychological assessment of his aggression; and the testimony of this one witness. While he may be a violent and deeply unpleasant character, he still deserved a fair trial and I doubted that the judge had called an expert witness to explain the fallibility of memory and eyewitness testimony to the jury. McCollins was clearly a wicked man and people were no doubt safer with him off the streets, but that is not how justice works.

I set to work on a press statement. My aim was to give a

balanced view; to highlight the potential issues with the witness statement that the jury may not have been made aware of. A clear and concise statement of facts without suggesting innocence or endorsing the need for a retrial. As the Dutch say, 'One witness is no witness.'

Excerpt from the chapter 'My Role as an Expert Witness'

Reproduced from The Minefield of Memory by Amanda Dunstan.

My role is to help the judge and jurors understand how memory works, specifically in the case of witness testimony. This is particularly important when there is no physical evidence – no DNA, shoe prints or fabric samples. When there is no corroborating evidence, the word of an eyewitness is the primary evidence against the defendant. So we need to be sure we can trust the memory of the person who saw or heard what happened.

I am often working for the defence team. Trying to see if the evidence holds up. Before attending court, I work through the case file and identify any possible causes of concern. For example, there may be issues with the way in which the initial interview was conducted. Did the investigators inadvertently lead the witness, influencing their recollection of events?

It is not my job in court to make any judgements on whether the eyewitness is telling 'the truth', or the defendant is guilty or innocent. I am there to give the facts about memory, the things that psychology researchers have proved to be true about the ways that memories are created and altered over time.

In the courtroom my role is to explain examples like this – to outline the relevant research findings and how they relate to the specific case under discussion. I am providing an expert opinion. It is then up to the judge and jury to weigh up the validity of the eyewitness evidence and form appropriate judgements.

[Chapter continues]

Chapter Thirteen
Aftermath

It doesn't take long before the recordings of my tantrum trend on social media and my overarm vegetable shots are made into a meme. It's worse than I recall. In the video clip, my face is screwed up with fury and my frenzied behaviour suggests a woman completely out of control. As I lob food products at the journalists, I'm screaming.

'Just (throw number 1 – an orange) leave (an apple, number 2) me (number 3 – a potato this time) alone (the one whole egg left in the carton)!' None of this was strategically aimed: in the recording I can see that the orange is caught by a tall woman who leaps for it as if in goal defence and the egg spatters over the trainers of one of the men, who doesn't jump back in time as it hits the ground beside him. It was both unbecoming and unprofessional.

The photos in the papers were a different type of embarrassment – in those I'm red-faced and near to tears, clearly vulnerable and in distress; not that that engendered any sympathy in the online response. *'She's a mad woman'; 'How can this woman be a respected academic?'; 'No wonder our graduates are not fit for employment if this is their role model'; 'She desperately needs mental health assistance'; 'Bat shit crazy!'* At this moment I wouldn't argue with the latter.

The straightforward, logical press statement I'd crafted seemed to raise even more ire. My careful words had been taken out of context and had been reproduced under headings like *'Mandy – the Memory Expert and Murderer's Mate', 'Expert Witness Blames Judge',* and *'Ex-Academic Claims Jurors Lack Common Sense.* The columnists demanded to know why I was supporting an aggressive murderer, as if I'd personally unlocked the door to his cell and set him loose to continue his spree of slaughter.

As chains of hostile posts build up online, I realise two things: I've under-estimated the lengths the press will go to in order to hype a story and massively over-estimated the ability of the general British public to understand nuance. It seems hard for people to grasp that lack of evidence of guilt does not necessarily mean a person is innocent, but it could still call a criminal conviction into doubt. I shake my head in despair. Evidence is needed for a conviction. If there is none, or what exists is called into doubt, then a conviction may be overturned. This is how the justice system works.

It's a day or two before my parents register the controversy that I've inadvertently become engaged in. Then the telephone barrage begins.

'You stupid, foolish girl!' My father's anger sears down the phone line.

I count to five under my breath. 'I'm not a child, Father.'

'Well, you behaved like one. You are a laughingstock.'

Mother joins in on the extension line. 'It wasn't very wise. We'd only spoken about gravitas when you last visited. I suppose we should be glad you didn't swear.'

I stay silent. There was no way to deny it. I'd overreacted and I'm now paying the price.

'And your press statement.' Father again. 'Did you not think to consult your agent, or anyone with a modicum of nous, before you issued that nonsense to the press?'

'I only commented on the evidence available in the public domain and made it very clear I've not had access to the court records.' I can feel myself becoming defensive, my hand gripping the phone cord, twirling it tightly round my fingers, the tip of which are turning white.

My father isn't ready to let the matter end there. 'But you as good as blamed the judge and said McCollins should have a retrial!'

'You're not one of the Twitterati, Father. You're intelligent enough to grasp the distinctions I made!' My voice sounds shrill. I stand up, my hand shaking as the anger builds.

'Pardon? What did you just say?'

'Read the words. Read the actual words I wrote!' I shout, then slam the phone down on the holder.

I start to cry. This isn't me: this depth of fury, this self-pity. Phillip wouldn't recognise me as the woman he'd loved and married: *'bat shit crazy'* a fair summary.

The phone rings again and again, each time it's a journalist seeking a quote or asking for an interview. I start the morning being polite and referring them to my statement. By lunchtime I've resorted to 'no comment'. After that I stop answering the phone.

Later that day, my agent contacts me by email. I skim read the contents – *publisher wants to cancel all publicity events... reputational risk...future contact with press to go through lawyer...consider this as notice of terminating our contractual relationship with one month's notice as per...we will continue to offer support at this difficult time...*

I print the email. My hand shakes as I add it to my contracts file. Emotionally exhausted, I search for solace in a large glass of wine. By the time I go to bed the bottle is empty.

Chapter Fourteen
A Friend

For the next few days I keep the lights off and the curtains drawn. My brain is stuck in a loop, running through the horror of the memory of my behaviour, analysing the course of events and trying to make sense of it all. I feel too sick to eat, my head hurts and while I'm exhausted, I can't sleep for more than an hour without waking up to toss and turn. I feel so bad I wonder if I've caught Covid, but after the allotted fifteen minutes the lateral flow test tells me no.

Don has phoned several times each day since it all kicked off, expressing how *appalled* he is by the actions of the media and offering his support, both moral and practical. The first time he called I was touched by his thoughtfulness and I thanked him politely. He offered to come round straight away, but I told him I wasn't ready to talk or to see anyone. But I knew that would have no impact – he is nothing if not persistent, convinced I just don't want to bother him. After that I'd ignored his voice messages, unable to deal with the concerned tone of his voice, not wanting to burst into tears in front of him.

Everything I've worked so hard for has gone. It's the end of my career.

I send Don a short email about the young lad, Tommy, his neighbour's son, explaining that I can clearly no longer act as an expert witness on the misidentification which was so critical to his case. My credibility now destroyed by recent events, I'd be of no help to him. The best I can do for Tommy is to step away and point him in the direction of another professional expert.

The fourth morning, I sit at my desk with my diary open before me, crossing through appointments for the coming months; everything I'd scheduled has now been cancelled by the promoters, the organisers, or by me, my confidence gone. Who is going to hire me as a professional speaker or expert witness when I seem so unhinged?

I try to think of a plan to rebuild my reputation, but at the end of an hour all I've got is a mug of cold coffee and an intricate doodle of a group of stick figures behind bars. A subconscious image of being trapped in my home? Or all the future clients I now can't represent, locked up without help?

The clang of the metal flap on the letterbox interrupts my thoughts. I'd intended to gaffer tape it shut but couldn't summon the energy to hunt around in the garage for the reel of tape. I'd already had one newspaper offer shoved through: a payment of more than my annual private pension for my 'exclusive' views on events. Whatever has just arrived on the doormat would follow that offer into the recycling bin.

I creak to standing, my joints complaining from sitting in the same position too long. Despite my intentions to head straight for the kitchen to make a fresh cup of coffee, my curiosity gets the better of me when I see the envelope on the mat by the front door. It's a pale blue Basildon Bond type envelope, like my mother used to give us for writing thank you letters after birthdays. There is no stamp and it is addressed *To Amanda* in cursive italic writing that I don't recognise.

I pick it up and walk to the kitchen, turning it this way and that, as if that will help me deduce what is inside. I lay the envelope on the counter top and go to the tap to fill the kettle. But my attention is diverted by it laying there and I end up soaking my hand and sleeve as the kettle overfills. Unable to locate the hand towel I wipe them ineffectually on my tracksuit bottoms and pick up the envelope, smearing the ink on the outside.

Inside is a handwritten note. I hold it by the edges so as not to smudge the writing before I've read it.

'Amanda, I hope I'm not intruding but you've been in my thoughts during these past few days. I can only imagine how hard it must be to be hounded like this. And you of all people do not deserve it. That man is merely using your good reputation to win himself publicity. If there is anything I can do to help – shopping etc or a listening ear – I am here. My best regards, Kathleen.'

Seeing it in writing like this I realise Kathleen is right. McCollins is out to get as much attention as he can for his case and I've inadvertently played my part in his plan. He wasn't seeking my expert help, rather he is riding on the back of the publicity my book has won, to get his case in the public eye. How could I have been so foolish? My professional career is now in pieces due to my shameful overreaction. All that I've worked so hard to achieve lost in a minute of uncontrolled frustration.

Ruminating on *what ifs* is doing me no good. I need to pull myself together.

As I pick up the phone receiver, the musty smell of stale sweat hits me. A shower and a change of clothes would help. But first I dial Kathleen's number.

She answers the call as I run my finger through the dust that's accumulated on the sideboard. 'Hi, Kathleen, it's Amanda. I just wanted to thank you for your note…I can't offer you dinner and I'm not ready to go out yet, but I do have some wine in the fridge.'

'Sounds great. How about this evening? I can drop by the curry house on my way over,' Kathleen says. 'What do you fancy?'

The smell of the tandoori chicken wafts into my (now dust free) hallway as I open the door, making me realise how hungry I am. Other than the odd bowl of cornflakes, I'd not eaten properly for days, too wound up to notice the complaints from my stomach.

We dish up and eat in companionable silence, perched at the kitchen counter. Kathleen eats with a relish Mother would approve of: spearing another potato from the Bombay aloo, forking it on to her plate before spooning on extra sauce; checking if I want the remains of the pilau rice before adding it to her plate. She doesn't ask questions about what has happened over the past few days since the door-stepping incident, and I feel no need to fill in the gaps.

Settling down in the lounge with our glasses of wine, I begin to relax. 'Do you live locally?' I ask her.

'A hop and a skip away in Stonebury. I'm hoping to buy a place, but I'm living above the shop while I save up some cash.'

'You run a shop?'

'I've got a café-come-bookshop: A Book and A Brew, it's called. You'd love it. It's all very informal. We have an after-school reading group and I run a book club there. That's how I originally came across your book – it was our monthly read. We had a great discussion that night – lots of food for thought. I can't believe how little we understood about memory.'

'It's been my passion for as long as I remember. I used to love teaching the students, seeing their faces as they realised it was a lot more complicated than they'd initially thought.'

'Do you miss working at the university?'

'Sometimes. Although there were a lot of frustrations.' I tell her a little about my struggles with the direction the college was going and the reasons I decided to leave.

'I guess that was pretty hard for you.'

'A bit...I miss the students. But the expert witness work is really interesting.'

'It must be lovely to have such a depth of knowledge. To have people asking for your advice and expertise and to know you can help.'

I take a sip of my wine. 'I'm not sure how much they'll be

asking my advice from now on,' I say. 'They might be scared I'll start lobbing fruit at the prosecution lawyer!'

'To be honest, your aim wasn't so good; they've not much to worry about!'

'But think of all that mess to clear up afterwards,' I say.

Kathleen laughs, her head on one side, one hand covering her mouth. It's a gesture that reminds me of someone, but I can't think who. 'Seriously,' she says. 'They'll soon forget about it. And you should too. Look forward, not backwards, that's my motto.'

'I'm sure I will in time.'

'You're a recognised name with an academic track record. And I'd bet money on it that your book is selling really well right now. Remember, there's no such thing as bad publicity.' She raises her glass in a salute before taking a drink. 'Hey, I just had a thought. You remember I mentioned my book group? You wouldn't consider joining us one evening for a Q and A–' She stops abruptly, reading my expression.

I know that she's trying to be nice, trying to encourage me to get back into the public eye in a safe environment, but I can't do it. I shake my head. 'No. Thank you, but not yet.'

'Sorry,' Kathleen says. 'Silly of me. I wasn't thinking.'

But it wasn't a thoughtless suggestion; it came from a good place. I haven't felt as relaxed with someone else for a long while.

'Even though the circumstances have been ...strange, I'm glad our paths crossed,' I tell her.

'The pleasure is mine,' she says.

Excerpt from chapter titled 'The reasons for Misidentification'

Reproduced from The Minefield of Memory by Amanda Dunstan

Without looking at your mobile phone, what is the third icon/app from the left on the second row of your home screen? Some people will know the answer immediately without needing to check, but most will not remember. Research suggests we look at our phones about 150 times a day and yet we don't always <u>see</u> what's in front of us.

Think back to a stranger you met recently for a brief interaction. Maybe the person who checked your ticket on the train, the cashier who served you in a supermarket or coffee shop, the individual who walked past you and said 'good morning'. Can you recall anything about their appearance? How confident are you that you'd recognise them again if shown a photograph?

There are a few things that research shows would help your memory:

- *The length of time you spent with the person – the longer the better;*
- *How long after the interaction you were asked to identify them – the sooner the better; and*
- *If the person has distinctive features which stick in your memory.*

When a crime happens there are many reasons that eyewitnesses may not have accurate recall of the perpetrator. It is an unusual situation, often of extreme stress particularly if there are weapons present. This has been shown to negatively impact our ability to recall details accurately. And of course, the criminal is not going to make the eyewitness' job easy: the perpetrator will probably have adapted their appearance in some way and disguised identifying features.

[Chapter continues]

Chapter Fifteen
Kit

The next time we arrange to meet I insist on buying dinner for Kathleen, a thank you for her kindness and support. We settle on a small but bustling bistro where there is less chance I might be recognised. The irony doesn't escape me – only a fortnight ago I was so flattered when a member of the public approached me to say they'd read my book. Now I'm hiding away, avoiding the possibility of someone wanting to harangue me about the McCollins case. In reality it's old news now; everyone – apart from me – has probably forgotten and moved on.

I arrive early and find a corner booth where I can see the room without being in the centre of the action. Once settled, handbag safely stashed, jacket folded, I scan my surroundings. No one is looking my way, so I relax and order a drink. There's a smell of garlic and spices wafting from the next table and when the waitress puts the still-warm bread on the table my stomach gurgles in anticipation.

It's a pleasant place, no doubt drawing trade from surrounding villages. Framed pictures are strung across one wall, probably by local artists. They're clustered close together from dado rail to ceiling, small labels under each giving the price. The way they're displayed reminds me of the paintings at the Summer Exhibition, at The RA in London. Phillip and I went to see the summer show once, the year Grayson Perry was curating – although that wasn't the particular attraction. We'd received a flyer from Don's ex-wife, Gita, who was thrilled that they'd accepted one of her paintings. Apparently, it was a huge accolade to be selected. Huge overblown flowers were generally her thing, thick paint and weird dark colours. I can't recall what her chosen painting looked like, but I do remember Phillip and I played 'guess the price', shocked by the ridiculous sums of money that quite badly executed works commanded.

'How much does a set of paints and brushes cost? We should invest twenty quid and both have a go at it. I'm sure I could knock up one like that,' Phillip had said, pointing at a painting that looked like it had been thrown together by an untalented child.

'Faux naïve,' I stated, as if I knew what I was talking about, when I'd actually heard the couple next to us discussing it in intelligent arty language.

'Art bollox,' Phillip had retorted.

Pulling myself back to the present, I keep an eye on the door as I sip my white wine spritzer, ready to hail Kathleen when she arrives. She's bang on time as I'd anticipated: she seems both organised and considerate from the little I've seen. I watch her shrug off her jacket, adding it to the coats on the rack by the door. She says something to the waiter, whatever it was causing him to beam a wide smile, before he points me out across the restaurant. She waves, smiling warmly, and edges her way between the crowded tables, before sliding onto the bench seat opposite me.

'It's good to see you looking more relaxed,' she says. She nods towards my wine glass. 'I hope you've not been waiting long. Have you had time to look at the menu?'

'Hmm. I was early. The salmon looks good. Specials are on the board.'

'Distance glasses for the board, reading glasses for the menu. The joys of middle age.' Kathleen checks out the chalkboard menu across the restaurant, then removes her glasses before searching in the large satchel she always carries. It's the first time I've seen her without glasses and there's something familiar about her face – a slight similarity to Jamie Lee Curtis maybe? But that could just be the cropped hair. And then there's her walk. As she crossed the restaurant, there was definitely something I recognised about the way she strode confidently towards me.

'This might sound odd but there's something about you that feels really familiar,' I say, 'I've had this feeling I know you from somewhere. Somewhere before all this. Were you one of my mature students when I taught at the university?'

'No.' Kathleen pulls out a leather purse, then a monogrammed glasses case, the LV of the brand shouting expensive. She continues to search for something in the depths of her bag. 'It was further back than that. Maybe that's *one* of the reasons you forgot. Hold on.' She pulls out an envelope which she passes across the table to me. 'I was going to raise it tonight.'

It's a small brown envelope, the glue on the flap no longer tacky. Curious, I open it carefully and peek inside. It holds a polaroid photo. I pull it out to look, turning it in the light to see better. It's a photo I've not seen before.

'The hairstyles weren't so flattering!' Kathleen says. I sense her watching me closely as I study the image.

There are three girls in their late teens or early twenties. The middle one has her arms slung casually round the shoulders of the other two, an open can of beer dangling in her right hand. It takes me a moment to recognise myself as the girl on the left. My face is almost obscured by an overlarge perm, reminiscent of Brian May from Queen. The hair style suggests university days – I would never have risked sporting such a style when I was still at home. This version of me from the past is half-turned away from the camera, distracted or averting her gaze it's hard to tell. But she looks uncomfortable, like she doesn't belong.

The other two girls have cigarettes hanging casually from their pouty lips, acting up for the photographer. On the far right with the Suzi Quatro haircut there's a flash of emotion as I recognise Lisa, the first person who'd befriended me when I went to University, who went on to become my closest friend, my first real crush. Lisa's trying to look tough, one eye closed to protect from the plume of cigarette smoke. She was never a natural smoker, often letting them burn out forgotten in an ash tray. It's clear she's acting a part. I turn my attention to the girl in the middle. Her head is on one side and she's staring straight at the camera with a look of challenge which conveys both confidence and cool.

Kit... It can't be.

I look from the photo to Kathleen. She rests her arms along the back of the bench dangling her wine glass in her right hand, pursing her lips, her head tipped sideways, adopting the same pose as the girl in the photo.

'Kit?' I study Kathleen's face, confused. 'You're Kit?'

'Yes. Well, Kathleen now. I'm sorry I didn't tell you before, but there's been so much going on in your life I thought I'd better give you some breathing space.'

'Oh goodness. You should have told me. It really is you!'

'Yes. It's been around thirty, thirty-five years... but yes, here we are.'

'Gosh. Give me a moment to think.' I look down at the photo again. 'When was this taken? I'm guessing when we were in second year?'

'I think so. Probably around 1987, '88 I guess, going by the hair,' Kathleen says.

'Thirty-five years. How did the time go so fast?' It's hard to relate this Kathleen in front of me with the young woman in the photo. I'm aware of a vague feeling of unease at this sudden arrival of the past in the present, but push it to one side. 'How did you find me?'

'I heard your talk on the radio and recognised your voice. I couldn't believe it was you at first. That's why I came to the book signing, to see for myself.'

'You should have introduced yourself then!'

'You were a bit busy with writing dedications at the time.'

The way her eyes crease as she smiles, her lips parting to show her teeth, suddenly seem more familiar.

I can't separate out the kaleidoscope of feelings I'm experiencing: a rush of curiosity, surprise – and an edge of discomfort – all tumbling over each other in a changing pattern that I can't process quickly enough in the moment. The shock of seeing Kit again after so many years; the realisation that this new friend was actually an old friend. Not recalling the fine details of our past, how or why exactly we lost touch.

'You've done really well for yourself, Amanda. You should be proud of all you've achieved. But then I'd have expected no less. You always were the bright one.'

'Oh, I don't know about that.'

'You were always in the library studying. Me and Lisa used to call you The Professor, don't you remember?'

'No. I didn't know that. Anyway, I never made it to the dizzy heights of professor so you overestimated my abilities I'm afraid.' A flash of memory comes back to me. 'Didn't Lisa used to call you Dodger? You were usually up to something or other, but always got away with it.'

'Not always,' Kathleen says ruefully.

I've so many questions bubbling up, I don't know where to start. 'Are you still in touch with Lisa? Do you know what she's doing now?' I try to sound casual, to keep the hopefulness out of my voice.

Kathleen shakes her head, no. She takes a sip of her wine, studying me over the glass. 'Not seen her since I left. If anyone would know where she is, I assumed it would be you.'

I'd not thought about those days for years, pushed them to the back of my mind, but now it's flooding back to me. A surge of emotions connected to that period of freedom: the thin slice of my life when I was away from parental demands and before the pressures of work, when I was free to indulge in the joy of learning and new experiences in their broadest sense. I'd learned a lot about the harshness of the real world and Kit had been a great driver of that.

When Kit had arrived at university, she was already a teenage mum with a toddler, Jed. She'd juggled her college studies with looking after him and working part-time in a local greasy spoon café. Luckily the college was supportive, rearranging some of the course elements to allow her flexibility. And of course, she was rarely short of a babysitter among the students wanting to earn a pound or two, or get her help with their course work. And the woman who lived in the flat upstairs didn't mind keeping an eye on him now and again. He was such a good-natured kid. I remember Jed well.

'And Jed. How's Jed?' I ask. He used to be like a windup toy, dashing about wildly before almost falling with exhaustion when the spring uncoiled. 'Do you remember I used to look after him sometimes when you and Lisa wanted to go clubbing? He was a sweet little chap. What's he doing now?'

Kathleen's smile disappears.

Something's wrong. 'He's okay, isn't he?'

Kathleen looks away, her eyes cast down.

'What is it? What's upset you?'

She sighs. 'Things didn't go well for me after I had to drop out of college.'

'But I thought you chose to leave? I assumed you just got fed up with the course.'

Kathleen leans forward, her elbows on the table, interlinking her fingers below her chin, staring directly at me, the intensity of her gaze unnerving. I try not to look away, waiting for her to say something. When she eventually speaks, the flat tone of her voice suggests statements rather than questions. 'You don't remember what happened. Didn't you and Lisa talk about it at the time? Do you really not remember…?'

My skin prickles with a dark feeling I've pushed to the

depths of my memory. She disappeared. One day there, gone the next. Even as I speak, I'm uncertain I want to hear what she has to say.

'Well...,' I start slowly. 'I remember we all lost touch at the end of second year. It was around the time of our exams.' I try to steer us to firmer ground. 'We were all going to share a flat in the final year, weren't we? But then you disappeared and Lisa failed her course and went home to her mum and dad...' I'm overcome by a heavy sense of sadness; a feeling of loneliness, of great loss and remorse. 'We should have kept in touch, but you left so suddenly and Lisa moved away...You know what it was like back then, before the internet, I had no way to track either of you down. I didn't know how to reach you – no phone number or address to write to... It was all a bit sudden as I recall.'

'That's pretty much what happened. But it was a bit more complicated than that. Don't you remember the last time you saw me, before I 'disappeared'?' Kit says.

Guilt rises in my throat. The buried memory of that afternoon clawing its way to the surface. I don't know what she knows. Did she see me watching through the window? Does she know what I witnessed?

'I'm sorry,' I say. 'I can't recall the details. Remind me what happened.'

Chapter Sixteen
And Then There Were Three

Before Kit had arrived on the scene, there had been me and Lisa.

I had never had a close friend at school: my goody-goody image coupled with introversion didn't make me the go-to playmate. Occasionally, nice-natured children would sit next to me at lunch, try to include me in their games, invite me to their homes after school, but inevitably, I would prove too quiet, too dull, too afraid of getting in trouble, and there'd be a reshuffle. At the time I'd never thought to question it. It was just how things were.

Nothing changed at secondary school, I just developed more hobbies. Immersed in my model railway I was quite happy, until my mother decided I was too solitary and enrolled me in Girl Guides. There I developed a schoolgirl obsession with the troop leader, a motherly figure who I wanted to impress. Conscious of my own mother's preferences in children, I became a silent helper and could be found stacking the chairs at the end of the meeting, handing out leaflets about the upcoming jumble sale, always watching for a chance to prove myself both capable and useful. It was a two-pronged tactic: the second arm of which required me to dedicate myself to badge collection and – thanks to the sheer number of badges I amassed – our Girl Guide Captain certainly noticed me, as she had to present them to me every other week.

Having fantasised for months about adoption, as unhappy children often do, my heart was broken when I found out the woman already had four children of her own – all girls – and no need for another. Instead of the hoped-for escape from my family, I was promoted to Patrol Second, a role which seemed to underline where I stood in life. Always second best.

It was a quiet, introverted teenager who arrived at university, knowing no one, knowing nothing about life, and with few expectations. So, when I met Lisa and we had something in common it was quite a shock. It took a while to realise we were of a type: both trying to keep the peace in our different ways, schooled in the art of complying/conforming (me) or kowtowing/ingratiating (Lisa). It felt like I'd found a soul-mate and I loved her for it – for the first time I'd found someone who appeared to be like me, and most importantly, liked me. We agreed on everything, never falling out about a decision: 'Shall we go to the library after lunch?' one would ask; 'Yes, that would be good,' the other would respond, immediately adapting their plans. To some it would have appeared dull, to me it was bliss: a partner in conformity rather than a partner in crime.

We had six months as best friends before Kit arrived on the scene.

Kit was different from the outset. Kit didn't ever talk about her past. She just arrived, landing part way through the first year with her young son, Jed, taking rooms in town, away from the watchful eyes of the academic advisors. She was several years older than the rest of us who'd come straight to university from school. Living away from our parents for the first time, we campus students wore each new experience like a badge, debating and comparing in excited voices. But Kit had no desire to play that game. She didn't need an audience, didn't seem to need others' acclaim, although people were often drawn to her.

Kit had grabbed life, sniffing out fun and new experiences, creating excitement when it didn't come to her; whereas I shied away, preferring my routines, doing as expected, determined to win my parents' approval by being the good girl; to reach at least a baseline of achievement, when my brother had already been deemed to have collected all the medals.

I was the type who kept inside my lane at the swimming pool, while Kit executed a perfect dive right under the 'NO splashing, NO running, NO diving' sign. I played it safe, leaving gigs early to get the last bus home, not taking up smoking because I knew the health risks and 'what if my parents found out'; not sleeping with boys because what if I'd got pregnant – I'd never have been forgiven. I was the studious 'Professor', my knowledge coming from hard work, my nose in a textbook at every opportunity, typed revision plans to help me learn and colour coded notebooks to help recall.

Meanwhile, Kit was naturally bright and just seemed to absorb the information by osmosis, hardly taking notes in lectures. She was 'Dodger', courting danger but usually avoiding any serious consequences.

It was in our second year that I started to notice changes in my relationship with Lisa. Small signs at first, but nonetheless heartbreaking. The seat I'd reserved for her in the optional evening lectures would remain empty. I'd be woken by the sound of stones hitting my bedroom window when she was locked out of our accommodation after the cut off time, then I'd creep down barefoot to let her in, to find her fizzing with excitement about the fun evening she'd had. Her clothes would smell of cigarette smoke and she'd started copying Kit in other ways, like drinking Guinness and getting her hair permed. While I didn't say anything, it felt like I was channelling a mute version of my mother, mentally criticising Lisa's every move, wound up in my envy of Lisa's closeness to Kit, my fear that she was pulling away from me.

It was when they started openly smoking dope in Kit's flat that I felt a line had been crossed. I wanted nothing to do with it. But it soon moved on from there. It became clear that Kit had the contacts, so other students started asking her to buy dope for them. She wasn't earning enough from her job in the café and the extra cash was a bonus. Ultimately, she'd said, it was all for Jed.

When I first found out about the dealing, I'd informed Lisa, expecting horror and outrage but Lisa merely went a bit red and said, 'You won't tell anyone, will you?'

That was when I knew I'd lost her. It was like losing a lover. Although there had never been anything physical between us, I'd found myself falling for Lisa, while wanting to *be* Kit: intelligent, free-spirited, loving and living life. Bottling my raging jealousy, I still hung out with them, pretending nothing was wrong, keeping a close eye on them as I played my role, trying to be one of the cool girls while unknowingly winning the accolade The Professor.

Chapter Seventeen
Misremembered

Kathleen suggests we go somewhere quieter for her to tell me why she disappeared. I assume it will be her story of that afternoon all those years ago, but I don't know if she was aware I was there. I pay for my drink and we leave the restaurant, our table quickly grabbed by a young couple who've been loitering by the door.

We walk in silence following a dirt track signposted to the Meadow Fields, a romantic name that leads to an open playground area surrounded by sparse trees, rather than the promised bucolic meadow. It isn't one of the modern open-air gyms, but more reminiscent of the simple parks of my childhood – a few swings, a slide, a climbing frame. The equipment looks tired, the paint worn through to the metal. I sit on the wooden bench at the side of the area ring-fenced for children, waiting for Kathleen to sit next to me and start her story, but she wanders over to the swings and lights a cigarette.

'I need to start out by saying I really don't blame you for anything that happened back then. I did for a while, but we were all young, we all made poor decisions at that time. There are no grudges – we're different people now. But you want to discuss it and I think we should clear the air so we can move on. I'd really hate for there to be a block between us.'

She inhales then tips her head back to blow a smoke ring above her head, where it rises like a cloudy halo. She's looking away from me, towards the trees as she says, 'Think back to thirty-five years ago. Do you remember the last time you saw me?'

Nothing comes to mind before that awful afternoon

when I saw her on the floor of her bedsit arguing with that man. For now, I'll assume she doesn't know I'd been there, watching. 'No,' I say. 'You just dropped out; one day you were there, the next gone.'

'Do you remember my bedsit?'

As she speaks, a mental map of the layout of Kit's flat pops into my head, the downstairs of a two up/two down. A street door to a shared hallway, stairs leading to the neighbour's upstairs flat, Kit's own door always on the latch as she kept losing the key. It's weird how much I can remember as I mentally walk through. A tiny toilet area was built in, crammed under the flight of stairs. There was an oven and cupboards in one corner; a patched sofa under the bay window, all squashed into the one room. Other than that, there was just a tiny backroom where Kit and Jed slept, his cot next to her bed, their clothes swinging on hangers from a washing line she'd strung up between the window and the door frame.

'Gosh yes.' I'm surprised by how much I recall. 'You had a lava lamp you'd rescued from a skip. It used to stand on the floor... I remember the red and purple swirling patterns on the TV screen when we tried to watch anything.' Strange what the brain chooses to store and spontaneously recall.

She takes another drag on her cigarette. She's standing up, leaning back against the seat of the swing. Seeing her like that, blowing smoke rings, backlit by the streetlight, she could almost be that young girl again. When she speaks her voice is emotionless, almost robotic. 'That was where you last saw me.'

How does she know I'd been there? Did she see me watching from across the road or does she know I witnessed the argument with that man?

'Saw you?'

She contemplates me in silence for a second and I try to hold her gaze as she says, 'I was lying on the floor.'

She knows. She must've seen me through the gap in the curtains. I cannot lie to her about being there. It's time to confess.

'Yes...,' I say. 'I remember now. I heard voices so I looked through the window.'

'What else do you remember?' Her tone is alarmingly casual.

'You were lying on the floor and...' It's uncomfortable to revisit that afternoon, to raise the details up from where I'd suppressed them decades ago. 'And Jed was crying. There was a man there. The two of you were arguing.' I'm recreating the scene as I speak, mentally outside the window of Kit's room. It's as if I'm directing a play, placing the actors and props in their correct places – not seeing exactly but more *knowing* where things were. There was Kit lying sprawled on the floor and Jed...

'Jed was there...on the floor next to you...' My heart beats faster as the memory crystallises and I begin to relive the fear I'd felt on that afternoon so many years ago.

'I was lying on the floor yes, but you've missed out the blood. You must have seen that. Head wounds bleed a lot.'

'Yes. Yes. That's right. At first I thought you were asleep. But then I realised you were hurt. It was such a shock, I couldn't work out what was going on.' Even as I say it, I know this is no excuse for my subsequent actions. 'The man... I assumed it was something to do with drugs.'

Kathleen says nothing, merely raising her eyebrows, encouraging me to continue.

'I didn't know what to do... You always kept that side of your life separate. I didn't want to interfere.'

She looks away, her eyes on the dried earth by her feet. 'I always wondered about why you didn't help me. Why you didn't come in and check I was okay after he'd left. Why you just abandoned me.'

I need her to understand that I'd truly wanted to help.

'I can't really remember the details...like I said, I think I didn't want to interfere. I know I ran to the phone box to get help.' I was mentally back there in the past, recalling the event as best I could: remembering the phone box, round the corner on the next street, the streetlamp above it always broken, sex workers' cards tucked around the sides of the framed dialling instructions.

'I phoned 999 but when the woman asked what service I didn't know what to say; whether to get an ambulance for you or ask for the police. I told her you'd been hurt, that there was a man in your flat and he was threatening you, but he'd gone now. I must've said I'd seen you moving so I thought you wouldn't need an ambulance...'

'So you asked for the police?'

'I don't recall. I think she said she was sending a police car straight away but that it didn't sound like you needed an ambulance...she said I should go back and check you were okay and wait with you until the police arrive.'

Kathleen throws the stub of her cigarette to the floor and grinds it out with her boot. She hooks her arms around the chains of the swing. 'But you didn't come back and check I was okay. You didn't sit with me, did you?' she speaks quietly. 'Things might have been so different if you'd come in and helped me.'

A sudden realisation hits me: she's right and I know why. I hadn't gone into the flat to help her as I should have – I'd feared guilt by association. I couldn't possibly be there with her when the police arrived. I couldn't be associated with a drug addict.

It's a shocking realisation, something I'd chosen to forget.

There's silence, a tightness in my chest and even as I ask the question – 'Can you tell me what happened?' – I don't want to hear what Kathleen will say next, fearing that it will be bad.

'Let me start by saying, you completely misinterpreted

what you saw that day. The man who was with me was my friend Miko from that greasy spoon where I'd been working. He'd just called round and found me in that state. I'd been hit by a cyclist on my way home, tripped and head butted the kerb, that's why my face was battered. I knew I had to collect Jed so I told the woman on the bike I was okay and limped back. But once I got inside the flat my head started spinning and I was seeing double. That's when Miko arrived and told me to lie on the floor with my legs up so I didn't faint.'

'That man was a friend? Then why was he going through all your cupboards and shouting at you?'

'He might have been shouting, I don't recall, but he wasn't shouting *at* me. He was probably panicking. He was looking for something to help me – I don't know, painkillers or ice or something to stop the bleeding.'

'But why did he suddenly run off like that?'

'He went to buy some bandages. I remember I asked him to take Jed with him because I wasn't safe to look after him in that state.'

'But... I waited outside... By the house opposite...' I've always believed I'd waited until I saw the police car pull up and knew Kit was safe. But now I'm not so sure. In my own carefully constructed memory of that afternoon I'd watched from across the street, willing the police to arrive before the man returned, thinking he was the person who had harmed Kit. In my version of events I'd stood there on guard, waiting for ages, constantly checking my watch unsure what to do if the man reappeared. And then the relief when the police eventually arrived: they would know how to help her. I believe I stayed there for another ten minutes or so, then, once I was sure she was safe, I'd caught the bus back, returning to my room. Never mentioning what had happened, or my inaction, to anyone. And as Kit hadn't seen me, she wouldn't recall me being there. Kit was safe and I was safe.

But I've actually no real recollection of what happened when the police arrived.

'So what did the police say?' I ask.

'They got there before Miko returned. They found me semiconscious still on the floor, Jed screaming the place down. All my stuff chucked out of the drawers on the floor... That's when things started to get worse.'

'What happened?'

'I won't bore you with details but they found some... gear. Miko had left his bag there and they assumed it was mine. They took me to the police station.'

I've no recollection of seeing her bundled into a police car. Had I actually been there when they arrived? If I had seen it happen, maybe I assumed they were taking her to hospital?

'They put me in a cell overnight after they got a doctor to check me over,' Kathleen continues. 'My mum was furious as she had to drive down to collect Jed and, to be honest, I think she encouraged them to keep me in. I was terrified I'd get a prison sentence... but they didn't press charges in the end. They were going to allocate me a social worker I think.'

'But why didn't you come back to university afterwards? Why did you just disappear?'

'I...' She lowers her head and I think she might be crying.

'Oh, Kathleen.'

'I just felt I'd messed up everything. I'd tried my hardest to earn money for me and Jed but I'd made such stupid decisions with the drugs and everything. And...and I thought maybe you'd called the police to get me in trouble. Then when you didn't come back to help me....Or to see me the next day to check I was okay, I...I felt so alone. Abandoned. It just felt like me and Jed against the world...I thought you'd tell everyone and it would turn them all against me and I just couldn't face it.'

'Oh God. I would never have done that,' I say. 'I'm so so sorry.'

Kathleen sniffs loudly and lifts her head to look at me, her eyes sad. 'We were just kids. You did your best. You couldn't have known the impact it would have… It still seems strange how the events of one afternoon can change so much. But a butterfly's wing flaps…'

I take a deep breath. 'What happened to you?' I'm unsure if I'm ready for what I might hear.

Chapter Eighteen
Kathleen's Story

'After I left University, my mum didn't think I was safe to look after Jed on my own. So, she took him for a couple of years to give me a chance to pull my life back together. But I wasted that chance. I'll admit, I was still taking drugs. Mum took charge of every decision about him as I wasn't deemed fit to look after him…And then Mum died – complications of her diabetes… Jed was five and I hardly knew him. He went into foster care.'

'Oh Kathleen.' I don't know what to say. I can only imagine how heart-broken she would have been. 'That must've been so tough. So much to deal with at such a young age.'

'I was a wreck for several years, completely off the rails – I'd lost everything that mattered to me: my mum, Jed, my only real friends, all hopes of a career that could help me pull myself up again and get Jed back.'

'What happened to Jed?'

'He was adopted in the end. I got in with a bad crowd and turned my back on him, figuring he'd be better off without me. I don't know where he is now.'

'Oh no. How awful.' I get up from the bench and walk over to kneel before her. 'I am so very sorry.'

That night I can't sleep, my mind running over the discussion we'd had that evening.

It completely recast the events of thirty-five years ago. Over the years I'd clearly edited my memory of the incident to fit in with my self-image, truly believing I'd waited until the police came to be sure Kit was in safe hands and wouldn't be further harmed by that man. Even though I now know this wasn't true, I can still conjure up the story of watching Kit's flat from across the road, imagine myself fidgeting from foot to foot, my arms wrapped around myself for comfort. But that wasn't what happened. Everything I thought about that afternoon is untrue.

Why hadn't I gone back to help Kit? Or to comfort poor Jed? It would have been the humane thing to do, let alone what a friend should do.

I realise now, that while I knew I *ought* to get help for Kit, I was *motivated* by self-protection. I'd not wanted to get involved: this was not my way of life, and as – I probably saw it then – should never have been my problem to resolve. Having heard Kathleen's story, with hindsight I can see that I'd done the minimum needed to salve my conscience, before scurrying back to the safety of my college room as quickly as I could. I'd needed to get as far away as possible, not wanting to risk being called in by the police who would undoubtedly want to investigate the evidence of drug selling. Questioning me on my involvement and what I knew.

And back then I'd had the tendency to spin everything into an impending disaster, predicting the bleakest outcome imaginable. Not happy with my imaginings of interrogation by the police, I'd no doubt have created an impending catastrophe: what if the man comes back and attacks her again while I'm still outside her flat? What if he kills her? What if a neighbour or someone has seen me watching? If they know I'm a witness I'll be called to court, to the inquest...

I could never have risked my parents finding out about any of it. They would have forced me to come home immediately, back under their watchful eyes. It would have been the end of my university days, the end of all my dreams.

But *why* had I misinterpreted what I saw and misremembered my role? Yes, it was decades ago but I'd clearly known the truth somewhere deep inside. Over the years I must've dusted off the story, changing it with each recall, until eventually I had a nicely polished version that I didn't need to think about anymore. In my version I'd done my best. But I'd fallen for that trick of memory that I schooled others to understand – I had rewritten history to fit my self-image.

At four in the morning I'm pacing my kitchen, a lukewarm cup of coffee in my hand. While I now understood *why* I'd behaved as I had all those years ago, I'm appalled by two things: that my constant need to win my parents approval had outweighed my humanity; and that the consequences of my self-serving actions had been life-changing for Kit and Jed.

All I'd needed to do was pop in and check she was okay, then I'd have known the true story and been able to do something practical to help her. Instead, far from helping, my actions had been the catalyst that damaged two lives irreversibly.

The flap of a butterfly's wings.

One thing I am sure of: now I know the truth, I have to make amends. I will do everything I can to be a supportive, loyal friend now. I have a lot to make up to Kathleen.

Excerpt from chapter titled 'The Controversy of Repressed Memory'

Reproduced from The Minefield of Memory by Amanda Dunstan

A repressed memory is defined as a memory which we <u>unconsciously</u> inhibit or suppress. Repressed memory is a highly contentious concept and researchers and clinical therapists can hold widely different opinions.

Some therapists believe that when we experience traumatic events we can be overwhelmed and so we subconsciously bury the memory. By doing this the individual doesn't recall the trauma ever happening. These therapists believe that therapy can help them to recover the original memories and previously unknown events can be discovered. This is believed to release the emotional pressure, by enabling the individual to work on their past with this new knowledge.

Scientists who conduct research in this area say there is no evidence to suggest this <u>unconscious</u> repression exists and while fine details of traumatic experiences are not always recalled, the event is remembered. Often the details of memories have simply been forgotten – someone may know an event occurred but only retain a vague idea of it. Alternatively, the individual may have <u>consciously</u> decided not to think about the memory, preferring to forget. They may edit their history to recall the event in a way which fits with their current self-image.

Scientific research has shown how easy it is to implant completely false memories, for example, of having committed a crime as a child, been attacked by an animal, or been abducted from a shopping centre. The subjects of these research studies start to believe the false memory they've been told and subsequently claim to 'remember' the events, embellishing the stories with surprising detail.

Imagine the consequences this could have in a court of law?

[Chapter continues.]

Chapter Nineteen
Photos

Kathleen filled me in on her life story in the days following that initial conversation in the park.

She'd managed to turn her life around in her mid-thirties when she had lived with a much older man for some years. Life had been good for her then, which was a relief to hear. No longer in touch with Jed, she'd decided not to have any more children, still carrying some guilt for how her behaviour had impacted his young life. Instead, she'd built on the experience she'd gained when she'd worked in the café: she enrolled in catering college and set up a small restaurant with her husband.

Eventually, they'd separated amicably and she never settled with anyone else, saying she preferred the single life. 'Cyndi Lauper had it right – girls just wanna have fun,' she told me. 'At least until the hips start giving out!'

It's strange to think back to that time so long ago, to recall how young and naïve we all were; how our lives were before us and we had no idea how things would turn out.

I'm surprised by how little I remember of those days at university. But if my head was always buried in a textbook maybe there was actually nothing much to recall outside of my psychology studies. I could define the Zeigarnik, Ovsiankina, and Barnum effects; the theories of attribution and cognitive dissonance; explain attachment theory and the work of Bowlby and Ainsworth – all these essential undergraduate psychology concepts remain lodged in my brain. But anything I'd experienced outside the academic requirements was long gone.

That photo Kathleen had shown me of the three of us together had sparked recognition, although no actual recall of the event: I had no idea where we'd been that day or who had taken the photo. But it did make me wonder if looking at old photographs could jog my memory further. Curious, I decided to test out my theory. On a mission to search out the past, I lower the loft ladder and clamber up into the attic to see what I can find.

Phillip had boarded the floor of the loft, so there was no risk of stepping in the wrong place and bringing the bedroom ceiling down, but I still move with caution. It smells like a library, not damp or mouldy, but of old paper; a familiar smell, comforting and safe. There are piles of dead cluster flies built up around the windows at either end of the building and I make a mental note to bring up the vacuum cleaner. That had been one of Phillip's annual jobs. But out of sight out of mind, I tend to forget about it until I make a foray to locate something stored in one of the boxes stacked floor to eaves along the sides of the loft.

The boxes are all labelled in black marker pen: MEDICAL; HOUSE PURCHASE; LEGAL (POA, WILLS, INSURANCE, ETC). I say a quiet thank you to Phillip for his organisation. When I'd had to deal with probate after his death it had made everything so much easier. Sadly, I've not maintained his administrative thoroughness; like cast off clothes around the laundry bin, the paperwork is now piled up near the relevant box, never quite making it into the files.

I find the archive box I'm looking for at the bottom of a stack of similar ones each marked with their contents, PHOTOS – holidays, PHOTOS – railway, PHOTOS – house. Moving them all to one side I pull out PHOTOS – Amanda's; the photographic history I'd brought with me to our relationship. Images featuring my family, my school and university days, the first home I'd ever bought, old friends and holidays. All those years before Phillip.

Unlike Phillip who had sorted and categorised, mine were still in the paper photo wallets, just as they'd been given to me at the chemist when they were developed. At best, I'd scribbled a date on the outside before stuffing them in plastic bags to join all my other photos in one huge jumble.

Sitting cross legged on the loft floor, I flick through the first few photos in each wallet as I take them from the box, quickly passing over childhood shots of beach holidays and Christmases with my family – too familiar to be of interest. I spend a while contemplating the shots of my first house when I find them, recalling my excitement at having a place of my own, with no one there to criticise or tell me what to do. There are 'before and after' shots of each room: completely empty (bar the patterned carpets) the day I moved in, and then furnished with my belongings, albeit in fairly bad taste in retrospect – largely second-hand pine standing on the previous owners' swirly/patterned carpets. It didn't matter to me one iota, I was just pleased it was mine. The years I spent there were happy ones.

The next set of photos causes conflicting jolts of emotion. Penny's "wedding". The first is the traditional group shot of the happy couple, flanked by all the guests. Everyone smiling as you'd expect, including me; third from the left in the back row.

Penny had been my second love. I loved her in a more mature, less angst-ridden way than Lisa. More grounded in reality. We were an unofficial couple for ten years living separately but seeing each other whenever we could. Occasionally we managed holidays abroad, went on day trips, accompanied each other as a 'plus one' to work events. But in all that time we never once shared Christmas together. That was ultimately the reason we split up; one final version of the long running December argument about logistics. It wasn't Christmas per se but what it represented – each year it underlined that I wouldn't (couldn't) introduce her to my parents and family.

She eventually decided she wanted 'a proper family life'

and within a year she had met Samantha and they were living together. There was, and is, no animosity between us, it was right for both of us and in due course I became a distant 'atheist godparent' to her eldest child.

Their unofficial pagan wedding ceremony was a surprise, in both the speed of their commitment and the nature of the event. A beautiful, romantic and very personal idea. It was actually a happy occasion for both of us, as I met Phillip at the reception. I scan the group photo to find him. He's slightly turned from the camera, half hidden behind some woman's hat, but I know it's him. He was an invitee on Samantha's side – a work friend as I recall. We were on the same table for the wedding feast. We chatted and when the barn dance started later that afternoon, he asked me to join him in the 'Hexam Reel', laughing with relief when I declined. It turned out he hated dancing as much as I do. We swapped phone numbers and agreed to get in touch. Our first date was afternoon tea in a railway carriage. So Penny's wedding nicely symbolised the shutting of one door and the opening of another.

I flick through the rest of this set and extract the photos with Phillip in, then place the others back in the box.

Ten minutes later after a few more detours, I'm a bit disappointed when I locate the relevant wallet for my undergraduate university days; its lack of thickness suggests there are fewer photos than I'd hoped. The first four or five are out of focus shots of buildings around the campus: the library, the halls of residence, one of the flight of steps to the students' union with two tiny people at the top of the stairs, who I assume are Kit and Lisa, although I'd need better light to be sure. There are photos of students in fancy dress, several of parties or in the halls of residence, but none of the people stand out in my memory. These strangers probably have similar photos of me that they can't place: *'Who's that girl there?' 'You know – she used to hang out at the library. What was her name?' 'Dunno. I don't think I've ever seen her before.'*

Casting these unknown people aside, my stomach flips as I turn over the next in the pack. It's a shot of Lisa and Kit. They are arm-in-arm, so close their perms look entangled, a mass of blonde and brown hair like some mad Medusa. But Lisa's face has been fiercely scribbled out with biro, the pressure so hard that the photo is ripped in places. I set this photo down beside me only to find the next is the same: a halo of blonde hair the only clue that it was Lisa standing with an armful of books outside the library. Her face has been obliterated. The third photo shows a group of students, including me. I'm sitting next to Kit both of us smiling broadly, but an unattached elbow shows that someone has been cut out from the side of the shot and I can guess who that would be. I don't recall the specific act that had been the catalyst for me to wreak this destruction, but this is an act of passionate emotion. Had my jealousy been that strong?

Looking at the photo of me sitting next to Kit, I remember how I'd secretly worshipped her. Her independence and wildness were traits I envied – back then I aspired to be like that. To speak my mind, to not care what others thought, to be proud of who I was. (Although given the feedback I'd received from my manager and colleagues when I worked at the university, maybe I took that a little too far as I got older.)

At first things had worked as gang of three, but soon it all changed. Lisa changed. Then the dope and drug dealing started and I was left by them both. Alone again (naturally) as Gilbert O'Sullivan sang in the 1970s.

The Professor with her textbooks.

Originally, I'd intended to show Kathleen the old photos when we next met up, but given how I'd defaced most of them, there aren't many to share.

A few days later, I invite her round for coffee and to my relief she readily agrees. It seems nothing has been changed by our conversation in the children's park and the subsequent sharing of her life story. 'Water under a bridge' she'd said and told me to stop apologising. But I am desperately aware of my need to make up for what I did – and didn't do – half a lifetime ago.

Once we're settled in my lounge, I hand over the photo of her and Lisa at the top of the flight of stairs outside the student union building.

'I might need a magnifying glass,' Kathleen says, 'Haven't you got any of us all together? It was always Leese, Kit and Mand wasn't it? The gang of three.'

I keep my thoughts to myself. It had been a 'uni' thing to shorten names to one syllable like that and while (to my face) they'd called me 'Mand', it was a role I played. In my head I'd always remained Amanda, a studious analytical girl, driven 'to achieve my potential' (Father's phrase) and make my parents as proud of me as they were of Dereck. In truth, once Kit came on the scene it was more often Leese and Kit, with me as an afterthought.

'Look,' I say, changing the subject, 'I found this. It's Jed as a baby.' I pass Kathleen a scuffed polaroid, the only one I have of the child.

The photo shows Kit hugging him. She's clutching him tight to her chest, her dark curls falling around her pale face. Her thin arm resting on Jed's chubby thigh.

'You look so young, Kathleen.'

'I was. We were.'

'You've never looked for him over all these years?'

'I had nothing to offer him.' She pauses. 'I suppose I was ashamed. And now too much time's gone by. He's got his life and I've got mine.'

'You couldn't have done more for him.' I'd admired the way she looked after him: the number of toys Jed had, how he always looked so smartly turned out, how Kit had worked so hard, juggling her university course with her job at the café and Jed's care. Now I realise that Kit had only started selling drugs to the other students when the café stopped her taking him into work with her. She'd had to give up her Saturday shift as she didn't have reliable childcare.

'You always put him first. You made sure he never went short.'

Kathleen snorts a laugh. 'Maybe I could've chosen a better way to do it.'

'He'd be proud of you. Getting on your feet and running your own business.'

She shrugs. 'Yes, I guess. I'm proud of my little shop and it's a lot of fun. But the business is hand to mouth. It's a struggle every month. I couldn't do it if I didn't get a huge rent reduction. Part of the council's scheme to stop high streets turning into charity run second hand clothes markets.'

'He'd probably be pleased if you found him and I bet he'd want to meet you. You could use one of those DNA sites. You know, make a connection through a common relative.' I was about to suggest maybe there was someone on his father's side of the family but stop myself in time. Kit had never mentioned the father when we were young and it had never been discussed. There probably was a good reason, but now was not the time to bring it up.

'No. I don't want to do the DNA thing.' Kathleen's tone is definite. 'I ruined Jed's life once and I don't want to disrupt whatever life he's made for himself…I'd be happy just to know he's okay. I don't want to meet him, but I suppose it would be nice to know how he's doing. That he's well and happy.'

'You've never thought to Google him? See if you can find a trace?' I have to admit that aside from my desire to bring them back together, I'm also curious to find out how things have worked out for him.

'Of course. But I always thought it best to leave well alone...

'We could do it now. Just take a look and see what we can find?'

She raises an eyebrow, shrugs slightly. 'I guess just looking wouldn't do any harm.'

I fetch notepaper and my laptop and we sit huddled at the kitchen table. I type *Jed Cooper* into the search bar.

I point at the screen, snorting a laugh. Google has pulled up pages about a 1960's movie. 'Marshall Jed Cooper? You named him after a character in a Clint Eastwood film?'

'No, he's named after my grandad Gerald.' Kit leans forward, peering at the screen, squinting to help her focus without her glasses. '*Hang 'Em High,*' she reads the title of the film aloud. Reaching over me, she moves the touch pad, clicking on the link. '"*When you hang a man, you better look at him*",' she reads the quote on the screen with an American drawl. 'Wise words. Hmm. Clint Eastwood didn't look too bad in those days that's for sure. Better with a hat on.' She sits back allowing me to take control of the search again.

'Well, who knew? *Hang 'Em High,*' she says to herself.

There are pages of sites relating to the film character, others for an actor called Jed Cooper, half a dozen on LinkedIn but no one of the right age; nothing for me to jot down on my pad of paper. On Facebook we try Ged, Gerard and Gerald with far more hits, Kathleen occasionally peering in to look more closely at a headshot. After half an hour Kathleen flops back in her chair, her expression resigned.

'He could've changed his name entirely. He's probably going by the name of his adopted family. We'll never find him.'

She rubs her forehead as if suddenly tired, and I wonder if I've upset her, forcing her to think about the past when she didn't want to go there. Making her think about all she's lost; not just time with Jed but maybe the chance for grandkids, a family life.

'Thank you for trying to help, but it's ok.' Kathleen puts her hand out and closes the top of the laptop. 'Maybe I'll look for him in my own time. Meanwhile, I'll choose to believe that was him – that man we just saw online. The one with the full head of hair. He was about the right age.' She nods her head firmly, a smile of acceptance on her lips. 'Yes. That's him in his smart suit and tie, a big look-at-me car in his own parking space outside his posh corner office, an efficient secretary that calls him Sir and a gorgeous wife who loves him to bits. That's him – a successful *Asset Manager*… whatever that means!'

Excerpt from chapter titled 'The process of forgetting'

Reproduced from The Minefield of Memory by Amanda Dunstan

Why do we forget? Unlike the proverbial elephant, we humans have a tendency to forget things we once knew. Some information we forget quickly – a phone number we don't need to remember, someone's name minutes after we've been introduced. Other facts we forget over time – the name of our junior school teacher, the postcode of a property we used to live in, how to do quadratic equations.

So, why does this happen? The inability to retrieve a memory is common. We know the answer we're striving for but it feels just out of reach. 'I know the word begins with S!' When this happens, a cue can help: a prompt from someone else, a relevant song or smell, or a photo to remind you. Active forgetting refers to the way in which the brain prunes information it has no use for. Akin to freeing space on a hard drive. We forget that which we rarely bother to retrieve.

Interference can also affect our ability to recall. This could be intrusion of another memory that is similar: either an old memory that gets confused with the new memory, or a new memory that makes it difficult to retrieve your original memory. For example, you may think you know the words of a poem or the lyrics of a song, but then you read the actual words and cannot now recall your mistaken version.

We also often fail to store the details accurately, remembering the gist of an experience rather than the complete story. We forget because we didn't attend to the full events at the time.

Forgetting irrelevant memories is a vital part of being human. In fact, Dr Andre Fenton describes forgetting as 'one of the most important things that brains will do'. Research suggests that by letting go of the information we don't need, we can become better at recalling the things that are more relevant to us!

[Chapter continues]

Chapter Twenty
Book Shop

Three weeks after the door-stepping incident the interest of the press has died down, a shoal of piranhas, all moving as one to focus on the latest scandal involving a social media influencer and a celebrity who should have known better. Consequently, my recently acquired antisocial habits – ignoring the doorbell, ducking behind the sofa at the sound of footsteps, and not picking up the phone – are currently focused on avoiding Don and his enthusiastic attentions, rather than hiding from journalists.

I'm planning another day of idleness and look out of the window to check the weather, my equivalent of a coin toss to decide what I might do that day. Sunshine equals walk into town (which I kid myself is part of my new daily exercise regime); clouds overhead equals clean the bathroom. My timing is lucky as I spot Don's car pulling up on the road outside my house. I don't have the energy to face him today. Fired up with a mission to get out of the house before he can get out of the car, I grab my handbag and coat and rush out of the front door. Busying myself with the lock, I hear his voice behind me.

'Oh. You're going out?'

I hold my arms wide and scan down my body as if surprised to find myself in outdoor garb rather than dressing gown and slippers. 'Gosh, yes! It appears so.'

'I didn't know.' His face is crestfallen and I almost feel sorry for him.

'No. But then you're not a mind reader.' Mentally I add *thankfully*.

'Where are you going? I could drive you there,' he says.

'Dentist.' I immediately regret furnishing him with a destination, even if a fabrication; it will only encourage him to ask again next time. 'That's fine thanks. I'm packed and ready to go as John Denver sang.'

'Ah yes. Leaving on a Jet Plane. I always preferred the Peter, Paul and Mary version. Did you know some people thought it was a protest song about the Vietnam war?'

His fascination with trivia is renowned and back in the day when we all used to go out for drinks together, we'd make a game of finding a topic he didn't know about. I think Phillip once stumped him with 'embroidery', but Don launched into a history of the Huguenots who may (or may not) have brought lace making to England in the 16th century.

'Vietnam war? Hmm, I'll remember that for the next pub quiz,' I say as I take a purposeful step towards my car. 'I really need to get on else I'll be late.

'Ah, yes. Are you in later?'

Bless him. It's his puppy dog enthusiasm that I find exhausting. He never gets the hint, like a dog keep returning with the ball long after the owner has lost the will. Don and I are not really friends, just two people whose paths have crossed many times over the years, our only connection through Phillip. And now Don is the only connection *to* the memories of Phillip, someone who knew him even better than I did. I don't dislike him and I guess I'm glad he's still in my life, but sometimes I'm bitter that he is here when Phillip isn't.

After reversing off the drive with a cheery conscience-salving wave goodbye, I have no idea where I'm really going to go. That's the problem when I have nothing to anchor my days – no court cases to work on in my role as an expert witness, no book signings or talks to promote *Minefield of Memory*...No one to chat to while sharing the cooking for lunch or dinner. I push the last thought from my mind, resolving to get back to my usual structured way of life. I will make a plan.

Driving aimlessly, I ponder options that could keep me busy.

There's the obvious activities: getting more involved with the railway museum; decorating the house; applying to give talks to the Women's Institute and University of the Third Age... Then there's entirely new avenues, like basket weaving or painting stained glass or studying medieval history...But there's a goalless element to these ideas. The big question is why? It's that Sunday afternoon feeling I had as a child: my homework and chores completed, nowhere to go, nothing on TV, just filling time. Just waiting for school the next day and the structure of timetables, the demands of bells, the safety of knowing what to wear and where to be. A place where the 'why' wasn't questioned.

Deep in thought and with no clear destination, I've been driving around the local area for almost an hour, before I find myself on the A-road out of town. I usually only come this way to go the retail park: my annual visit to M&S for a new winter coat or underwear; a trip to the garden centre to stock up on hardy annuals. It's the wrong time of year for either of those and I really don't need more summer clothes. At the next roundabout I decide to take a right turn for no reason other than I've never been that way before – there's spontaneity for you. It's then I clock the road sign, 'Ackleston, Stonebury , Upper Greenfield, Stanston.'

Stonebury. That's where Kathleen said she lives, in a flat above her shop. It's barely mid-morning, she is bound to be there. Half an hour to browse her stock of books, then maybe we could both go for a quick lunch. I have a plan! Spotting the next road sign to Stonebury, I pull off sharp left, earning a hoot from the car behind for failing to signal. Ever polite, I raise my hand in the typical British gesture of both thanks and sorry, rather than a V sign.

Stonebury is a bigger town than I'd envisaged. When Kathleen mentioned her bookshop I'd assumed a village environment. I drive around for a while scanning the store fronts for Kathleen's shop-cum-cafe, finally admitting defeat and stopping to type *bookshops* into Google maps. I'd assumed I would recognise the name of the shop if I saw it, but disappointingly nothing comes up apart from W H Smith. In the end, with nothing better to do, I tour the side roads, zig zagging across the main street until eventually I come across *A Book and A Brew*, tucked away at the end of a short alley that leads to the exit of a car park.

It is only once I've parked and walked back to the shop that I see it properly. It's nothing like I imagined. One side of the bay window is splattered with bird poo from roosting pigeons, clattering about in the gutter. The brown paint is peeling to expose the tan colour undercoat. A hand-painted wooden sign nailed above the window reads 'A Book & A Brew'. Beneath it the window display reminds me of a charity shop: stacks of used paperbacks, their spines broken, their pages flared. Handmade tent cards are propped at the bottom of each pile for identification – CRIME (with a template image of a gun); LOVE STORIES (a heart); ADVENTURE (a cowboy with a lasso)… In the centre stands a tray holding a coffee pot, china cups and a large vase of fresh lilies, this oasis of calm seemingly out of place; an island in a sea of yellow tinged paper.

Maybe this is a bad idea, dropping in unannounced. Kathleen may feel uncomfortable about me just turning up like this; not want me to see that everything is not as shipshape as she'd implied. It certainly doesn't look like a thriving business. As I'm contemplating what to do, there's a movement behind the window bay and I think I may have been spotted. Decision made.

The door needs a shove to open properly, warped by sun or rain, and I almost stumble into the shop when it gives. The ting of a hanging bell above the door announces my arrival and I catch a glimpse of a brown-haired woman as she rushes away from me, disappearing behind a curtain at the back of the room. A door slams.

I catch a flurry of movement in my peripheral vision and turn to see Kathleen. She's sitting behind a counter, some paperwork in her hand. She stands and takes a step towards me.

'Can I help? You can see we're in a bit of a state –' She stops suddenly, removing her reading glasses to peer at me. 'Amanda?'

'Sorry for arriving unannounced.' I feel strangely awkward, like I've caught someone in an inappropriate situation. The shop is best described as shabby: the floor tiles lifting, a bare bulb in the light fitting, a couple of Formica tables skirted by white plastic garden chairs. The sign on the till reads 'Cash only'. I look at anything rather than Kathleen, not wanting to see her embarrassment as I witness the truth of her business.

'I was passing and thought I might pop in,' I say.

'Passing?' she says, and I realise too late that one can't inadvertently drive past unless exiting the car park.

'I was on my way to the retail park and thought I'd take a short detour to say hello.'

There's a pause while we both register that she hadn't ever given me the address. I can see a flash of something in her eyes – wariness? – but it's gone in an instant.

'Yes, of course. Gosh. Well, welcome. It's good to see you. It was on my 'to do' list to give you a call for a return match after we met at your place.' She is burbling, filling the silence. 'What can I get you? Tea? Coffee? Only instant I'm afraid.'

Kathleen fusses over the kettle and mugs which she retrieves from under the counter, asking twice if I take sugar when she knows I don't. We sit at one of the tables and she pushes an open box of books to one side to make space for our cups.

'It's all a bit of a mess. There was a major water leak a

week or so ago and all the books were ruined. I'm waiting for the new stock to arrive but they can't confirm when it will be delivered.' She waves her hand towards the boxes. 'I've bought some second-hand books to keep us ticking over.'

'How awful,' I say.

'I've had to cancel all the events I had planned. It's so disappointing for us and the customers. Not to mention the authors. I know how much these publicity events mean to them.'

I mentally flinch, remembering how many of my promotional opportunities were suddenly cancelled after the McCollins tantrum incident.

Kathleen gets up to fetch a teaspoon to remove the teabags which have sunk to the bottom of the mugs. I don't recall ever seeing her disorganised and fidgety like this and I'm not sure if she's unsettled by my presence or the state the place is in. To my right, cardboard boxes are balanced awkwardly on top of each other, looking like they could spill their contents at any moment. Black rubbish sacks are piled in the far corner. Things appear so haphazard I'm unsure which is the new temporary stock coming and which the ruined stock waiting to be transported to the dump. A major leak flooding the place could explain the mess inside, but not the lack of care over the shopfront. I know she'd described the place as informal, but this is a shambles.

'I've sorted things out a bit. You should've seen it when it first happened,' Kathleen says, reading the expression on my face when she returns with a teaspoon and a damp cloth. She wipes down the tabletop, avoiding eye contact.

'You should've told me. I didn't know you were dealing with all this.' I gesticulate to our chaotic surroundings. 'It's a hell of a lot to sort out on your own.'

'You've had enough on your plate. You don't need my troubles too.'

'Seriously, I'd like to help. Let me do some sweeping up or

take stuff to the recycling centre for you. And I'm not bad with a paint brush either.'

Kathleen shakes her head. 'You're too kind. It's okay. I've got an offer of help from someone.' She crosses her fingers. 'Between us we'll soon get the job done. She's not here today but you'll probably meet her another time.'

I drink my tea as quickly as I can, planning to leave as soon as politely feasible, my idea of a lunch together abandoned. She'd sounded so proud of her plans for her business when we first spoke. All those dreams, all that hard work, swept away by a flood of water and bad luck.

Driving home I ponder this friend who is going to help her with the clean-up, surprised to experience a nip of jealousy. 'The past driving the present' as the therapists say, a familiar feeling from childhood popping up unbidden. A memory of always feeling the second-best friend in every relationship, passed over for someone less prickly, more easy-going, more fun.

But my adult head reminds me of the circumstances. Of course she has closer friends. And why should Kathleen see me as someone she can rely on for help after so many years? Particularly given the awful way our previous friendship had ended.

Chapter Twenty-One
Memorial Event

Don paces back and forth in my kitchen having caught me at home before I had time to fashion an excuse. The memorial event in Phillip's honour is now confirmed and Don is buzzing with nervous excitement as he explains the plans to me. It's as if he was the one being recognised in the ceremony at the Bridgeton Railway Museum. I wish he'd sit down and not keep bobbing back and forth across my field of vision.

'You will come along, won't you? The Mayor will be there and they've arranged quite a do.' He takes his glasses off and rubs them on his jumper, probably not wanting to see my reaction. He just told me Phillip's name is to be on the building and then slipped in the news that it is definite about the ribbon cutting ceremony. They want me to do it.

I widen my eyes at him, hoping this conveys everything I'm restraining myself from saying.

Don puts his glasses back on in that clumsy schoolboy way he has: gripping the frames with two hands, his fingers smearing the lenses he's just wiped and still managing to end up with them sitting lopsided on his nose. His awkwardness is probably endearing to some people, the motherly types who would wipe a child's face with a spit soaked hanky, or straighten their partner's tie before brushing lint from their shoulder. It just makes me irrationally irritated and I try to summon Phillip's level of tolerance.

'Why now?' I say.

Don stares at me, his head on one side like a curious sparrow. 'Wh.. wh.. what do you mean? It's to open the memorial.'

'Why do they want to hold a memorial now? Phillip's been dead five years. Why now?'

'I don't –'

'Publicity. An article in the local press. That's why. They need money for their planned museum extension and they're trying to drag more people in. I bet their visitor numbers have crashed since Covid. It's nothing to do with Phillip, or celebrating all he did for them over the years.'

Don's mouth hangs open and he runs his hand through his hair so it stands cockatoo-like, flustered by my response. 'But you will come? You must come.'

'There's no *must* about it. But I will come. I will shake hands and smile and be gracious, just as everyone would expect.' Although given my earlier tantrum with the press I'm not sure that such pleasantness *is* what people would expect from me.

But I'll do it. For Phillip.

I hadn't intended to tell Kathleen, knowing she's still immersed in all the work to clean up and relaunch the bookshop. But it comes up in one of those 'are you free for coffee on Thursday?' phone conversations, and I feel obliged to confess to my true whereabouts rather than just hide behind a shield of feigned busyness, like I frequently do with Don.

'To be honest, I'm not even sure what will happen at the ceremony. I'm guessing a bit of a speech, followed by luke-warm tea and digestives. Maybe a selection of Mother's Pride sandwiches cut into quarters – your choice of ham, cheese, or for those who like the more exotic, cheese *and* ham. Possibly crisps if they really push the boat out.'

'You didn't tell me about all this. I love a cheese and ham sandwich.'

'I didn't mention it – the railway stuff – because most people aren't interested. Most normal people that is.'

'I could think of plenty of more boring hobbies... Stamp

collecting, fishing, making crocheted hats. Railway memorabilia is interesting – it's part of our history after all.'

'I'll be glad when it's over to be honest.'

'Are you going with a friend?' she asks.

'I'll know people there…'

'Your tone suggests they aren't people you'd usually choose to spend time with.' She laughs.

'My husband's old friend, Don, will be there. I know him better than most of them, but he's a bit…' I pause, unsure whether to describe Don's unwanted attentions: how to convey the anxious looks, the concerned questions, the feeling of being hounded that he induces. 'I guess he worries about me. But he fusses too much…He means well, but to be honest it's going to be stressful enough for me… I could do without him following me around acting as a chaperone.'

'I'm free on Thursday. I could come with you if you like. Maybe act as a buffer? Keep this Don chap busy so you can dunk your digestive without hassle. It would be interesting – a new experience for me. And a break from paperwork.' Kathleen's smile is encouraging. 'And who knows, I might get to chat to the Mayor. I'd love to get her involved in some sort of publicity for the bookshop – once I've got everything sorted out again.'

On the morning of the event, I change three times before I feel comfortable with my outfit. I cycle through a smart skirt and jacket that I used to wear to court, but reject that as too formal; then the dress I'd worn on my first proper date with Phillip, brought out for our anniversary celebrations every year since – this railway event was in his honour after all and it seems fitting. But smoothing down the patterned fabric of the skirt, the prick of sadness behind my eyes makes me put it back on the hanger without even looking at myself in the mirror. I finally settle on understated black trousers, a plain cotton top and M&S jacket, my go-to comfort clothing. My invisibility cloak.

Kathleen and I travel together. The car is filled with companionable silence rather than the anxious running commentary I would have suffered with Don. Kathleen's presence is calming.

True to my word, at the Museum I shake hands, smile, and make small talk. I admire the new model railway layout, a loop of tracks meandering around most of one of the sheds. I compliment the arrangement of old signage, one of which has been restored by Will of 'The Repair Shop' fame apparently. *'He's very good with wood as well as being easy on the eye – made for TV'* as the Treasurer informs me, her foghorn level aside resulting in an unhappy glance from her husband. I agree a date to deliver some of the memorabilia Phillip kept stored in our garage, as I'd promised years ago before Covid shut everything down. Meanwhile, Kathleen does a spectacular job of keeping Don at bay, towing him round the museum to show her various exhibits, her face animated as she interrogates him on provenance, history and purpose.

The ribbon cutting is as arduous as I imagined. In front of a small crowd of staff and visitors, the Mayor and I are required to pose for 'official' photos. I can imagine the resulting montage, carefully labelled and mounted in the ticket area: both of us clutching the red velvet cushion on which the scissors sit; the Mayor lifting the scissors and presenting them to me so I can officially open the building which we've all been looking round for the past hour; and then everyone duly celebrating that the ribbon has been successfully cut without incident, toasting our efforts with thimble-size portions of warm Prosecco. Who would have thought snipping a bit of fabric in two could be such a performance?

'I'm surprised we weren't asked to do a risk assessment and a rehearsal beforehand,' I whisper to Kathleen.

The building named, we return inside where the clingfilm barrier is removed from the refreshments. 'Cheese and ham, my favourite,' Kathleen says loudly and I stifle a laugh as she winks at me.

We've all been socialising for a while, evidenced by the empty crisp bowls, and my thoughts have turned to how to make an exit, when I'm unexpectedly called on for one more task. It's time to unveil a plaque installed in the hallway of the newly named building. A party of people cluster behind me, cameras once more at the ready as I reach for the cord which will draw the curtain aside. I've not seen the plaque and I'm anticipating a few short lines of text, (probably written by Don), describing Phillip's contribution to the Museum. Something in general terms:

> In Memory of Phillip Brownfield.
>
> Trustee from 2000 to 2019
>
> Valued colleague and friend

What I hadn't expected is a photo of Phillip.

Don must've given them a copy.

In the shot Phillip is grinning widely, his favourite blue v-neck jumper over a checked shirt, the collar unbuttoned. His hand rests on a red wooden sign which reads 'WHISTLE UNTIL CROSSING REACHED' in large hand-painted white letters. I'd found that sign in a junk yard, a quirky gift for his 65th birthday, knowing he'd be pleased with this memorabilia from the age of steam travel. He'd hung it in our back garden, near the railway-sleeper bridge that spanned the pond, jokingly whistling as he took me to inspect his work. I'd taken this photo of him myself. The weather had been glorious. We'd linked arms and walked around the garden, admiring the orange roses, the yellow laburnum, the purple buddleia. We'd opened a bottle of wine and sat on the patio, drinking until the sun spread a red glow on the horizon. Needing nothing more in our lives than that.

I become aware of clapping behind me. How many seconds have I been standing frozen, lost in my memory of Phillip? Tears in my eyes, I swallow hard, unable to turn around and face an audience and unsure of my next move. Sensing someone beside me, I lower my head to wipe my eyes, not wanting anyone to see my emotional reaction.

There's a quiet whisper in my ear, 'It's okay. Stay there.' It's Kathleen. Then louder, for the benefit of those around us, Kathleen continues, 'Gosh, I'd not realised he was a trustee for nearly twenty years. Imagine that! He must've seen some changes. When was the Museum first opened?' The latter comment directed to the Chair who's been itching for a chance to address the group since the sandwiches and crisps were passed round. As he expands on the history of the venue and answers questions from the assembled crowd, Kathleen gently steers me to the side of the room.

'Can I get you anything, or do you want to use this as an excuse to leave?'

'Could you thank them but say I've got a migraine and have to go?'

Minutes later the two of us slip out through a side door just as the Chair was segueing into a speech about 'the need to find new opportunities for ongoing finance in these challenging times'.

'Thank you. Thank you for rescuing me. I couldn't...' I tail off.

'It's okay. I get it,' Kathleen says. 'I know you'd rescue me if I needed it. It's what friends are for. To be there when you need help.'

Chapter Twenty-Two
Flashback

A lot has been stirred up for me in the past few weeks what with the memorial for Phillip and getting to know Kathleen again after so many years. I've been getting more of those spontaneous flashbacks recently, most of them small reminders of our time at college. Inconsequential memories, popping up unbidden and gone in an instant: the Charles and Diana biscuit tin in Lisa's room on campus; the leather jacket Kit customised to be more fitting for a New Romantic; the narrow corridor which led to my bedroom/study.

One morning at my kitchen table I sit contemplating the few photos I'd found from those university days. Even though I know it's unlikely, I wonder if there could be another way into my memories. On a large sheet of paper I map out a timeline, hoping the concrete dates and events might form a scaffold for me to jog more detailed recollections from the dusty alcoves where they might lay hidden.

1985 – First year.

Arriving at the University. I know I travelled by train, lugging a huge suitcase and rucksack containing everything Mother told me I'd need. I remember other students in the carpark, hugging their parents and crying, but I don't recall feeling any sadness myself at leaving home. More likely relief.

My room on campus. I pause trying to recall the spatial layout of the room. A narrow bed. Wardrobe. Desk and chair. Was there a sink? I'd left my walls bare, until I saw that all the other girls had pinned up posters. Then I made a trip to Athena and bought a poster of a Victorian steam train… in the line drawing the bridge has collapsed and the train has been jettisoned into a river below, a crowd of bowler hatted men pointing at the wreck. It was only when I'd hung it on my wall that I noticed the words 'Oh shit!' in tiny print. It felt slightly rebellious – I would never have had a poster like that at home.

I continue jotting down anything that comes into my head in a kind of mind map.

Lectures. Studying. Having studied science subjects and enjoyed biology and maths, I'd found the lack of concrete answers in psychology frustrating. Why were there six theories of memory? Why couldn't they settle on one? I'd turned up on time for every lecture, attended every seminar discussion but it took most of the first term for my frustration to abate.

I realise I'm skirting around the most important event that happened to me in that first term.

Meeting Lisa.

I'd noticed Lisa in the lectures before I knew her name. She was taking copious notes and I liked the way she chewed on the end of her biro when she was thinking. Strange to look back, but that's what made me decide Lisa seemed the type of girl I could befriend: studious, but not perfect. Of course, not being a natural at friendships I'd watched and waited for an opening. It came in the form of a campus cat. Lisa was walking ahead of me and stopped to look up into a tree. Following her gaze I could see she was looking at a cat. She'd said something to the effect of, 'I think it's stuck.' She wanted to call the porter to rescue it. I can't recall what happened to the cat – it probably jumped down while we were talking – but I still remember Lisa's green/grey eyes, how I'd watched Lisa's lips as she spoke, how it felt like we were meant to be friends for ever.

1986 First year, 2nd term.
  Kit.

Kit was like no one I'd ever met before; single mothers didn't feature in my middle-class upbringing. Although we didn't know about Jed in the beginning. We'd taken pity on Kit arriving in January, three months after everyone else had settled in and got used to the rhythm of student life. Lisa and I had shown her how to register for the library, helped her sign up for the student union, photocopied our notes from the first term for her. Kit had been really touched by these gestures of kindness and we'd quickly become a gang of three – well, three and a half if you counted Jed.

Those few months were the happiest terms of all. The three of us just seemed to slot together so easily then. Just as we helped Kit to find her way, she was equally kind and thoughtful to us. When it was coming up to the May Ball, Kit was excited for all of us to go, but I wasn't at all sure it was my thing, the whole idea of getting dressed up in fancy frocks being my main objection; I had no idea what to wear.

When Kit heard, she took me under her wing. 'Come on,' she said. 'We're going dress shopping. It will be fun.'

She wouldn't hear 'no'.

She took me to shops I'd never been in before – Chelsea Girl, Tammy Girl, C&A – Mother having always selected most of my clothes from the outlets where she bought her own. (I was an M&S woman way before my time.) It was daunting: not understanding what would suit me and being confronted with so much choice. Kit pulled things off the racks and held them against me giving a running commentary: 'Nope, makes you look too mousey with your hair'; 'Not bad at all, brings out your eyes'; 'Hmm, okay we should go for more of this colour, that works with your skin tones.' She'd spin me round to the mirror so I could see anything she thought 'might work', fluffing out my hair around my shoulders, giving me instructions on how to stand, before accompanying me to the changing rooms with arm loads of outfits for us both to try on. It was like having my own personal stylist.

In the end we stood side-by-side in front of the mirror and agreed we'd found the perfect dresses. Mine was grey/black, loose fitting and sleeveless ('lovely arms, but better shave your pits!'), fell just below the knee, with an appliquéd long cream jacket. Kit had selected something surprisingly elegant, when I'd have expected something more Madonna or New Romantic: a long emerald green dress with a square neckline.

'Gorgeous,' she said, blowing a kiss at our reflections in the mirror. And for once, I actually felt it.

But when we came out of the changing rooms she left her dress on the rack. 'But it looked lovely. Don't you like it?' I asked her.

'No, it's not that. I can't afford these prices. Don't worry, I'll get something from the church jumble sale on Saturday. They'll have some good stuff I can easily alter. I'll be the belle of the ball!'

It took some arguing but in the end I bought the dress for her: I had money left at the end of each term as I rarely spent my full allowance. I couldn't have her being Cinderella after she'd gone out of her way to help me.

The evening before the May Ball Lisa coloured our hair red with a temporary dye that Kit had bought in the market. She practised fashioning our hair in a punky version of an up do and all three of us looked so happy, so young and full of promise. I was the happiest I could remember, there, in that moment having fun with my two best friends.

On the night itself we wandered around the building, chatting, eating, dancing (Kit) or swaying to the music (me and Lisa), or just sitting and people watching...the evening passed so quickly. At midnight, giddy on excitement, laughter and alcohol, we took our shoes off and Kit led us away from the crowds, down to the river to watch the fireworks, Lisa bouncing between us, assuring us in slurred tones, 'I lurve you. I really really lurve you two. You're my very best f'ends.'

She lay down on the grass and promptly fell into a snoring sleep, while Kit and I sat on the bank near a moored rowing boat and she pointed out stars. I can't now recall why but for some reason I suggested we get in the boat. Maybe I thought it would be nice to feel the gentle rocking as we stargazed? Maybe I wanted to appear adventurous, a little reckless? Or most likely I'd just had more than my personal limit of two alcoholic drinks?

Kit had shrugged her agreement and started tying up her long frock with a ribbon from her hair so she could attempt the venture more easily. Meanwhile, I set off full of enthusiasm. I edged my way into the boat but hadn't expected it to rock about so much and soon lost my balance. With all my flailing about I managed to overturn it and ended up tipped out into the freezing cold water. As I tried to stand my feet sank in silt, sinking further the more I struggled. I started to panic, tears rolling down my face. 'Help me! Help me!'

Kit didn't hesitate: she strode straight into the water towards me and wrapped me in her arms. 'Shhh. It's okay, Mand. I'm here too. We're okay. We're going to be okay.'

The commotion brought a small knot of people from the main building, including one of the security guards. They quickly got us out of the river but then there was a lecture about us having messed about with the boat. 'I, I, I'm ssssorry,' I stuttered through chattering teeth.

Kit stepped forward. 'It's my fault. It was my idea. The stars are so bright tonight and I just thought it would be so lovely to see them from the river. It's been such a perfect evening and I thought it would be a beautiful way to round it off. We really didn't mean any harm.' Already charming them, she switched on a soft apologetic expression. 'I am so sorry.'

As I recall, the security man ended up almost apologising himself he was so bewitched. He walked Kit back to the main building, Kit chatting all the while. One of the other men put his jacket round my shoulders and his girlfriend woke Lisa who promptly sung a slurred, hiccoughing version of 'Happy Birthday to You' for no apparent reason.

The next day, the three of us took our dresses down to the campus laundry and sat there recapping our memories of the evening, polishing and embellishing every event until my five seconds in the river became an attack by an overgrown trout. We laughed so much we didn't care when the dresses came out of the wash shrunken and miscoloured because we'd not read the washing instructions for delicates.

'Life is a bowl of cherries,' Kit said.

If only everything could have stayed like that.

1986 Oct onwards, 2nd year.

This is where my memory is even vaguer. Knowing that second year exam results counted towards the final grade, whereas first year didn't, I suspect I was laser-focused on my studies.

Things must have been okay between the three of us for the initial months of that second academic year, as we'd definitely planned to rent a place together in the final year. Maybe it was my obsession with my studies – saying 'no' to one too many suggested nights out? Offering to babysit when I should have joined the two of them? Maybe that was what led to Lisa and Kit becoming so close?

Before I get maudlin, I decide I've spent long enough in the past for one day. I have my tax return to complete. It's time to return to the present. Stretching, I shake the past from my bones and go to put the kettle on.

It's a couple of days later – in the hairdresser of all places – that I have a more disturbing memory, prompted by a record I hear out of the blue. I'm getting my hair tidied up and Stacey, my hairdresser, is just trimming my fringe when a song comes on the radio and flips me right back to the past.

With the prompt of the music, a whole memory unfolds unbidden.

It had been a wet and miserable afternoon and I couldn't find Lisa in the library, so I got the bus to Kit's assuming she'd be there. The door to Kit's bedsit was unlocked as usual and I could hear music – this song – coming from the small bedroom which Kit shared with Jed. But that day she was in there with Lisa. They were lying next to each other on the bed. Both were leaning back against the headboard, Kit's denim clad leg casually resting over Lisa's as they passed a joint between them, giggling and singing along to the record. They were so wrapped up in the lyrics and each other that they were completely unaware of me; spying silently through the crack in the door, needing to watch but not wanting to see. When the song finished Kit kissed Lisa on the lips. I was so shocked I gasped out loud. I turned and ran, not worrying whether they heard me. And I didn't stop running all the way back to campus, my tears mingling with the rain.

Second year. That must've been second year. When Kit started on the drugs.

'What was that song?' I ask Stacey as the record finishes.

'Madonna. Open Your Heart. I saw her at Wembley. Can't believe she's still going strong.'

The nail technician chips in, 'More energy than I've got and I'm half her age.'

Against my better judgement, I look up the lyrics on my

phone, discover it's a song about passion and love and getting what you want. I'm hit by the same wall of pain that I'd experienced all those years ago. The gang of three was really two plus one. As usual I had been on the outside looking in.

But that was long ago. We're different people now. All jealousy must be left behind, where it belongs.

Excerpt from chapter titled 'Jealous Minds'

Reproduced from The Minefield of Memory by Amanda Dunstan

Our emotions are subjective. You may watch the same film as a friend but both come away with a different reaction – one bored to tears by it, the other having enjoyed every moment. Objectively you experienced the same event, but you each bring a different personal history to the situation, hold different values and beliefs, and experience different emotions.

How does this impact memory? When we have an experience, we pay attention to the things that interest us and matter most to us. Research shows that emotional experiences are easier to remember and will impact how well and how much we can recall after the event. Notice what you notice, as that's what you'll remember.

Let's take a specific emotion as an example: Jealousy. Jealousy is often defined as a perceived threat causing a fear of losing what you have.

Imagine a situation: A is often jealous and witnesses their partner, B talking with C at a party. A's jealousy causes them to focus on the interaction between B and C, looking for evidence to support their suspicions. Are they flirting? Are they showing too much interest in each other?

Their fear of losing their partner will result in a jealous reaction and they will recall any relevant evidence which backs up their interpretation, remembering these comments or behaviours better than other events that occurred at the party.

As a witness to the event, A's memory of what they saw and heard will <u>not</u> be impartial.

[Chapter continues]

Chapter Twenty-Three
Memorabilia

It is only a few days after the memorial ceremony when Don gets in touch again. He wants to come round to collect the rest of the railway memorabilia. Over all these years I've never got round to looking through it, never feeling quite ready to sort Phillip's collection. But with recent events it seems like a good time.

Kathleen is surprisingly upbeat when I phone to see how she's getting on with 'the great clear up' (as she terms it). 'I've sorted more of the ruined stock and I'm one step nearer to getting rid of it, even though it breaks my heart. Anyways, I've got a plan to make a plan to take it to the recycling centre sometime this week,' she jokes. 'What are you up to?'

I casually mention that Don is coming round that afternoon to sort the wheat from the chaff in my garage and she seems keen to join us to help.

'You fancy *another* afternoon with Don?' I say, laughing.

'Beats an afternoon digging through paperwork for the shop. I've got to sort out the insurance and you know I'm not one for numbers and detail.'

'Okay, if you're sure. He'll be more manageable if you lend a hand. But there will definitely be spiders and maybe mice – so you've been warned.'

'They hold no fear for me!' Kathleen says.

'Wear your old clothes,' I say. 'Come round the back. I'll be out in the garage getting started.'

While Kathleen follows my advice on what to wear, she turns up looking like she's stepped out of the pages of a DIY article in the Sunday supplements. An open shirt with the sleeves rolled up over a vest top; faded jeans with the odd telltale paint spot; her hair tousled and a light touch of make-up. It is effortless chic, whereas I look more like a street sleeper: my hair in a makeshift turban to keep it out of my eyes; one of Phillip's old t-shirts paired with my gardening shorts; my feet clad in battered crocs. We are like the before and after on a restyling TV programme.

As we sort the memorabilia I hold things up to show Don, seeking his advice on the items the Bridgeton Museum might want.

'Definitely these,' he says, having flicked through several albums of photos of the rebuild of Liverpool Street Station. '1986 these were taken. They knocked down Broad Street Station to build the shopping complex and refurbish the platforms.' I catch a glimpse of Kathleen's expression and roll my eyes as he continues describing the finer details of the rebuild.

'Surely this isn't worth keeping?' Kathleen asks as she passes Don a metal sign for the Gentlemen's toilets. He expounds on the value of all old signage as if on the Antiques Roadshow, although to be fair he does know his stuff. He seems to puff up when she asks him a question, chest out like a pigeon strutting around a potential mate.

Through the afternoon I notice that Don manages to spot every opportunity to help Kathleen; she only has to look at a heavy crate or manoeuvre an awkward object and he is at her side offering to assist. His display of manliness is only spoilt when several mice skitter from under some boxes and he lets out a yelp like a character in a cartoon as he leaps to his feet.

Kathleen offers him moral support by telling an anecdote about how she'd tried to herd a rat from the back of the shop with a broom. 'I made a Heath Robinson barrier from an old draft excluder and a roll of kitchen towel. But the damn thing launched itself from the dark, leaping over my barricade like it was in a steeplechase. And it was coming straight towards me!'

Don shudders. 'Why didn't you hit it with the broom?'

'Aw, no. That would be cruel. It was probably just scared. Anyway, I was so shocked to see it coming straight at me that I fell on my backside and whacked myself on the head with the broom handle. I swear it did a jaunty flick of its tail as it darted out of the door.'

'Horrid things.' Don has his back pressed to the wall, his eyes scanning the floor. I'm half tempted to screech and jump in the air pretending to see another mouse, but given his panic I don't want to risk upsetting him further.

'They're quite cute really, but I wouldn't want them in my home again,' Kathleen says lifting a box, not noticing Don visibly recoiling at the off chance of another encounter with a dislodged rodent. 'They nibble everything and don't get me started on the droppings.'

Despite her good-humoured attempts to jolly him along, Don still seems all of a tither over the mice and offers to fetch soft drinks from the kitchen before steeling himself to re-enter the garage.

'He's nice,' Kathleen says, watching as he heads for my kitchen.

'He's good hearted.' I can't deny that. I'm so used to him by now that it's hard for me to see him through her eyes. 'He'd do anything for anyone.'

Kathleen watches until he disappears through the kitchen door, then turns her attention back to a black plastic bin liner that she'd been about to lift down before the mouse incident.

'What's in this?' she says.

It's quite bulky but the contents are obviously light as she easily lifts it down, holding it with one hand to cover her mouth as she starts coughing from the disturbance of dust. Opening the bag, she peers inside. 'I think it's a kite.'

'Gosh. I've not seen that for years.' I hold out my hands to take the bag. 'We were on a driving holiday around Wales and came across this kite flying festival. Phillip bought it for a bit of fun.'

'A kite festival? Who knew there was such a thing!' I hold the bag while Kathleen disinters the multicoloured kite, its long tail trailing in loops on the ground at her feet.

'I'd forgotten all about it. They had really fancy versions at the festival. All sorts of shapes. Dragons, an octopus… that kind of thing. They even had one like a train. We bought this from a stall – the fanciest one they had for sale.'

'Shall we give it a go?' Kathleen asks, grinning as she unravels the strings. 'Come and help me. If you hold the tail up, I can run down the road with it and see if I can get it flying.'

I wince, thinking of the impression the neighbours already have of me. 'Maybe the back garden rather than the road!'

By the time Don returns with glasses of iced orange juice, Kathleen is running barefoot down the lawn with the kite trailing behind her. He breaks into a broad grin and his eyes light up as he watches her and we both applaud her efforts.

'Come on, Don. It's your turn!' she says, holding out the kite to him. He pulls a fake look of horror, miming Munch's The Scream, but allows himself to be enticed into having a go as Kathleen places his hands on the cross bars of the kite and explains what he needs to do. Watching the two of them, a sense of warmth and well-being envelops me. We all laugh ourselves silly at their attempts to get the thing flying and it's the most fun I've had in years.

Later, when we've loaded Don's car with items for the museum and made two piles for the charity shops and the dump, I thank Kathleen before she leaves.

On her way out, she hugs Don, standing on tiptoe to give

him a kiss on both cheeks. Unaccustomed to this type of affection, there's an awkward clash in the middle and a smear of lipstick left on the tip of his nose. Kathleen laughs, reaching up to rub the pink cosmetic off his face. 'You're a gem,' she says.

'Would you like me to see you out as you reverse onto the road?' he asks.

'What a gent. But I think I can manage thanks. I've been driving a good long while now.'

All the same, he watches from the doorway until she's backed out safely, sending her on her way with a wave.

'What a charming woman she is,' he says, shutting the front door. 'You didn't say how you know each other. Is she someone you worked with?'

'No. We were undergraduates together and met up again recently.'

Don raises his eyebrows. 'She doesn't look that old… Not that you do. I didn't mean it like that.'

'No. Of course.'

'Anyway. I'd best be going in a moment. Unless there's anything else I can do for you while I'm here?'

'No thank you. You've been a tremendous help.' I pick up the tray of glasses from where he'd put it on the hall table. 'I just need to get these washed up and then I'll put my feet up with a book.'

'There is one more thing. My neighbour's son. You remember? You said you'd look at the files.'

'Ah yes.'

Don retrieves a cardboard wallet file from the passenger footwell of his car. He hands it to me. It's labelled *Tommy Brown*.

'I just got the information from the family. I know you can't help as an expert witness, but could you just take a look?'

'Yes. Yes, of course. I'll do whatever I can.'

Don bends down and leans in to kiss me on the cheek – a

spontaneous gesture, no doubt prompted by Kathleen's goodbye kiss. I flinch and he snaps away, surprised by his own unusually familiar move, his face reddening. 'Thank you. It's very kind of you,' he burbles, covering his embarrassment. 'Catch up soon. I'll be off.'

Later Don emails a short video of our attempts to get the kite flying. I laugh out loud as I watch it, surprised by the amount of good-humoured banter in the film clip, how happy and relaxed I look. There's something addictive about Kathleen's enthusiasm; she still has it – that energy that draws you in.

Chapter Twenty-Four
Bad News

The following evening, I read through the case file Don has given me, then draft a rough statement for Tommy Brown and his family to hand to his defence team, pointing out the places where the witness testimony is weakest. It looks as if the police have inadvertently led the witness, introducing facts that have then coloured their version of what happened.

People don't realise how easy it is to corrupt memory.

Back in my days at the university, I designed a lecture to get this point across to my students. Firstly, I arranged an undergraduate get-together involving several different classes of my students, about fifty people in all. Declan was my stooge – a popular student who everyone knew. I made sure that he told people he was going, but secretly we had arranged that on the day he wouldn't turn up. My second co-conspirator was his close friend Jamila; she was to attend the event and deliberately circulate around the group making sure she was seen by as many people as possible. While Declan hadn't been there, I wanted to see if I could use leading questions to instil a belief that he had been present.

I divided the students into four groups. When I asked the first group an open question –

"Who was at the party that night?" – no one mentioned Declan in the list of people they'd seen. With the next group I used a slight change to the wording – *"Was Declan at the party that night?"* This led most students to correctly answer "No" or "I don't know/I don't think so/I didn't see him."

I changed the question again for the third group and asked, *"At the party, did you see Declan talking to Jamila?"* By phrasing the question this way, I planted the idea that Declan was there. And since Declan and Jamila are friends, it would be quite likely they would speak with each other. Many people answered, "I think so, yes", or "Yes, I definitely saw Jamila." These people weren't deliberately lying but, given my prompt, they may have recalled other times they'd seen them together. By imagining Declan and Jamila together, they start to form a picture of seeing Declan at the party. The more they think about it, the more convinced they become that Declan was there.

The final group was given a statement of fact followed by a leading question: *"Declan often wears a rugby shirt. Can you remember if Declan was wearing it that night?"* This phrasing implies he was at the party. By asking them to think specifically about what he was wearing, many will conjure up an image of Declan in his rugby shirt. They then create a memory of him wearing it that evening.

When I presented the findings to the students, sometimes they would ask, why does this matter? And I would point out, 'What if a crime had been committed at the party and Declan was in the frame for it? There are now witnesses willing to state that they saw him there – and these people are even willing to describe what he was wearing. Their memories have been corrupted purely by the way the questions were asked.'

I could see from the interview transcript that Tommy Brown's case was similar. The interviewers had phrased their questions in a way that appeared to inadvertently lead the witnesses. Satisfied that I may be able to give useful advice to Tommy Brown's family, I put the file aside. I'll give Don the good news tomorrow. And I'll take him the biscuits I bought earlier as a thank you for helping with sorting the railway memorabilia. Phillip would be pleased it was all going to a good home.

I settle down to watch one of my regular TV programmes. It's only one of those *Abandoned Engineering* episodes, nothing mind blowing, but Phillip used to love the series and I still look forward to watching them. I've just found the channel and arranged a comfy nest out of the cushions when my mobile rings. It's out of reach on the table and I can't be bothered to get up. The mobile stops ringing and I vow once again to change the ringtone: Phillip had set it up as a joke – the opening bars of some song by Simon and Garfunkel because its lyrics were about memory. I've never actually heard the words because it cuts off after the guitar chords, but one day I'll check them out.

The phone starts ringing again. Reluctantly, I stretch to grab it from the coffee table so I can see the caller's name and I'm surprised to see it's Kathleen. What on earth can she want at this time in the evening? Pressing the button to accept the call all I can hear is crying.

'Kathleen. Speak to me. What's happened?' I reach for the remote to mute the TV.

'There's been an accident –' The rest of the sentence gets lost in her sobs.

'Are you okay? Tell me where you are and I'll come now.' I sit forward on the settee, scanning round for my shoes and handbag.

'It's not me. It's El.' There's a loud sniff. 'I'm sorry, I shouldn't have bothered you. I'm just shaken up. I'm not sure I should drive…'

Holding the question of whom El is, I ask, 'Are you at home? I can come right away if that's helpful.'

'Yes, I'm at home waiting to hear from the hospital. Would you come? I… I'd really appreciate it… I'm a bit flustered…I don't know what to do.'

When I pull up outside the shop forty minutes later there's a light on downstairs. I've never been here in the evening before and the interior looks dark, the single lamp casting long shadows. I suspect the leak must have damaged the central light socket and Kathleen's not had time to get it fixed.

Kathleen opens the door and hugs me to her. Not used to such physical closeness, I stifle my immediate desire to pull away, patting Kathleen's back in a parental 'there there' kind of way. Over her shoulder, in the shadows at the back of the shop, I can just make out someone sitting in a wheelchair. It's a woman. She is wreathed in bandages and sits slumped in the wheelchair with her head hanging down.

Releasing me from the hug, Kathleen takes my arm. 'I was such a bag of nerves. I was going to ask you to run me to the hospital, but they just brought El home in an ambulance,' she says, 'I'm so sorry I dragged you all the way over here for no reason.'

'That's fine. I'm glad you called me.'

She steers me round the tables and between the teetering piles of boxes still framing the room; the narrow space is just wide enough for us to pass through. As we near the woman in the wheelchair, I can see that both her feet are in the large blue hospital boots used for sprains and breaks. Long gone are the days of the plaster casts we used to enthusiastically sign as kids. The knees of her jeans are scuffed and stained and her right arm is in a sling. Her head is bandaged and her brown hair matted with blood and mud. Kathleen rests her hand tentatively on the woman's shoulder.

'Amanda, this is El... My half-sister. El this is Amanda, my friend from university days.' The woman raises her eyes but not her head, a quick glance of acknowledgement before she looks away again.

I was unaware Kathleen had a half-sister. 'Pleased to meet you, although obviously not in these circumstances,' I say to her. 'Are you in pain?'

El just shakes her head a little, a small, controlled movement.

'She's on strong pain killers,' Kathleen says. 'They dosed her up at the hospital.'

'What happened?' I ask.

'She was driving home on the dual carriageway when a car pulled in ahead of her and slammed on its brakes for no reason.' She looks to El, confirming it's okay to talk about the accident. It is a caring, thoughtful gesture: concern that it may upset her sister to hear the events discussed, not wanting to remind her of the fear she must've felt. El just keeps her head down, fixing her gaze on her lap, her good hand fiddling with the hem of the sling.

'El tried to avoid hitting him, but she must've caught the rear side of his vehicle and then her car span round into the embankment.' Kathleen covers her mouth with both hands. 'She rolled the car. She could've died...'

'These things happen in a split second when you're travelling at speed.' I'm not at all sure what I should say to help: my stock responses to grief not that helpful: *That must be very sad; That must be very frightening; I'm sorry for your loss.* Empathy is a head-based thing for me – something I can understand logically when I have time to process, but in the moment, I usually don't know how to pitch the right emotional response. I'd once explained this to Phillip. 'I'm surprised enough when my neurotransmitters hijack *my own* emotions, let alone when I'm trying to understand others' feelings.' He'd laughed out loud. 'You don't need to tell me!' he'd said then gave me a hug. He always understood me.

Kathleen rubs her eyes. 'I suppose it could've been so much worse. What if her car had rolled back onto the dual carriageway.'

'And the other driver?' I ask.

Kathleen speaks for El who is still zoned out, barely listening to what we are saying. 'El said that he seemed okay – whiplash probably. But obviously they exchanged details for the insurance. I expect we'll hear from him in the next week or so. He said a deer ran out in front of him.'

'You do see them dead sometimes on the A-road. I can

imagine you'd have to brake fairly hard if one ran in front of you. They're sizeable animals.'

'I think... I need... to lie down,' El mumbles, her voice a whisper.

'Do you feel lightheaded?' Kathleen asks, concerned. 'It will be the shock. I'll take you through to the back room.' She turns to me. 'We've got a sofa bed made up. Give me five minutes to get El comfortable.'

I sit heavily on the chair behind the desk looking at the state of the place – no better than when I last saw it. For want of something better to do, I make a mental list of all that needs to be sorted out to get the shop ready to re-open. To start with: clearing all the boxes of ruined stock; repairing the floor where the lino's lifted; painting over the watermarks on the walls. She ought to arrange to get the electrics checked if she can't use the main light socket – maybe that's why there's such an ad hoc arrangement for teas and coffees? Given she runs this as a café as well as a book shop, there must be a kitchen out the back she would usually use...Then there's the window display, new stock, labelling, publicity materials for rebooked events. It all adds up...

But now is not the time to discuss it.

Kathleen interrupts my thoughts as she returns, shutting the door firmly behind her and rearranging the thick curtain that hides this private area from customers.

She looks tired as she walks slowly towards me, her shoulders rounded, her expression grim.

'Are *you* okay?' I ask her.

She nods. 'As long as El is safe. That's all that matters to me at the moment. Thank you for coming over. Everything's okay now I've got El home again.'

'I didn't know you had a sister, Kathleen.'

'Neither did I, until a few years ago. There could even be more. Our dad travelled a lot. She's all I have. The only *family* I have.'

It was one of those moments when I'm pleased that my face naturally settles into a benign friendly look without me having to move a muscle; my brain is working overtime to process this new information about her half-sister.

'Can I do anything practical to help now I'm here?' I ask.

'No. I'm so sorry for calling you to come all this way, but I didn't think I'd be safe to drive to the hospital on my own... I wasn't expecting them to bring her home so soon, but I guess they need the beds.'

'It's not a problem. I'm glad you phoned me. Thank goodness she's okay.'

Kathleen's discrete yawn tells me it's time to go and I arrange that I will phone her in a couple of days to find out how things are going.

Driving home I keep thinking about her. All her plans for the business ruined. So much bad luck – first the flood in the bookshop and now this awful accident. I mentally repeat my vow to do everything I can to help her.

Chapter Twenty-Five
Fragile Ego

Working on Tommy Brown's case has made me curious to know if there have been any developments in the Mac McCollins situation. I search on the BBC news website but there is no information and nothing I can find in any of the press. A few more weeks have gone by since I last checked and it seems it has all blown over and everyone has moved on. I appear to be the only one whose life has been thrown up in the air because of it.

Looking at the calendar, I realise I can no longer avoid calling my parents. We've not spoken since the argument over my press statement and it's nearly time for the next 'last Sunday of the month lunch' ritual. I'd missed the last one, not ready to face them, but bridges must be built. With a heavy sigh, I pick up the phone and dial the number.

'Good morning, Mother.'

'Oh. It's you.'

'Don't sound too disappointed.'

'I was expecting a call from your cousin Diana,' my mother says, 'She's coming round for dinner and she's going to let me know what time she can escape work. She's always in such demand – hardly ever in the country. We were lucky we got a slot in her diary. I thought I'd make the monkfish dish she likes–'

'That's one of the reasons for my call.' I interrupt before Mother can describe where to buy the best fish and give me the details of the benefits of Jamie Oliver's recipe over Delia's.

'Monkfish?' she says.

'No, dinner. I wanted to check whether it's okay for me to come for Sunday lunch this month as usual.'

There's a silence.

'Mother?'

'Mummy,' she corrects me, 'Mother is so ageing.'

'I asked you about coming for dinner,' I prompt.

She sighs heavily, then says, 'I'm not sure about Daddy.'

'What's wrong with him?'

'You as good as accused him of being ignorant. He's still very upset.'

'On the contrary, as I recall I said he was intelligent enough to know better.'

'That's not how he remembers it.'

'Shall I come round and talk to him then? Just pop in briefly rather than come for lunch?'

'No. I don't think that's a good idea just yet.' The tap of her fingernails on the phone receiver her own morse code, the rhythm sending a clear message she's uncomfortable about the conversation. 'You know how long Daddy can hold offence. You remember we had to get rid of the window cleaner after he criticised Daddy's choice of new car. And he'd been coming here years. It took months to find someone else to take us on. Daddy takes these things to heart. The two of you are so alike. You both appear tough as old boots, but you can't cope with criticism. Fragile ego identity.'

'Where did you get that phrase? It doesn't sound like one of yours.'

'I heard it in an interview on Radio 4 and I thought 'that sums them up'. Now let me tell you what your brother's been up to...'

I doodle the words *fragile ego* on an envelope, outlining them in concentric circles, only half listening to the update on my brother's latest career achievements, the progress of his daughter's PhD on migration patterns. Pushing away the feelings of being second best.

Diana and Dereck. The family favourites.

Family legend has it that I was always a couple of steps

behind my brother, wanting to play, desperate for his attention, but ultimately just happy to be near him and watch what he was up to. That adoration quickly faded, around the time of Felix-Felix's untimely end, but even then – aware as I was of his lies, his callousness – I still harboured hope.

Diana was our only cousin on Daddy's side of the family, the daughter of his brother. (Formally known as Uncle Sidney, but more commonly referred to as The Gold Digger by Daddy. Something to do with the split of assets in a will. Or possibly the way he always claimed he was 'about to strike oil' with each of his new ventures. I never found out for sure.) Luckily, our cousin Diana seemed to have struck lucky in the gene pool and took after her mother.

One day Uncle Sidney had come to visit and was soon ensconced in the study with Daddy, no doubt attempting to convince him to invest in his latest money-making scheme. He'd brought Diana with him on the pretext she wanted to see us, her cousins, but we knew the real reason: her presence brought the temperature between the two adult brothers down to an acceptable level. There would be no raised voices, no storming out, no huffs or tantrums if she was there.

When I'd tired of listening at the keyhole of Father's study, I went in search of Diana and Dereck. Diana was fifteen that summer, a year older than Dereck, six years older than me.

I guessed they'd have gone over to the fields. I followed the trampled path through the long grass, until I heard faint voices down near the river where we weren't supposed to go. I ducked low and slowed my pace to a creep. When I reached the cover of some wild Rhododendrons I squatted down on my haunches to watch them.

They were in a clearing. Diana was sitting on a fallen tree, her knees turned to one side, legs crossed at the ankle as if perched on a sofa partaking of afternoon tea with the vicar.

Dereck was facing her, leaning back against a tree, looking like a plump unstable stork as he stood on one leg, the other foot against the bark of the oak. He'd done something strange with his hair, parting it on the side with a weird quiff effect and he had to keep running his hand through it to stop it from returning to its preferred helmet shape. They made an odd couple: he, still the rounded schoolboy, all soft at the edges not having grown into his body yet; she, a young woman, long haired, long limbed, the type that would be the first selected for the netball team, first to sign up for the Duke of Edinburgh Award, first chosen to represent the school (or the family) in the wider world.

Dereck was pontificating about King Canute, having just completed a history project for school. He was describing how the King had tried to hold back the waves to prove his power. I'd heard this story before, over supper last night: he was hoping to impress Diana in the same way he had Mother, who had clapped and smiled her enthusiasm and offered him more pudding.

Diana listened in polite silence, a gentle smile on her face. 'There are – as you know – other interpretations of that event,' she said when he'd finished.

'Well, yes of course.' Dereck's cheeks flushed and he did that pouty thing with his mouth. It made him look like he was preparing to inflate a balloon, but was usually the precursor to a sulk. He clearly had no idea what she meant, but was saved from the further embarrassment of having to debate these other interpretations when Diana said, 'Why don't you come out and join us?' to the Rhododendron bush.

Thrilled I bounced out of the bush and skipped over to them, full of nine-year-old eagerness, not worried about wrecking Dereck's chance at flirtation.

Dereck petulantly attempted to whittle a stick with his Swiss army knife, whistling in that annoying way men do when they want to appear casual about something. Meanwhile, Diana joined me, sitting cross legged on the grass, to show me how to extract the tiny yellow fairy ring from deep inside the flowers of bind weed.

'Here, look. The yellow bit at the base of the stamen and stigmas,' she told me. I repeated the words silently in my head, taking them as precious gifts while not knowing what they meant.

It turned out to be a project that required faith, patience and dexterity in equal measure, but I was determined to do it, even more so when she told me each fairy ring could be used to make a wish. While I laboured at my task, she made me a daisy chain crown, holding it up against my hair at intervals to check the length.

Eventually, I set out my five fairy rings on a flat stone – so tiny, so fragile, so precious – a wish for each of us: Diana and me, Mummy and Daddy, and Dereck. Diana placed the daisy crown carefully on my head then bent to kiss my forehead calling me 'sweet child', and I thought I would melt with happiness.

But then Dereck returned. He'd broken his stick while whittling and gone off to find another, more suited to the task. He strode into the clearing swinging a long skinny branch from a sapling, swishing it over his head then along the ground, in the type of display only a fourteen-year-old boy would ever use to show his manliness and impress a female. Diana laughed, thinking he was trying to be amusing, but this clearly wasn't the desired response as Dereck's swings became faster and more aggressive, forcing me to roll to the side to avoid being hit. He dropped the branch in front of Diana and stormed off.

'Well!' she said, raising her eyebrows as she watched him go.

I burst into tears. 'My wishes!' The stone where I'd carefully laid out my afternoon's work was empty. On all fours I scrabbled around in the leaves trying to find them. Diana came to hug me as I clenched into a tight ball of fury, unable to be consoled.

Later that day, back in my room, she showed me how to press my daisy chain in a book so I could have it as a keepsake. She kissed me goodbye before they left and whispered, 'Stay strong, precious girl,' in my ear. Years later I used to run my finger over the imprint in the pages of the book recalling how happy she'd made me that day.

Of course, I didn't tell Mummy any of this.

The next day, Dereck offered to help me search for the fairy rings. His hair was back to normal and I took that as a good sign. Maybe he was pleased that I'd put a wish aside for him.

He strode ahead down to the river clearing and I gambolled along behind him, singing 'Yellow Submarine' under my breath. When we got there, he kicked over the leaves as I knelt to explore. 'They're *very* tiny. You have to look closely,' I explained to him.

'Listen,' he said, 'Did you hear it?'

I sat back on my haunches. 'What?'

'Frogs. Didn't you hear the croaking?' He walked over to the river and peered down. 'Ah! There they are. Come quietly so you don't disturb them.'

He pointed down into the depths as I stood next to him. 'One just jumped from the side there.'

'Where is it? I can't see.'

'Over there. Lean forward a bit.'

I squatted down to be closer. 'I wonder if–' My sentence was cut short by a shove in the centre of my back and I fell forward into the filthy water. I spluttered to the surface, wiping mud from my eyes. Dereck was gone.

Luckily the water was slow running and only came up to my armpits, as I wasn't a strong swimmer. The banks were very steep at that point and the ground level was about a foot above my head. Maybe Dereck had gone for help, but given the shove that I'd felt I doubted it. I waded along the river seeking a shallower stretch of water and a lower bank so I could climb out, muttering the only bad words I knew under my breath, 'Bum, shit. Bum, shit.'

When I got back to the house, I dripped into the kitchen looking for Mummy.

My bottom lip trembled as I puddled on the wooden floorboards in front of her, holding back tears. 'He pushed me in the river. He told me there were frogs.'

She frowned at me as if I was talking in tongues. 'Who pushed you in?' She grabbed a towel from the aga and wrapped it round my shoulders. 'What were you doing at the river?'

I started crying, fully aware the river was out of bounds. 'Dereck. Dereck said there were frogs and he pushed me in.'

Mummy clasped my shoulders and held me at arms' length, her eyes flicking over my face. 'What nonsense. Don't lie to me child.'

'I'm not. I'm really not. We went to look for my fairy rings.'

'Dereck has been in his room studying all morning.' She spun around towards the hallway, turning to beckon me to follow. 'Come.'

From the bottom of the stairs the muffled chords of classical music could be heard.

'Dereck,' Mummy called up the stairs.

A door opened and the music became louder. 'Yes, Mummy?'

'Come down here, please.'

Of course, Dereck had planned it all along. He'd put a tape in his cassette player and left it playing in his room all the time we were outside at the river; his homemade 'Do Not Disturb' sign in place on the door, as always when he was (theoretically) engaged in his schoolwork.

I was sent to my room, still wrapped in the damp towel,

to think about my lies and instructed to come down when I was ready to tell the truth. Needless to say, I thought about running away, even checked the drop from the window, but I eventually cried myself to sleep. The next morning, stomach complaining about having missed supper, I cautiously came down for breakfast. Dereck was halfway through his porridge and smirked at me as he spotted me hovering in the doorway, before ladling another spoonful of sugar into his bowl.

'Are you ready to apologise for lying to your mother?' Daddy asked.

'Yes, Daddy. I'm sorry I went to the river and told a lie.'

I was permitted to eat breakfast, but I was then sent back to my room to write an apology to Mummy for lying, an apology to Dereck for blaming him and a one-page essay on why lying is bad. The fulsomeness of the sorrow expressed was to be judged by Daddy.

Outside in the yellow warmth of the summer sun Dereck kicked a ball against the wall beneath my window for most of the morning.

Chapter Twenty-Six
Insurance

Later that week I arrange to call in to the bookshop to see Kathleen and her sister El and find out how they're both doing. From outside it looks like everything has taken a turn for the worse. The flowers that were central to the display in the window are now decayed, slumped over in the vase in an inch of green water, and the whole window display gives off a feeling of exhaustion, as if mirroring Kathleen: deflated by events and given up caring.

As I push open the door I'm hit by a pungent odour, a combination of woody herbs and patchouli. Marijuana – a smell I still recognise from those times years ago in Kit's room. Not that I had ever smoked it. The thought of losing control like that fills me with horror. But no doubt there was an element of passive smoking as we now call it. My clothes and hair would always stink of it after an evening with Kit.

Kathleen spots me sniffing the air. 'I'm sorry. It's El. She's been in so much pain, she just can't get comfortable. I said I'd get her some of that CBD stuff from the health food shop – you know, the non-active stuff – but she wouldn't wait. I don't approve but she says it's helping.'

'You should have phoned me. I could have popped in and got the CBD while I was shopping.' I hold out a full carrier bag to Kathleen. 'I got you some essential bits and bobs. I thought you may not want to leave El to go out.'

It's the first chance I've had to look at Kathleen properly. Dark circles ring her eyes, her hair looks lank and her cheeks sunken.

'You don't look well,' I say, then realise this could be construed as rude, but Kathleen doesn't react.

'No. Probably not.' Her voice is flat. 'I'm not sleeping

more than a few hours a night myself. Listening out for El in case she needs anything.'

'She's not worse is she? Or is it the shop that's worrying you?'

'I suppose it relates to both in a way...' She appears anxious, her hands clenched together, her foot jiggling; her body communicating the things she isn't expressing in words.

This isn't like the Kathleen I have come to know again over the past few months. Her can-do, upbeat approach seems to have drained away. Something else must be wrong. 'What is it? You can tell me.'

Kathleen takes a deep breath before speaking, her eyes cast down to her lap where she is smoothing the hem of her sweatshirt. 'I hate to ask...but...could you lend me some money?'

'I haven't got much cash but you can borrow whatever's in my purse,' I say. 'I usually use my cards but I've probably got about fifty pounds. You're welcome to that to tide you over.'

'No. I... It's...' Kathleen pauses. It's obvious something is wrong.

When she doesn't continue, I say. 'Speak to me. You know I want to help.'

She looks up at me and her expression is so sad, I actually register a twinge of emotion in response. 'It's more serious than that. You remember I told you that the bookshop doesn't earn much money? It was hand to mouth each month even before we had the leak...'

I nod, encouraging her to say more.

'Well. I contacted the landlord about the insurance and there is none.'

'How can that be? They must have buildings insurance?'

'It's my fault. I didn't register that isn't the same as contents' insurance. I didn't even think about it to be honest

– there was nothing valuable worth stealing... I just never imagined we might lose all that stock...' She tapers off, closing her eyes before she begins speaking again as if unable to face the truth. 'I'm at my wits end. What with El's accident. And now there's no insurance money and El can't help me and I can't afford to get someone in...' She lowers her head, covering her face with both hands. Hiding from the world. 'I can't even afford the paint.'

'Oh, Kathleen. It's so unfair. It's just been one thing on top of another.' I'm struck by an idea. 'Look, don't worry. I can help you. We can get the place sorted. We'll do it together. I've various tins of paint in the garage we could use, as long as you're not too fussy about matching Pantone's colour of the year. We could have it ship shape in a few days.'

Something flashes across her face but before I can register the expression it's gone and she smiles wanly. 'I couldn't ask that of you.'

'But you don't need to ask. I'm offering. Now, you'd better put this milk and eggs in the fridge and then we can make a plan.'

The next day I arrive at the bookshop early, a box full of paint tins and brushes in my arms. I shove the shop door open with my hip, the 'OPEN' sign still swinging on its hook even though it was unlikely any customer would venture into such an uninviting place. Above the tinging of the bell, I catch the sound of a woman's voice from the back room.

'I just don't think it's right.' It's not Kathleen so I guess it must be El. She sounds angry.

'Just leave it to me. It will be fine.' Kathleen's response is terse. 'I know what I'm doing.'

Feeling guilty and not wanting to eavesdrop, I bang the entrance door loudly, put down the box and shout, 'Hello.' There are sounds of movement from the back of the shop but my view is obstructed by the floor-length curtain that keeps the backroom from prying eyes when the connecting door is open. Kathleen appears from behind the curtain and calls back over her shoulder, 'Get some rest.' She shuts the dividing door firmly behind her.

'El's fussing. She thinks I'm taking on too much. We're both so grateful for all your help.'

'She's probably frustrated that she can't do anything.'

'Hmm. I guess. I just want her to focus on getting well again.' Kathleen brightens as she sees the range of paint tins. 'Wow, that's quite a selection.'

'They were all stashed in the shed. I can offer you Sunshine Yellow, Cornflower Blue, or Fresh Cotton – more commonly known as Magnolia.' I point to each tin in turn where Phillip had sensibly painted a sample of the colour on each lid.

'Yellow. Definitely yellow. Let's brighten this place up.'

'It's your shop. Whatever suits the atmosphere you want to create.'

We chat as we work, Kathleen asking question after question – first book you remember loving as a child (I go with *The Secret Garden*, Kathleen says she'd loved that too); a book we'd recommend from the past year ('Yours of course', Kathleen says smiling); favourite subject at school (English Literature for both of us). Again we get on so well; all good humour and playfulness, just like the day we flew the kite.

Kathleen tears a stripy piece of fabric to use as a rag then squats back on her heels to wipe paint splashes from the skirting board. 'Remember that pyjama party after the exams at the end of first year?'

'Was I there?'

'Yes for sure. I've got a photo of it somewhere. A bunch of us all dressed up. Us three girls wore striped pyjamas.' She holds up the striped fabric. 'That's what reminded me. The boys went a bit over the top. Do you remember Miko?'

I frown trying to place the forgotten name. 'Remind me?'

'He wore a babydoll over rugby shorts. I'm surprised you don't remember that! Once seen never forgotten. Very hairy legs.' Seeing my blank expression, she continues. 'He was friends with Ray, that bloke who had a crush on you.'

'He didn't, did he?' I say, vaguely able to recall Ray but not the evidence of his crush.

'Duh! He pitched up everywhere you went. A total obsession. He walked into a bollard once, he was so intent on following you.'

I pull a horrified expression. 'Sounds like stalking to me.'

'He bought you a teddy bear for Valentine's Day.'

I laugh at the sudden flash of memory. 'God, yes. It played some sort of tune when you pressed its stomach. He clearly knew me well!'

As she entertains me with anecdotes from our college days, it's like the intervening decades have faded away. We manage to cover three walls before we run out of stories and the yellow paint.

'Shall we do the last wall blue for contrast?' I suggest. 'Don't the Sunday supplements call it "a feature wall"?'

'I've got an idea. How about we paper that wall with the pages of some of these old books? Like decoupage.'

'Oooookay.' I'm slightly taken aback. 'I guess that could work.'

'We just need to make sure we avoid pages from *50 Shades of Grey* – that would definitely be the wrong vibe. There's loads of copies in the boxes – the charity shops can't get rid of them they've got so many.'

'Shall I make us a cup of tea while you look through for something suitable? Do you think El would want a cup?'

'No.' Her tone is abrupt and I wonder if she is still cross with El after the argument I overheard when I arrived. 'Let's leave her be. It's best she sleeps as much as possible. You'll find the kettle and things under the counter.' She waves her hand towards the unit, already opening the flaps of one of the boxes. 'Tea bags are in the tin.'

'This one?' I hold up a tea caddy plastered with Charles and Diana's photos. 'Didn't you have one like this at college?'

'Did I? I thought we all had them. An ironic statement on the eighties.' Kathleen shrugs. 'I don't know where I got it. Maybe someone gave it to me? Before we start papering these pages up I'm going to write something on the wall. A secret message from the past to the future.'

By the time I've made two mugs of tea, Kathleen has painted the words 'Remember the good times' across the wall in blue paint, the brush strokes so thick that the letters start to run like tears.

She turns to me, beaming proudly. 'Thank you for being such a good friend,' she says.

Chapter Twenty-Seven
Outing

Kathleen is still her high energy bubbly self when I next hear from her. Her moods fluctuate from day to day in a way I don't recall from our time at college, when she always seemed upbeat. I wonder if it's to do with the trauma of her life since then – she hasn't had it easy.

'Musicals,' she says on the phone. 'Love 'em or loathe 'em: there's no halfway measure. Where do you stand?'

Needing some kind of context, I hold back my gut reaction of loathe. 'Why do you ask?'

'I've three free tickets – gosh that's hard to say – three, free, tickets. Mamma Mia!' Her voice is excitable, I can imagine her wide grin. 'Since El can't join us, I thought you and Don might like to come with me. An outing to London to say thank you for your support and friendship. What do you say?'

She's good. I walked into that one...

'When is it?' I say, rueing that I'd blocked my initial reaction. Musicals, karaoke, sing-alongs, children's choirs, Christmas carols, to my mind they're all an assault on the ears.

The tickets have been provided by a customer who felt sorry for Kathleen after the water leak destroyed the shop. She always did have that impact on people – the lecturers at college extending the essay deadlines for her, her landlady providing pots and pans when she first moved in, me typing all her college reports – people like her and want to help. Things always seem to go wrong for her, but she doesn't give in to self-pity, and ultimately she seems to find a way through. She has a lot of admirable qualities.

To my surprise, when Don next calls and I pass on the invitation, he is extremely enthusiastic.

'I didn't have you down as a musical fan,' I say.

'It's important to embrace new experiences. I've been reading a book Kathleen lent me. *'Say Yes to the New'*, something like that.' He frowns as he tries to recall the title, mumbling to himself, *'Say Yes to the New You'? 'Don't say No to the New'?'*

This is news to me. I'm curious as to the how, when and why of this book sharing, but knowing Don will undoubtedly spill all the details in due course, I merely say, 'Oh?'

'Not the sort of thing I'd normally read at all. A *new experience* in itself!' He grins and rubs his hands together, pleased with his observation. 'Kathleen was so enthusiastic about it. She said it changed her outlook. The chapter on moving outside your comfort zone was inspiring…'

He elaborates on the contents of the book, which sounds like one of those self-help paperbacks whose key points could easily be condensed into a fridge magnet. It seems Kathleen raved about the book when the three of us were clearing out Phillip's railway memorabilia. Don had apparently invited her to come to one of the museum open days when he could show her behind the scenes; that had led her to expound on the importance of embracing new experiences; and in turn, to her recommendation of the book. She'd 'popped in' to Don's with it last week. 'A lovely surprise' apparently.

'I could lend it to you. I'm sure she wouldn't mind,' he finishes off.

'You've not seen my 'to be read' pile. I feel you've summarised the key points for me so I'll pass thanks.'

'Mamma Mia! Who'd have thought I'd ever be going to see that?' he says.

'Indeed,' I say. 'Who would have thought it?'

It's a matinee performance. While I've been expecting to hate the whole experience, the cast are so professional and energised that I'm reluctantly impressed. Not an outing I would have chosen, but far pleasanter than I'd anticipated. And sitting between Kathleen and me, Don is wide-eyed throughout, his expression no different to the child further along the row. A new experience for us all.

In the interval, Kathleen insists on queueing for ice cream tubs for the three of us, while I join the absurdly long queue for the ladies' loo. The woman ahead of me is singing *Money, Money, Money* under her breath. The Abba songs are so catchy that I know I'll have ear worms for the next few days – '*here I go again*'. But despite this, despite myself, I realise I'm actually enjoying the afternoon. I definitely need to say yes to the new more often.

Returning to my seat, I see Kathleen has got back already. Standing in the aisle as I wait for someone ahead of me to take their seat, I have time to watch her and Don. She's leaning in towards him, helping him locate the small spoon in the lid of the ice cream – another new experience by the look of it as he fumbles to extricate it. She takes it from him, swapping his tub for hers which she's already opened, the spoon standing proud in the vanilla ice cream. He says something to her, their heads close together, animated in quiet conversation. And for the first time, it strikes me that they may be interested in each other.

Through the second half of the show and the journey back I look for further signs. Leaving the theatre, he chaperones us both through the crowd, but it's Kathleen he checks on when she falls behind. She weaves her way towards us and links her arm through his, joking that we mustn't lose her as she wouldn't be able to find her way home. On the train, I deliberately sit opposite Kathleen and note that Don slides in next to her, not me. As he looks through the programme he bought, he points out occasional items to Kathleen and she shows animated interest.

We say goodbye to Don at the station and he gives Kathleen a hug. 'Thank you so much for inviting me,' he says.

As I drive Kathleen back to the shop she asks if I've anything planned for Don's birthday, which is apparently coming up.

'He's a Leo,' she says, which is meaningless news to me. 'Why don't we make him a cake and have a little do for him at yours? Nothing expensive. Just something to mark the occasion.' She starts searching on her mobile. 'We can play music from the year he was born and have a little party. I could make some paper chains we could hang up and get some balloons. It will be fun.'

By the time I've dropped her off she's reined back her ideas, deciding she will make him a card and we can decorate some shop bought cupcakes for him. 'It's not a five or a zero birthday after all,' she says.

While my observations throughout the day are clearly far from conclusive, it would seem there may be a romance brewing between Kathleen and Don. And while I should be pleased for them both, there's something gnawing at me and I have to admit I'm being a bit of a dog in the manger with regard to his friendship and attention: not wanting it myself but not wanting to cede to someone else. I vow not to stand in their way if it looks like love is blossoming. It's about time Kathleen had some luck.

Excerpt from chapter titled 'You Cannot Witness What You Don't Observe?'

Reproduced from The Minefield of Memory by Amanda Dunstan

You cannot witness what you don't observe. Now I recognise that sounds like a statement of the obvious – of course you can't witness what you don't see. But think of the number of times you have been at an event or watching a film and someone later points out something you didn't see yourself. You were there, you were watching, but you just didn't notice that particular thing.

Is it surprising that witnesses may have very different perceptions of what they saw, even though they experienced the same event? If we're focusing on one specific thing we can completely miss something else that's in our frame of vision. It's called selective attention. In some circumstances selective attention is a good thing. It enables us to focus on one aspect of our environment: we can pay attention to the football on TV while other activities are happening in the same room; or we can listen to what a friend is saying, tuning out others in a crowded pub. Our brains divert attention to the thing that is deemed most important at that time.

If people are asked to watch a video and to observe something specific they will frequently fail to notice something that should have grabbed their attention. You can test this out for yourself. Search online for Test of Selective Attention, an awareness test developed by scientists Daniel Simons and Christopher Chabris. You may be surprised at what you miss!

Chapter Twenty-Eight
Threat

Kathleen's mood seems to have changed again over the past week. The fun-loving, energetic Kathleen who taught Don the lyrics to *Gimme! Gimme! Gimme! (A Man After Midnight)* has been replaced by her monosyllabic twin; her warm laughing self, vanished again. It's hard to keep up with, but I can excuse it as I know how much she's going through at the moment.

When I call her to check she's okay, it sounds as if she might have been crying, her voice catching as she speaks. 'Can I see you?' she says.

'I can come over tonight if you like.'

'No. Can I come to you? I won't stay long... There's something I want to discuss, but not in front of El.'

It's clearly an evening for tea rather than wine. Kathleen turns down the slice of M&S lemon drizzle cake I offer and cradles her mug in both hands, hunching forward with her head hanging down. She's so unlike her usual self that I wonder if she is seriously ill and that's what she wants to discuss. I mentally list all the things that might be upsetting her: maybe she's had bad news about El's injuries; concerns about the shop; cash flow issues; man troubles. I pause on the latter. She's not mentioned any current partners. Does she think I'm upset about her flirting with Don? Is she falling for him and imagines I'm in some sort of relationship with him? But she's a tough cookie and I can't believe that would lead to tears. While I'm naturally good at long silences, eventually I have to ask.

'What is it Kathleen? What's wrong?'

Her hands are shaking, her knee jittering up and down as

it always does when she's anxious. She sniffs loudly but doesn't speak.

'Is it something to do with El?' I start with the first thing on my mental list. It's clear how much she always worries about her; frequently calling home when the two of us have been out together, buying her a magazine from the shops in case she's bored, or getting a slice of cake if we go out for coffee so she doesn't feel left out. Kathleen must've been pleased to find out she had a younger sister that she didn't know about for all those years. Which makes me wonder how much Kathleen's shared with El about her own past.

'El's not in a good place right now...' Kathleen stops and I allow the silence. Okay, so it's something to do with El.

When she continues, it's in a whisper. 'But it's worse than that. I... I can't believe how bad things are...'

I move closer to hear what she's saying. 'How? What's happened?'

'The man. The other driver. The one whose car El hit. He's contacted El.' She stops.

'Did he need more information for the insurance company?'

'No.' She raises her eyes to look at me. 'He's demanding money... He says the electrics on his fancy car have been damaged and it's going to cost a fortune.'

'But that's what the insurance is for. They'll sort it out. You don't have to pay anything.'

Kathleen shakes her head. 'You don't understand. He's phoned El shouting about loss of earnings, claimed he can't drive his car...He wants cash to get it sorted. He says he can't wait. He's got a quote from some garage already.'

'Have you seen this quote?'

'No, but he's told El she needs to pay him five thousand pounds.'

'He can't do that!'

'I don't know what to do. We don't have that kind of money.' Kathleen lowers her head and covers her face. 'We don't have anything. The shop's in ruins and we've no income, just bills coming in and money going out every month... Even if I sold my car it's not enough to pay him... I don't know what to do.'

I'm incensed on her behalf. The cheek of some people. 'You shouldn't even consider paying him. He has no right to ask for money like that.'

'I know...But...'

'Just tell him he'll have to wait.'

There's something she's not saying. She shudders. 'I've got to get the money somehow...He's got El's phone number. He knows our address. He's...he's threatened us. El's so frightened.'

'If he's threatening you then you must go straight to the police. They'll stop him.'

'El won't involve the police.' Kathleen's voice is quiet but firm, implying there is no discussion.

'Why ever not?'

'She was in an abusive relationship. She reported her boyfriend to the police but that made it worse.'

'Worse?'

'They did a 'wellness check' – called in at the house to check she was okay – and as soon as they left he beat her up again. Eventually she ran away from him. That's when she came to find me. She had nowhere else to go. She's been living with me ever since.'

Suddenly it makes sense why she is so protective of El: the calls to check on her, the thoughtful tokens of affection. She's the big sister looking out for her sibling, making up for all those times she wasn't able to protect her in the past.

'She could take out a restraining order,' I say.

'She doesn't have the money for lawyers. And what evidence does she have? It would end up being his word against hers. She's okay, she's safe with me. But this has rocked her. She's right back to how she was.'

'I can see why El's reluctant to go to the police. But I still think you should report this man for demanding money. It's outrageous to ask for five thousand pounds. He should wait for the insurance to be settled. Do you want me to come with you to report his behaviour?'

'No. No, that's alright. I'll sort it out.' Worry flits across her face. 'I'm sorry I bothered you with this.' She pulls up her sleeve to look at her watch and I catch sight of a mark on her forearm.

'Kathleen, what's that bruise? How did you do that?'

She tugs down her sleeve, hiding the injury from sight, cradling her arm protectively.

'Kathleen?'

She breathes in deeply, slowly exhaling before speaking. 'He did it... The man who El crashed into...He turned up outside the bookshop and shouted at me about his car and the money... I don't think he really meant to hurt me, he just grabbed me in temper when I tried to walk away.'

'You must tell the police. That is assault.'

Kathleen keeps her eyes averted. 'I better go. El's so frightened about being on her own in our flat right now.'

'Let me think about it,' I say. 'See if I can come up with something that could help. I'll speak to you tomorrow.'

As I clear up the tea things I start to ruminate. I can't bear to think of the two of them in this dire situation. I may be able to find the money if I draw out some of my cash assets, but equally I know that paying up is not the answer. Once you submit to a bully they rarely go away but make you their project, finding never-ending ways to victimise. Quite likely he'd inflate the bill, claim it's not just the electrics but the whole car must be written off... It could be never ending. Maybe she just needs to stand up to him, to show she's not going to kowtow to his every demand. Or imply she'll go to the police if he doesn't leave them alone. But El's terrified. And realistically Kathleen's not strong enough at the moment to take him on...

There must be something else. What can I offer to do to help? Then it strikes me: what if go I with her to meet him? I'm more experienced at dealing with challenging people. I've experienced the full range of the scale – from students who want to argue against an established psychological theory, to the prosecution trying to tear holes in my expert advice in a court of law. I'm well used to standing my ground. If we can go to see him together, we can try to convince him it's best for everyone if he waits for the insurance pay out.

The next day I phone Kathleen to tell her my plan. She's anxious at first, but I convince her that he may see reason if we reassure him that the money will be paid in due course. To be honest, I am not so sure that he sounds like a reasonable man, but it's the first thing we should try.

I'm sitting next to Kathleen as she dials his number to arrange a meeting. 'What's his name?' I ask.

'Turner. He calls himself JT Turner.' She puts the mobile on speaker and I hope he picks up as she seems so nervous I may not be able to persuade her to try again later. And it would ruin everything if he rang her back when I'm not with her.

'Turner speaking,' he says. He is unexpectedly well-spoken in that accentless way of some boarding school alumni, neither overly posh nor regionally intoned.

'This is Kathleen Cooper. I'm phoning about the car accident you had with my sister.' I notice that she doesn't refer to El by name, subconsciously keeping her out of it as much as she can; the protective older sister.

'Yes?' he says. 'I assume this about the money you owe me.'

'We'd like to meet up... to discuss things.'

'Any things in particular? The state of the government?

Global warming?' He's clearly enjoying this. Kathleen flashes a look at me as if unsure what to say next. I mouth *just repeat what you said.*

'We'd like to meet up,' she says and glances at me. I nod encouragingly. 'We want to have a chance to talk with you. And I want to bring a friend.'

'A friend? How delightful,' he chuckles. 'You could bring more and we could make it a party.' His tone changes, suddenly serious, as he says, 'I'll be at The West Street tomorrow night from eight. Come then or not at all.'

Kathleen's hands are shaking as the call ends. 'Thank you,' she says, reaching for my hand. 'I don't know what I'd do without you.'

Twenty-Nine
Meeting

When I search online, The West Street turns out to be an upmarket wine bar. The next night when I drive us there my stomach feels jittery. For all I purport to be more experienced dealing with difficult people, I was thinking more of the likes of my ex-manager, Debbie. Or at worst, a tough defence lawyer, interrogating me on the witness stand when I outline memory research. Situations I'm confident I can handle. I've never had to deal with someone potentially physically dangerous before. I reassure myself that it's a public place so we should be relatively safe; he'll be unlikely to do anything with others around.

The wine bar is dimly lit, in a way that suggests it's designed for anonymity, affairs and secret deals. White leather sofas are arranged around artfully mismatched coffee tables and huge ferns. The walls are dotted with clusters of abstract paintings. Uplit alcoves house sculptures that look like modern interpretations of classic art works, identifiable only by their labels. The one nearest us is labelled DAVID and features a life-size sculpture of a naked young man, sporting a baseball hat instead of laurel leaves, a leather jacket casually thrown over his left shoulder, and a porn star erection. In the next alcove LADY JUSTICE is a model of a woman wearing dark glasses and a tracksuit, holding aloft weighing scales with stems of marijuana leaves in one of the pans. Statement pieces. Although what statement they are trying to make is unclear to me. Money can't buy taste?

I scan the room to see if I can spot any single men who look like they may be waiting for someone. 'Can you see him?' I ask Kathleen, concerned he may not be here. I want this over with as soon as possible.

She discreetly points to a young-ish man sitting on one of the sofas. He's engrossed in conversation with an elegantly dressed older woman, probably about our age. I'm shocked when I see him. I'd expected a thug like you see on TV – rugby player's nose, jutting stubbled jaw and drug dealer swagger, and I'd been eyeing a chap with a crew cut and tattoos leaning on the bar talking on an earpiece. But the man Kathleen picks out looks so normal. He could be an accountant or an entrepreneur – and in some ways I guess maybe he is a bit of both. He certainly understands money and seems to have an eye for ways of getting it. On closer inspection he is in his late-thirties, early forties. Short blond hair, well-groomed in a way that implies he cares about his appearance. He's wearing a tailored black jacket over a close-fitting t-shirt that shows off his hours in the gym. Smart black jeans and the type of trainers you see in the Sunday supplements, the ones that cost more than my entire wardrobe.

He spots us walking towards him and says something to the woman he's talking with. She glances at us, nods and gets up to leave, her walk as elegant as her clothing which – if it wasn't for the circumstances – would usually make me want to straighten my jacket, check my hair and suck in my stomach. I watch her until she disappears through double doors at the back of the bar. As we approach, Turner stands. He is shorter than I expected, around five foot nine. He smiles pleasantly and gestures to the huge armchairs on the opposite side of the table. It feels like an interview or a business meeting and I'm on guard, uncertain what to expect.

'Good evening, ladies. Sorry that we have to meet in these circumstances, otherwise it would have been a pleasure. Can I get you a drink?' Without waiting for an answer, Turner raises one hand and a member of the bar staff appears at his side.

'Your usual, sir?' the waiter asks.

'Thank you. And whatever the ladies would like.'

I perch on the edge of my chair, the seat too deep to sit comfortably unless you're considerably taller than us. Kathleen sits ramrod straight, her expression as if waiting to be called into see the headmaster. Nobody speaks as we wait for the drinks but I use the time to watch Turner closely, trying to weigh him up, curious as to how he will play this. He doesn't seem particularly interested in us and in no rush to get to the discussion as he reaches into his jacket pocket and retrieves a packet of chewing gum. He slowly opens the outer wrapper, then peels the silver foil with infinite care before holding the packet out wordlessly towards me, his eyebrows raised as he offers me a strip of gum.

'No, thank you,' I say.

He waves the packet towards Kathleen who shakes her head without looking at him. He shrugs, then casually unwraps a strip for himself and places the packet back in his pocket. He smooths down the flap of his pocket as he slowly chews the gum making it a strangely sensual act. It is mesmerising.

'Cigarettes are a disgusting habit. And don't get me started on the ecological impact of vapes. We will live to regret the cynical ploys of the tobacco industry,' he says. 'You wanted to see me.'

Knowing Kathleen is anxious about this conversation, I speak first. 'We just want to understand why you can't wait for this to be resolved through the insurance. We'd like to reassure you that you'll get your money in good time.'

'*In good time.*' He shakes his head, leaning back in his seat. 'And meanwhile my favourite car sits idle in a garage somewhere.' Without speaking, the waiter sets a lime and soda and a dish of large green olives in front of him, places our coffees on the table, then ducks away. Turner pushes the ceramic bowl of sugar lumps towards us.

'Caffeine at this time of day? Not recommended if you

want a good night's sleep. You look tired.' The latter comment is addressed to Kathleen who doesn't react. She's doing her best to avoid all eye contact with him. Unperturbed at her lack of response he continues, 'Me, I sleep like a well-fed baby.'

He removes his chewing gum discreetly, placing it in a tissue and then selects an olive.

'Yoga,' he says. 'That's another thing I'd suggest. No blue screens an hour before bed. And I can recommend a meditation app if that's your bag.'

From the corner of my eye, I can see that the elegant woman Turner was talking to when we arrived has now returned and is talking to one of the female bar staff. The woman hands her a piece of paper, nodding towards Turner then ducks through the door at the back of the bar room. The waitress places the piece of paper on a tray and approaches us, just as Turner is banging on about how he paid for sound proofing in his grandparents' house so they had peace and quiet at night. 'Silence is so conducive to sleep,' he concludes, with an expression on his face that implies this is an earth-shattering statement. He is used to a receptive audience.

The waitress waits at a polite distance for him to finish, before she steps forward and lowers the tray so Turner can take the message. 'Thank you, Cassie,' he says, before unfolding the piece of paper and reading it. He glances at his no-doubt-expensive watch, before smiling at the waitress saying, 'Please tell her I'll resolve it later.'

'New stock arrived earlier than expected,' he says to us in explanation. Kathleen turns her head away, not wanting to engage. He seems polite, courteous even, and I wonder why he is being so difficult when he clearly doesn't need the money.

He leans forward, resting his elbow on the table, his chin

in his hand, studying me. He is suddenly focused. 'I recognise you.'

He hasn't asked a question and so I wait for him to add more if he's going to.

'You're the woman who wrote that book. The one that was in the paper. You were on TV.' He has a discomforting stare: it's not a cold expression, but like he knows something you don't and you'd be wise not to push him. I try to hold his gaze.

'Mac McCollins,' he says, eventually. 'One of your biggest fans I gather.'

'I've never met the man.'

'And why would you? You don't look the type to hang out with murders. Personally I'd give him a wide berth. A nasty piece of work.'

'Thank you for the advice,' I say.

He laughs, sits back on the sofa. He taps out a rhythm on the leather arm rest with the fingers of one hand, still contemplating me as I try not to move a muscle. This feels like a battle of wills and I'm not sure where it's going.

'I've got a plan,' he says. 'I think you'll like it.' He raises his hand to summon the waiter again, turning to me and Kathleen. 'Would either of you ladies like to join me in a glass of wine? Which one of you is the designated driver? Safety should always be our watch word when on the road, but one of you will have a drink with me surely.'

Kathleen speaks for the first time, her voice quiet but firm. 'No, thank you. I don't think we need to draw this out longer than necessary.'

'Let's get straight to the point then.' He waves the waiter away, having placed his own order. 'I have a proposition. If you accept it I'm prepared to forget the money, maybe the whole matter of your sister driving her car into mine.' He flicks his fingers. 'Gone. Forgiven and forgotten, if you agree to what I suggest.'

Kathleen grasps my forearm under the table, an expression of hope on her face.

'Go on,' I say.

'I have an impending trial – I won't bore you with the details at the moment – let's just say if things don't go to plan it may not end well for me. I want you to help with something related to this case. What's good enough for Mac McCollins is good enough for me.'

I'm surprised by his audacity. 'I didn't help McCollins – one of his witnesses recanted their testimony.' Kathleen's hand tightens on my arm which I take as a signal to keep calm and not antagonise him. 'I can't help you.'

'Can't?' Turner raises his eyebrows. 'Or won't?'

'If you're looking for an expert witness for your case, there's no way I can support you after all the media coverage around McCollins. No one is hiring me now.'

'I could be your first client.' He smirks as he takes a sip of wine.

'It wouldn't help you. My professional credibility was trashed by the media and the controversy around McCollins. I couldn't even consider acting as an expert witness in court, even if I wanted to.'

'Actually, I'm thinking more behind the scenes…'

'My work is on eye and ear-witness testimony. The best I could offer is to look at any witness evidence and provide a report for your barrister. But there has to be something questionable about their recall of the event from a scientific basis. The way the evidence was gathered, how long after the experience, the circumstances of the event they witnessed – time of day, weather conditions, how near they were…that kind of thing.' I pause, checking he's understood and he nods. 'And it also depends on what the case is.'

He raises his eyebrows. 'Depends? In what way?'

'There are certain cases I won't defend –'

'Ah! Morals.' He steeples his hands, a cynical smile on his lips. 'A point of principle. That could be where we differ.'

His overconfident arrogance is starting to annoy me. I register my quickening pulse and try to rein in my snappiness as I ask, 'What is the case *actually* about?'

He pauses, studying me as he judges how much to say, how much to trust me. 'An eagle-eyed witness saw some people that I – for want of a better term – 'employ', doing something they shouldn't. They are due to go to court very soon. Now, I cannot afford to be associated with them in *any way* as it would have major repercussions for my own case if I'm tied to their…misdemeanour. It would join the dots, shall we say. But Ms Eagle-eye has told police she saw the three of us together. Her description of the man she saw is surprisingly accurate – and I'd be pleasantly flattered if it was me.' He winks at me, trying to include me in his jokey comments. 'Which of course it is not.' He pulls on the cuff of his jacket to straighten the sleeve, a smug smile showing how pleased he is with himself.

'Go on,' I say. 'What is it you want from me?'

He reaches for his wine and swirls it slowly around the glass before taking a sip. 'Specifically, I need you to discredit her evidence.'

'And how do you propose I do that?'

'I rather think that's your problem,' he says. 'Isn't that what you do?'

Discrediting a witness! Furious, I grab my handbag and stand to leave: my problem indeed. But Kathleen pulls on my arm, trying to stop me. I've been so wrapped up in the moment, I'd forgotten that the whole purpose of this meeting was to help Kathleen and El get this man off their backs, and I won't achieve that by storming out.

I stay standing, making it clear that I am ready to walk out if he makes any more disparaging remarks. 'I cannot discredit a witness just because you want me to. I can't possibly do that.'

'Your friend might have a different opinion.' He nods toward Kathleen who looks up at me, her eyes imploring. 'There is no can't. Anything is possible.' He looks at his watch again. It seems our time is up. 'I suggest we all three go away and think about it. Say the word and I'll get my lawyer to send the eyewitness testimony for this other case over to you. I'm going away for a few days on business, but I'll be in touch if I've not heard from you...Let's say, by the end of the week. I'm a reasonable man.' Grinning, he taps the side of his nose, deliberately overacting the part like a stage villain. 'Meanwhile, remember 'careless talk costs lives'! Not a word to anyone.'

We drive back in silence but there is no peacefulness. Kathleen leans her head on the passenger window as soon as we get in the car, staring into space, her eyes unfocused. My mind is churning, searching for workable solutions that will get this man out of Kathleen's life. As I pull up outside the bookshop there's a faint light from the back room. Seeing it, Kathleen seems reassured: El is home and safe. Without looking at me, she speaks, 'Please say you will do it. I just want all this to go away. I just want everything to be back how it was.'

'I'll work something out. Don't worry,' I say. But I honestly have no idea how I will resolve this.

Chapter Thirty
Alibi

This is so beyond my experience and I am in too deep. Sure, I've dealt with cases involving people like this before, but it's never been so personal.

And I can't abandon Kathleen now. She has no one else to turn to.

I'm trying to think of a way out of this mess. Maybe I should just give him the cash. Kathleen will pay me back in the future if she can. Maybe that's the best idea to get it over for all of us. That night I get out my banking folder and check my different accounts to see if I can access the five thousand pounds he demanded, but even as I'm adding up figures I know that if we go down this path it will only be the start. More demands will follow. I tear up the sheet of paper with my calculations and throw it in the bin.

Could I go to the police? In reality I don't have a shred of evidence: it would all be dependent on Kathleen and El providing their story. And Kathleen is adamant that they don't want the police involved. Maybe I could go to see the police myself and leave Kathleen and El out of it; not mention the threats and assault. What if I just tell the police what I know. But in truth it doesn't add up to much: a man called J T Turner (no, I don't know where he lives or even if that's his real name) has committed some kind of crime (but I don't know what or where or when), and he's asked me to discredit a witness (and no, I can't explain what hold he has over me that he would ask me to do that).

Okay, that's ruled out.

I think through the implications of what he's asked me to do.

He wants me to discredit the witness, the woman who saw him with these two other people. As I've already told him, that would only be possible if there's a problem with the way the testimony was gathered or something else that would suggest the witness' recall of the event was faulty. That *could* be possible but I'd need to look at the case file to see her statement and the validity of her testimony against him to know for sure.

Surely it would be easier to build up his own alibi? Convince people he wasn't at the scene.

He could go for misidentification – it was just a man who looked a lot like him. Build up his story so that the witness' claim to have seen him can't possibly be true, as A.N.Other can vouch for the fact he was elsewhere at the time… Why hasn't he taken this route? Or maybe he has and his story isn't strong enough? Given his impending court case for his own alleged crime, he would need someone trustworthy, ideally not connected to him in any way; a professional, someone the courts would look on favourably…

Oh, my God. Surely he isn't thinking of me? Does he want me to say I was with him at that time: to vouch for his innocence with regard to this specific accusation.

My mind is racing. I wonder what date it was that this event took place. Would I know where I actually was that day? I search for my diary amongst the piles of paper on my desk, abandoned as it's so rarely used now. Looking back over previous weeks and months, there's nothing recorded other than seeing Don or Kathleen, cancelled book promotion events, and the commemorative memorial for Phillip at Bridgeton Railway Museum. Other than that, empty pages.

Wait…back up a minute. Book promotions. What if I was doing a promotion on the day the witness says she saw him? He could say he was there at the event where I was speaking. And I could give him a signed copy of my book to prove he was there... I'd need to date my signature and make the message relevant...and brief him on the content of my talk... But it would be possible *if* the dates work.

What am I thinking? This is crazy.

To start with, as an alibi witness I'd need to provide my name, address and date of birth so Turner would easily be able to track me down. Given the link to the other court case Turner mentioned, there'd no doubt be a police investigation to confirm the validity of my statement. I'd have to swear that I don't actually know him personally, but he approached me when he realised he'd been at my talk on the relevant day and so I could vouch for him. I'd have to say I remembered him because he asked me some interesting questions about memory...

The Prosecuting advocate would interview me and Turner's solicitor would be there, both of them listening to my bald face lies. Then, if there was any doubt, I'd be called to court and the prosecutor would cross examine my evidence on the stand... I've been the subject of their haranguing enough times before: questioning my expertise, my practical experience, my competence. All of that was hard enough to handle, but if I were to offer an alibi to Turner they would have dug around in search engines looking for evidence to discredit me and my reputation, and no doubt come across the meme of my tantrum and the links to Mac McCollins.

I shake my head as I realise I've barely got started on all the reasons why this would be the most foolish thing I could ever do. There was that recent case in Birmingham where the woman was given a three year sentence for providing a fake alibi for her husband. Three years! And even the attempted use of a fake alibi can be deemed an offence. Or there's aiding and abetting which could result in a sentence of up to seven years.

I shudder at the thought of having to swear in a court of law on oath to defend him, to perjure myself by telling such outrageous lies. To break the laws I've upheld all my life. If the truth came out, that would be the end of everything. How would I survive if I was sent to prison?

I have until the end of the week to come up with a solution to this problem, but providing Turner with a fake alibi is not it.

Chapter Thirty-One
Disturbance

It's a couple of days after we met with Turner when Kathleen messages me. I know it's her as she's the only person I know who uses WhatsApp. She'd set it up on my phone raving about how easy it makes it to exchange messages with friends, share photos, forward messages, ignoring the fact I'm unlikely to do any of these things. Hearing the ping of an incoming message, I immediately assume she's calling to chase me for my response to Turner's request. Our deadline of the end of the week is approaching and I'm still stuck in the cleft stick formed by my reluctance to do *anything* to assist that man while also wanting to help Kathleen.

When I open the message it just says, 'Can you come round? There's something I need to show you.' No hello or other greeting, no sign off xxx. Gone are the dancing girl, wine glass or ROFL emoji she'd typically use when she's on one of her highs. While part of me hopes she wants to show me how well El is doing with her recovery, some progress she's made on the shop, or an idea she's come up with to resolve this problem, I doubt that it's such positive news.

I message back to say I'll be with her in an hour. I shunt my rough notes and mind maps into the paper recycling bin, then change out of my slobbing-around-the-house stretch pants into something more suitable to face the world.

When I arrive bang on time, there's no space immediately outside the shop so I park a few doors down. I'd not really registered before how rundown this street is. I park next to a charity shop, but either side of that the premises are empty: one with graffitied metal shuttering rolled down and padlocked; the window of the other plastered with red paper banners declaring a long ago closing down sale.

Kathleen is watching through the window of the book shop as I walk down the street. She opens the door, flips the closed sign round, steps out and locks up behind her.

'Hi,' I say, 'I thought there was something you wanted to show me.'

'It's not in there,' she says, her tone and face serious.

I nod towards the door she's just locked. 'Are we going far? I can drive us if you like.'

'No. Round the back,' she says. 'I just don't want anyone going in and disturbing El.' She turns and paces ahead of me towards the car park at the end of the street, clearly expecting me to follow.

I walk quickly to catch up with her. 'Is everything alright?'

'No. Not really.' She doesn't turn to look at me but keeps walking, her eyes focused on the filthy pavement, thick with scattered litter, cigarette ends and other detritus. I wonder if the street cleaners ever get this far as it certainly doesn't look like it.

We enter the car park, passing a pay and display ticket machine with a fading 'out of order' sticker. There are four or five parked cars, one with a flat tyre and I doubt anyone ever checks for tickets. I follow Kathleen around the metal flow control plates designed to stop vehicles entering through the exit. After a few yards Kathleen turns left, marching towards an alleyway that appears to lead down behind the small row of shops.

It's a dark dank passage, not wide enough for two people, so I fall behind her. She gets to a six-foot wooden gate which she shoves open with her hip and it squeals loudly in response. She goes through, stepping to one side to allow me to enter and then pushing the gate shut behind us. It hits the frame with a loud bang enclosing us in a small yard area which I assume is behind her book shop. There's clutter all around: a grey wheelie bin with a green food recycling bucket laying open next to it; the wheel of a bike with weeds growing through the spokes; some damp cardboard boxes leaning against the wall, no doubt part of the ruined stock waiting for their final journey to the dump.

The back wall of the shop faces us: the door to the left side is padlocked in three places on the outside. Next to that are two windows with cross hatch security bars, the glass covered with newspaper on the inside to stop people looking in. On the floor above, the curtains are pulled shut. I'm guessing all these security procedures were put in place by the previous occupants as traces of rust on the window bars suggest they've been there for a while. I can't imagine Kathleen taking these measures to secure such run-down premises.

Kathleen interrupts my thoughts. 'Last night,' she says. 'There was someone here. In the yard.'

'Did you see who it was?'

'No. El heard the noise of the gate but couldn't reach her crutches quick enough to get to the window. By the time she woke me up there was nothing to see – just the gate swinging open.'

'Probably just some local kids messing about,' I say, more in hope than belief.

'Not unless they're the type to leave veiled threats,' she says. 'This is what I wanted to show you.'

She takes a step backwards allowing me to fully see the back door. The door that would allow access to the shop if it wasn't barricaded so securely. On the backstep there's a green plastic petrol can. There's something hanging from the handle; a small object, bright red and yellow. I can't quite make out what I'm looking at so I step nearer to see more clearly. It's actually a children's plastic toy. It's so incongruous, almost comical, it takes me a while to work it out. Bending closer I can see it's a model of Noddy in his car. A wheel is missing and the plastic front bumper is broken. A length of string has been tied round the back wheels to attach it to the handle of the can. It would be comical in any other circumstance.

I straighten up. 'Is there petrol in it?' I ask pointing to the can.

'No. But there doesn't need to be. The point has been made.'

'Do you think it's connected to Turner?'

'What do you think?' Her tone is cynical and tired. 'But of course there's no way to prove anything. He'll have sent one of his underlings.'

'Do you believe it's a threat? Surely he wouldn't go that far? He wouldn't risk your lives by setting fire to the shop.' The thought is horrific.

'That's the trouble. We don't know. El is terrified. We're both terrified.'

'You could go to the police. Show them this.'

'Really? A children's toy and an empty petrol can? Are you mad?'

I take a deep breath as I think what to say, what to do. He's playing with us: a cat with a mouse. He's threatening Kathleen and El knowing he can get to me this way. To push me to do his bidding, to manipulate me through threats to the people I care about and want to help.

'Surely he won't make any move until the end of the week. He gave us that long. He won't do anything before then.'

'Amanda, this isn't a game of bluff. This is serious.' I don't recall the last time she's called me by my full name and it jars.

'Yes, I realise that.'

'El's really panicking. She was asking me if you could you lend us some money to stay in a hotel for a few days.' She looks directly at me for the first time since we entered the courtyard as she says, 'Or maybe we could come and stay with you?'

The now familiar churning of my stomach serves to underline what I already know: I'm not prepared to run the risk of Turner or his acolytes turning up at my house. I can't jump every time the fox knocks the bin over; cringe in fear if the neighbour's cat trips the movement detector and turns the lights on in the garden. I don't want to have to find the code for the house alarm and start setting it every evening, priming my brain for a sleepless night of worry. For my sanity I have to keep Turner at arm's length.

While I'm gathering my thoughts Kathleen adds, 'Or we could ask Don. I'm sure he must have a spare room we could stay in for a while. Turner would never find us there. And I expect this threat is just the start. If you're not going to do what Turner asks, I guess we'll need to sort out somewhere we can disappear to longer term... And to be honest you may need to do the same. I don't know what he's accused of, but I wouldn't trust what he may do if you get on the wrong side of him.'

I can't have Don dragged into this. Poor, naïve Don, who would feel guilty if he accidentally posted a letter without a stamp. He'd never understand this situation. He'd probably have a heart attack if he knew about all this. And what if she's right about Turner? That he'd come after us for vengeance? She's right in that we don't know how far he would go; how far he's gone in the past. The thought of uprooting my life to escape Turner makes me shudder. Always looking back over my shoulder in case he was tracking me down. I can't imagine how awful that would be.

'No, that's not necessary,' I say, my voice surprisingly firm: the decision is made. This can't go on. 'Tell Turner I'll do what he asks. Tell him to get the files to you and I'll look through the witness evidence and – while I can't promise anything – I'll see what I can do to help.'

'Thank you,' she says coldly. 'I'll tell El.' Without another word she yanks open the back gate and strides out.

Chapter Thirty-Two
Disclosure

As soon as Kathleen gives me the information from Turner's lawyer I can feel my shoulders tighten. There's a slight tremor in my hands as I take the box file, a pounding in my chest as if I'm holding a bomb that could explode any second. My whole body is telling me not to touch it, to run as far away as possible from his toxic world.

I cough before I speak, unsure how steady my voice will be. 'Has he said when he wants to hear back?' I can't bear to say his name.

'He said the end of the week would be reasonable.'

Reasonable. I think of him sitting in that poseurs' wine bar issuing his commands, a typical macho posture – manspreading, his hands behind his head, taking up space to underline his importance – *'I'm a reasonable man.'* There is a flicker of anger within me. This is a good sign: rage is better than fear.

There is nothing for us to discuss and Kathleen leaves as soon as she's handed over the box. I shut the door firmly behind her, locking it top and bottom as if that will keep me safe.

I'm familiar with these files of Disclosure documents. They will contain all the evidence to date relating to the case against his two employees, including the witness statements, which is what I want to see. As I lay out the paperwork to identify the priority items there's a sense of familiarity, a feeling of reassurance now I'm in my area of expertise.

I can do this.

My focus is on the statement from the only eyewitness, the woman Turner is concerned about; the only thing that links him to the two accused men.

"I, Rita Kaur, Office Manager, of Dragnet Alarms, Mandela Trading Estate, East Binholt, will say as follows:"

I scan down to the numbered section where she introduces herself, giving any personal information that she needs to disclose so she doesn't risk her evidence being challenged in court. *"I have worked in the office of Dragnet Alarms on the Mandela Trading Estate for five years. My mother is on the board of the company. My father is a Detective Inspector in the local police service. He is not involved in this case."* Ah. That explains why Turner hasn't tried to use any of his strong-arm tactics against her as the main witness. He couldn't risk his attempts at witness manipulation coming to the attention of the police.

I read on.

Background

10 The office where I work is located on the edge of the Mandela Trading Estate, alongside the main road. My desk sits under windows at the front of the building on the first floor and I look out onto the road where it runs up to the roundabout. Windows at the back look out over the carpark. As this statement relates to things I witnessed, I wish to state that I have 20:20 vision without the aid of glasses. **WS01**

I flick through to find the exhibit this code refers to. WS01 is a map of the area showing the location of her office relative to the road, which runs west to east. From the first floor it looks like she would have a clear view of anything that happened on the roads coming up to the roundabout, but I decide to drive out there and see for myself later today. Unless there are side windows, she wouldn't be able to see vehicles after they drive into the trading estate without getting up and moving to the back of the office, which faces south.

11 Between July and October 2022 I have witnessed four car crashes at the same roundabout. To my knowledge there were no accidents in the previous five years that I have worked at Dragnet Alarms in this office.

12 The first accident occurred on 4th July 2022. I recall the date as we always have a delivery on the first Monday of the month and I hoped that the accident was not going to block the road and delay our delivery lorry. A blue Honda Civic stopped suddenly at the roundabout for no obvious reason and a white Ford Fiesta ran into the back of it. Both drivers got out of their vehicles and spoke to each other. The Honda was driven by a woman and a man was driving the Fiesta that hit her. They seemed relaxed and friendly, barely chatting for a minute or two. They didn't inspect the damage nor did they exchange anything as far as I could see. The woman who had driven the blue Honda took a photo of the cars as they had ended up after the accident but as she was standing at the passenger door of her own car it is unlikely, given the angle, that the photo would show details of any damage.

Conjecture, I write on my note pad. She doesn't know this for sure.

*After that they both drove off. The position of the vehicles is shown in **WS02/1***

13 The next accident happened two weeks later on 18th July 2022. I made a note of the date as the incident was a repeat of the first. The woman that I have since identified as Defendant A stopped her car unexpectedly at the roundabout. She was driving a red Toyota Corolla. A blue Honda Civic drove into the back of her when she was stationary. The driver of the Honda was the man that I subsequently identified as Defendant B. They looked like the man and woman I had seen in a similar accident on 4th July 2022 and I believe the blue Honda was the same vehicle as used previously. Although I couldn't see the number plate, there was a large dent in the driver's door of the Honda which I recognised. Given the similarity of the events I thought it likely they were the same people which seemed very suspicious. I made a note of the date, the partial number plates of the vehicles and their description. The *position of the vehicles with registrations is shown in **WS02/2**. My descriptions of the two drivers are exhibit **WS03/1 and WS03/2***

14 The third incident occurred a week later[...]

Again she says she saw the same man and woman, but this time they were driving two other vehicles.

*15 The fourth time the events were different. The woman and the man (now known to be Defendant A and B) were travelling together in a silver Ford Seirra which the woman, Defendant A, was driving. She stopped the vehicle at the roundabout and a red Vauxhall that had been driving behind slowed right down and gently rolled forward into their back bumper. The position of the vehicles is shown in **WS02/4**. I didn't recognise the man who got out of the red Vauxhall. He walked forward to the woman's Ford Sierra and passed a small package through the driver's window to the woman. The woman then drove her car into the trading estate and the red Vauxhall drove away.*

What was in this package I wonder. Money? Drugs? Rita's statement continued.

*16 I went to the rear of the building to check if I could see the Ford Sierra as it pulled into the public car park behind my office. Having parked their car, Defendants A and B got out of the vehicle. They approached a man I hadn't seen before who was standing beside a parked BMW where they all chatted for a few minutes. The BMW driver has subsequently been identified as Man C. The woman then returned to her vehicle and placed something on the passenger side car tyre but I couldn't see what. Defendant B handed over the package they'd been given by the man in the red Vauxhall to Man C, who opened it and pulled out a bundle of notes. He put these in a brief case and then gave Defendant B a large box in exchange. All three then left in their separate vehicles. **WS03/3** is my eyewitness description of Man C.*

I flick to the description of Man C, the driver of the BMW who was handed the mysterious parcel. Under six foot, muscular build, blond hair, wearing jeans and a suit jacket.

Turner.

17 I continued watching and five minutes later another unidentified man walked into the car park and headed directly to the silver Ford Sierra that the couple had left behind. He took something from the top of the tyre which I believe to be hidden keys for the vehicle because he then unlocked the car and drove off.

I don't need to look through the other materials to confirm my suspicions: Turner is Man C. Crash for cash. That's what he and his team are up to. Causing accidents that enable them to make fraudulent insurance claims for major damage to the vehicle and for personal injury – anything from whiplash through to post traumatic stress – and subsequent loss of earnings. You read about it in the local press sometimes. A driver brakes suddenly and the innocent target in the car behind runs into them and is subsequently blamed for the accident.

It's one huge scam and it seems poor El has also been one of Turner's unwitting victims and came off worse than most. That's why he wants cash rather than to go through an insurance claim. Why didn't I think of that before?

I look up information on crash for cash. It seems Defendants A and B could face criminal charges of fraud as well as road traffic offences. They probably aren't the type to be overly concerned by the threat of a driving ban, but reading further, it looks as if they could get a seven year sentence. Surely that would cause them to implicate Turner? Unless he has a much bigger hold over them.

I look through the file supplied by Turner, searching for the statements they gave in their initial interviews with the police. Neither admit to knowing who Turner is, claiming the accidents were their own idea. Their stories are completely aligned, almost word for word identical – a sign they have colluded. They both claim they had arranged to meet Man C in the carpark as they were buying an old vehicle off him, which is why they handed him a bundle of cash. They'd never seen him before or since and he was nothing to do with their operation.

Causing 'accidents' that put innocent drivers at risk – that's Turner's business; although in this instance he seems to also be staging fake accidents with people he controls. I remember his words when we met in the wine bar: *'An eagle-eyed witness saw some people that I – for want of a better term – 'employ', doing something they shouldn't.'* He pulls the strings. And, if he is on trial for anything even tangentially related, it's no wonder he can't have anything tying him to the crimes of Defendants A and B.

I get my mobile phone and my keys and head for the door. I'm on my way to check out the road layout at the Mandela Trading Estate to see if she would really have been able to witness all she has described. It looks like this could be my one hope of challenging Rita Kaur's witness statement.

Chapter Thirty-Three
Checking

The trading estate is typical of those out-of-town industrial parks, primarily made up of low budget offices and small businesses. I pull up in the carpark, behind the office block where Rita Kaur works. A burger van is stationed near the entrance, a hand painted sign offering 'The best cheeseburgers in East Anglia' which I somehow doubt. Behind the burger van, amassed like estate agents' boards outside a block of flats, a confusion of signs direct visitors to Unit 16, Van'sRUs, Repairs and Parts, Vanessa's Home-Made Products, and a building that offers custom made posters. There aren't any people around at this time of day and I wonder how most of these places actually make a living.

I walk around the side of the office block, passing a sign that reads 'No Fork Lift's Past This Point' (which the pedant in me mentally corrects). I head for the road that runs in front of Dragnet Alarms. It's a two lane road, spotted with potholes, surprisingly quiet given the proximity of the estate. I cross to the other side of the road to stand near the roundabout in the approximate position where the accidents occurred. Looking up, I can see the first-floor windows of the Dragnet Alarms offices quite clearly. Anyone looking out on the traffic would have an unrestricted view. Unless it was a torrential downpour...

I momentarily consider checking the weather for the dates of the incidents but realise I'm clutching at straws. I cannot fault Rita Kaur's testimony with regard to the three accidents she witnessed and the fourth incident when a parcel of cash was handed over: she would clearly have been able to see everything from her office.

But it's really her eyewitness evidence placing Turner at

the scene that I need to challenge. With faint hope, I head back to the carpark to check the actual layout of the parking of their vehicles against her diagram.

The man in the burger van is leaning on his counter reading a copy of The Sun and it takes him a while to acknowledge that I'm there as I approach. He slides the hatch window open slowly, reluctant to be disturbed, and raises an eyebrow in an unspoken question.

'Hi,' I say. 'Are you here every day?'

'Nah, sometimes I go to Marbella just for a change of scenery.'

'I meant most weeks, are you here every day?'

He scowls. 'I'm here now. You want anything or not?' His hand is already on the sliding hatch window.

'No, thank you. I –' But he has already slammed the window shut and turned his back on me. Given Rita Kaur didn't mention him in her statement, I'm probably safe in assuming he wasn't another witness to the carpark exchange.

All I've learnt today is that there are no grounds to challenge her evidence.

Driving back home, I pull into a passing bay to give way to another driver as we both negotiate a stretch of road narrowed by parked cars and a string of potholes along the gutter. I'm so lost in thought it takes me a moment to realise it's Don. As we pass each other, he lowers his window and I do the same.

'Hi, how are you?' I say, affecting a cheery tone.

'I'm well, thank you. I wanted to see you because I've just been to the Museum and we've been unpacking all the boxes you donated.' I'm trying to place what he is talking about, the leap from criminal gangs to my real day-to-day life too big to make. I must look confused, because he continues. 'The railway memorabilia. The volunteers have been deciding where best to display things and it's going to really add to the collection. You must come down to see it.'

'Yes, that would be great.' I smile at him, for once loving his innocence, almost jealous of the pleasure he takes in his safe, familiar life. 'Yes, let's do that.'

'I wonder if Kathleen would like to come too? She's shown a lot of interest.'

'Yes. I'm sure she'd be thrilled. But I know she's a bit tied up with things to do with her sister and the shop at the moment, so maybe leave it a couple of weeks? I'll be speaking to her later and I'll get a date and give you a call. Is that okay?'

'Perfect. I was –' Whatever he was about to say is cut off by the hoot of a car that's pulled up behind him and has lost patience waiting for us to move on. 'Oh,' he says, 'better go.'

'I'll call you,' I say, noticing that I feel strangely protective towards him.

That night, once again I toss and turn, waking in a sweat at four in the morning after a nightmarish dream involving Turner. He was driving a dodgem car around a theatre stage, laughing like a maniac as he crashed into other vehicles in his path, the cars overturning and people scurrying to get out of his way in order not to be crushed or mown down. I untangle myself from the duvet which is twisted around my legs and go downstairs for a glass of water. Standing at the kitchen sink I rinse my wrists in cold water and dab some on my temples to calm my pulse. As I rejoin the real world and come to sanity, the dream seems comical in many respects. Dodgem cars are obvious – designed to crash into things – my dreaming brain being fairly literal. But why did my subconscious place them on a stage, rather than the more obvious fairground setting?

Ha! Stage = staging. He was staging accidents.

It's pointless to go back to bed, so I fetch some paper and start to jot notes as I think through the eyewitness testimony of Rita Kaur and the other information in the file. The case against Defendants A and B is watertight. Aside from everything Rita witnessed, they have both made insurance claims in different names for the four crashes they were involved in. They had the cheek to claim for personal injury, loss of earnings, damage to their vehicles, passengers who weren't in the vehicles and garage storage of the wrecked cars. But they were caught out by the partial number plates Rita had recorded which match those for the cars in their insurance claims. She was an ideal witness – a dream for the prosecution – and had identified both of them from a photo line-up and was able to describe in detail the role each had played in the four events.

However, both Defendant A and B claim not to know the identity of Man C.

They agree one hundred percent on their story: both say Man C was selling cars to them for parts, hence the exchange of cash. They claim that the box he handed over contained the logbook and some other car parts.

There is nothing I can fault in Rita Kaur's statement: she had recorded all the details that she observed in real time, taking notes as she saw the events. She even took a photo of the three of them in the car park together, but – fortunately for Turner – it's not good enough to say for sure that it is him, his face half turned away and out of focus. Her notes were made in real time as she watched from the window, so there is nothing for me to challenge as a professional expert on memory – she wasn't relying on memory when she described him.

It appears that Turner was already under investigation for something related and it was no doubt Rita's description of Man C and the suspicious circumstances that led the detectives to draw a potential link between the two cases. A link that Turner is concerned could blow things wider in his own case, whatever that is. But Rita's description is the only thing connecting him to *this* crash for cash case and Turner claims it wasn't him. Having read the whole file now, I know he's using his wife as a convenient alibi. But obviously the police have doubts and are still investigating.

That's when it hits me. This is the only link between Turner and this crash for cash case, a link he fears: *'It may not end well for me'... 'I cannot afford to be associated with them in any way... it would have major repercussions for my own case.'*

Maybe I'm approaching this from the wrong angle. What if he had to face those 'further repercussions'? What if there was another strong link between him and this case? What if rather than discrediting the evidence, I could create more evidence against him?

A plan is beginning to form. I have a couple of days to put it into action before Turner will start chasing me for my solution to his problems. But he definitely won't be expecting the solution that I have in mind.

Excerpt from chapter titled 'What's the difference between a guilty memory and a shameful one?'

Reproduced from The Minefield of Memory by Amanda Dunstan

*We've all done things which caused us to feel guilt to varying degrees. Feeling guilty tells us that we've done something which is against our beliefs, values or ethics. While others may not know what we did, **we** know and we don't feel good about our behaviour. We may feel regret and wish we could rewind events and often we will try to put things right in some way: doing something nice for someone, taking responsibility for the outcome, maybe confessing and saying sorry. By doing this, we bring ourselves back to equilibrium.*

If we haven't had a chance to atone, apologise or repair the wrong that we feel we did, the memory of our behaviour can eat away at us and lead to shame. Some definitions suggest that shame is a fear of public embarrassment, of others knowing what we did, resulting in feelings of humiliation or loss of standing.

Shame relates to your identity, how you see yourself as a person – who you are; whereas guilt is linked to a specific behavioural event – something that you did.

Shame is a more complex emotion linked to cultural and social factors and comparison of ourselves to an idealised standard. When we feel shame we may try to hide the full truth, destroy evidence or tell an outright lie. In turn, this can lead to low self-esteem and feelings of worthlessness.

If we build shameful memories into our autobiographical

narrative, we make them a key element of our identity and this can result in long term mental health problems like depression, anxiety and Post Traumatic Stress Disorder.

[Chapter continues]

Chapter Thirty-Four
Plan

Through Kathleen I've arranged a meeting with Turner in two days' time, supposedly to return the file and talk through my thoughts on how to negate the witness evidence. However, even Kathleen doesn't know what I really plan. It's best that way. The less she knows, the less likely it is she will inadvertently give something away. And if all goes wrong and I'm caught out, she is kept well out of it as she genuinely knows nothing of what I have in mind. I have to protect her at all costs.

I put the two days before we're due to meet to good use. Given how well the staff know him, it's clear The West Street wine bar is one place that Turner frequents and, I suspect, has a financial interest in. I hope to spot him leaving and tail him to find out where he lives. It's a long shot I know, but it would make my plan of action easier to execute.

The first night, I pull my Nissan in to the far end of the car park under the cover of some trees, the bonnet to the wall. It's a busy car park with a lot of coming and going, but I don't want to risk being seen peering over the steering wheel as I keep watch, so I intend to sit low in the seat and use the rearview mirror. I have a clear view of the entrance from here so can observe people as they arrive or leave. And if someone does spot me, well what could be more normal than a woman looking in the mirror to check her make up?

I have a full tank of petrol, a flask of coffee and a fully charged mobile. There's nothing for me to do but wait.

It's not cold but I feel stiff just sitting here, constrained like a jack-in-the-box just waiting for the button to be pushed before I can leap into action. Pent up energy, waiting for the release that means I can resolve this issue for good.

The curiosity of people-watching begins to pall after the first couple of hours and there may be a long time to go. I pull my coat tight around me. My hair feels uncomfortable, my fringe sprayed off my face with Elnett Extra Strong Hold. The rest of my hair is pulled up in a high ponytail – a style I've not sported since infant school, more suited to young girls or female footballers than middle-aged women. The elastic band I used is too tight, but I don't want to fiddle with it in case it comes loose. It's a token effort at disguise, along with the heavy make-up and the glasses (an old pair of Phillip's with the lenses popped out).

There's a lot of action around seven that evening, but no sign of Turner and I'm starting to get a bit bored. It puts me in mind of sitting on the riverbank with Phillip when he was in his fishing phase. Luckily it was short lived, else our marriage may not have lasted as long as it did. It was one of those dull hobbies I couldn't see the point of: sit for hours, catch a fish, weigh it and put it back. Nothing to show for all that effort apart from some scratchy pencil marks in a notebook, recording the date, time, bait and other pointless information. Bless him. I was relieved when he went back to train spotting. While I never understood that either, at least he had other friends he could go with, meaning he didn't rely on me for company, so we could do more enjoyable things together.

I wonder what he would think of all this? I like to think he'd understand. If he'd known about younger-me abandoning poor Kathleen unconscious in her room, I don't think he would immediately judge me. He'd consider the reasons I might have behaved so badly and try to understand that twenty-year-old girl. And he'd definitely recognise my desire to atone, to make it up to Kathleen in any way I can. While he may not condone what I'm planning now – too fearful of the risks I'm considering taking, the possible repercussions – he'd see that it wasn't entirely out of character: there are times rules need to be broken. And I've come to realise that *sometimes* the law is an ass and needs a helping hand to get things right. If there's such a thing as an afterlife, I'd like to think he's there rooting for me: 'That's my girl!'

I stay half an hour after the wine bar closes as the last stragglers and staff leave, but there is no sign of Turner. But as I'm about to set off I register the cluster of young women who exit the bar as a group. Clearly not patrons despite their high heels and low-cut tops; they appear sober, silent and morose. They are shepherded by a chubby white man in a t-shirt and jeans who doesn't even look at them, too wrapped up in the conversation he's having on his mobile. A chill runs through me as he hurries them to the back of a windowless transit van, parked to the side of the venue. They clamber in and he shuts the door firmly, before driving off.

What is going on behind the scenes at this supposedly upmarket wine bar?

The next day I turn up half an hour after the place opens, selecting a spot on the opposite side of the carpark. There are already quite a few vehicles there, most of them expensive. There's a flashy BMW parked not far from the entrance. I try to read the number plate to compare it to the partial registration that Rita Kaur gave to the police, but the angle is wrong and I don't want to get out of my car to check in case I'm spotted. If it is Turner's car then he's already here, but I don't want to get my hopes up. I settle down to begin my watch.

Through the late afternoon the sky transitions from faded-shirt blue to dishwater grey, to one of those drizzles that don't look like much but can soak you right through when you step out in them. Puddles form as I sit, and sit some more. I tell myself not to pay attention to my rising fear that this won't work. In truth I have no Plan B to put into action if Turner is not already in the wine bar, or if he doesn't show up tonight. But I can't bear to think about that yet.

The sky's darkening when the door to the wine bar opens and a few people exit to run through the pelting rain, heads down, across the car park to their cars. Having confirmed Turner is not among them, I return my gaze to the entrance, not allowing myself to be distracted. Two women walk past me completely unaware they're being watched. They huddle under a multicoloured golf umbrella as they head towards the venue, hobbling round the pools of water in their too high heels which make them walk in short flat pigeon steps. As they reach the door it opens and a man steps out.

It's him. Turner.

My hand reaches to check that the key is in the ignition, but I restrain my urge to start my Nissan not wanting to risk him looking my way when he hears the engine. I mustn't draw attention to myself. All three of them stand under the awning, the tall dark woman shaking out the huge umbrella, the other laughing at something Turner says. As he holds the door open for them I hold my breath, waiting to see if he will follow them back inside. The second woman stops to kiss him on the cheek as she passes and he leans in to whisper in her ear, causing her to throw her head back in exaggerated laughter. The door swings shut behind the women and Turner steps to the side of the awning. Watching him in the mirror, I squint to see what he's doing.

He takes something from his top pocket and lights it – a joint? It didn't appear to be in a packet and given his tirade against smoking when we met him here a week ago I doubt it's a cigarette. He takes a long inhale and then cups the lit end in his hand as he jogs through the rain towards the BMW I'd spotted earlier. Wait, be patient, I tell myself, he could be fetching something from the car. My fingers ache to turn my ignition key. What is he doing? Wait.

Five minutes later, the low growl of his engine is my cue. I watch as he sets off, see his profile in my mirror as he drives past. The glow of the joint in his hand, fingers tapping on the top of the steering wheel to some unknown beat as he passes. So close to me that I hold my breath. He is completely unaware.

I slowly reverse out of my parking space and follow him at a discreet distance.

Game on.

Chapter Thirty-Five
Accident

The window is fogged up by my breath and I reach forward to wipe it clear. I've been sitting in the car so long I feel I've moulded to the seat. It's that type of night when I least like to drive, the light fading too quickly, the rain blurring my vision. But tonight I'm focused; all my energy is targeted on keeping up with Turner. I have to find out where he goes.

He drives out of town at a leisurely pace, at one stage flicking the stub of his joint from the window to join the tide of mashed up detritus building up in the gutters. We turn onto the ring road. After a mile or so he swings off onto the dual carriageway and I follow, ceding to allow a silver-grey Vauxhall to swing in between us until I can overtake. A young woman driver, both hands at ten to two on the steering wheel. She's talking to herself or arguing with someone on her mobile as I can't see any passengers. She thanks me with a flash of her hazard lights (when did that become a thing?) and after a minute or so I pull out steadily to overtake her, being sure to signal each manoeuvre and allow plenty of time.

Despite the adverse conditions, Turner picks up speed and I stick with him: sixty, seventy. The Vauxhall is now some distance behind me. I turn my windscreen wipers up to full speed although it doesn't really help. Turner pulls out to overtake a red van in front of him before shooting back into my lane. The van is signalling left and leaves the dual carriageway before I need to overtake so I'm directly behind Turner again. While he'd be able to see me in his rear-view mirror if he looked, I can't actually see him because of the head rest. I imagine him singing along to some music as he heads for home, probably something hip hop or grunge, whatever was in fashion when he was a teenager.

Following behind him at a safe distance, I imagine what his home is like. For some reason I think there'll be high walls and a security gate to keep prying eyes out, one of those gates that slides to one side at the touch of a control panel. Once inside the fortress, there'll be floor to ceiling windows like you see in films. Inside, lots of chrome and white; maybe a stone and cement kitchen as portrayed in last week's Sunday magazine; modern art and huge flower displays like in the foyers of posh office blocks. An alien world.

I guess I'll soon see for myself, at least whether I'm right about the high walls and security gate.

But what if he's not going home? I push the thought from my mind, but it keeps creeping back: what if he's not going home? What do I do then? I have no other plan.

There's a sign for a roundabout up ahead. And it strikes me: why not now? I don't need to wait until tomorrow as I'd intended. Why not put my plan into action now while the conditions are ideal?

Turner has to give way to a motorcyclist on the roundabout and brakes sharply as he reaches the give way lines. Before I can debate the pros and cons, I've decided. The silver-grey Vauxhall is far enough back for this crazy plan to work. I slow down just enough to allow my car to run into the back of his, aiming for a gentle collision. Even though I've tried to judge the speed there is still a jolt as my Nissan hits his BMW and I'm momentarily shaken, but I need to stay focused. It's imperative that I act quickly. I grab the door handle and leap from my car.

Without looking towards Turner's vehicle, I run back towards the Vauxhall which has skidded slightly and come to a stop twenty feet behind me, the bonnet angled towards the hard shoulder. Thank goodness the woman driver was still at a safe distance behind.

It's vital I give her my version of events before she has time to process what's happened. My aim is to steer her memory the way I want.

The rain pounds on my head as I tap on her passenger window, mouthing at her unheard until she lowers it so she can hear what I'm saying.

'Oh my goodness, are <u>you</u> okay?' I pant breathlessly leaning down to speak to her, my expression all anxiety and concern. 'Did you see the crazy way that man was driving? Really dangerous in these conditions. Swerving all over the road like that. I swear he was way above seventy! He just did an emergency stop in front of me for no reason and I couldn't avoid hitting him.'

'Yes, he was going far too fast –' She stops abruptly, frowning as she stares behind me, looking towards Turner's BMW. I turn to see what's happening. There's a petite brown-haired woman stumbling towards us in the pelting rain, staggering along the verge, a look of panic on her face. It's as if she's appeared from nowhere. She glances back over her shoulder, back to where Turner is clambering out of his car.

'Get back here you dumb bitch,' he shouts into the wind. 'Come back here!'

The brown-haired woman starts to run blindly, but she trips on the uneven grass and discarded rubbish which lines the roadside and falls to her knees. Before she can get to her feet, or I can make a move to help her, Turner catches up with her. He grabs her upper arm trying to drag her back to the BMW where the passenger door hangs open, but she uses her weight against him, refusing to stand. He raises his fist and I run towards him as he starts to punch her.

It's only as I get close I realise I know who the woman is –

it's Kathleen's sister El. But it can't be! Last time I saw her she could hardly walk... But no, it is her. It's El.

Thoughts tumble over each other. What is she doing here with Turner? Was she in the car all along? Has he kidnapped her? Is he planning to hold her to ransom for the money he claims she owes him?

'Stop!' I shout. 'Leave her alone.'

He straightens up and looks towards me, his face tight with fury.

'You?' he says. 'What the hell –' The rest of his words are carried away by the wind and the blaring of horns and thunder of two passing vehicles as they pull out to avoid our three cars blocking the inside lane.

Focused on me he lets go of El's arm, but as he takes a stride towards me, she grabs his leg. He kicks at her trying to make her let go, landing several blows on her ribs as I run towards the two of them.

Things seem to move in slow motion, a series of images flashing in front of me like a slide projection. Turner so intent on reaching me he stumbles on the remnants of a ripped tyre on the verge. Turner losing his balance, his arms windmilling as tries to right himself. The sound of a horn screeching. Turner, half-turned, falling sideways onto the main road. Falling into the path of the traffic. A lorry passing in the outside lane. Blazing horns, the screech of brakes. And screaming; screaming loud in my head, so loud I can't tell if it's me or someone else...

Turner lying in a pool of blood not far from his car.

The young woman driver shouting into her mobile. 'WE NEED AN AMBULANCE. NOW.'

El sitting on the ground, hugging her knees to her chest as she rocks backwards and forwards, weeping in silence. Us clutching each other in the torrential rain, no words for what has happened.

I don't need to look to know that Turner is dead. That wasn't part of my plan.

Chapter Thirty-Six
Hospital

The sound of sirens in the distance confirm help is on its way. El pulls back from my arms to look at me. Her eyes lock to mine, frightened and vulnerable, and I feel her tremble as she reaches up, briefly touching my face with her fingertips. Instinctively, I take her hand and she shakes her head, quickly withdrawing her hand.

'Act like you don't know me,' she whispers. 'Promise me. It's for all our sakes. Promise me.'

I nod. I don't question it. I don't know why, but I trust her.

There's no time to talk to her properly as the police and ambulances arrive. El is wrapped in a silver blanket and whisked off to hospital after the police have taken her details. Meanwhile another policewoman wants to speak to me. The young woman in the silver-grey Vauxhall is shaken by events but doesn't need medical treatment. We will both be required to give a full statement, but our initial summary is aligned: it all started because the man in the BMW was driving recklessly, too fast for these conditions.

That had been my plan.

To stage an accident that looked like Turner had engineered it, an action completely in line with his crash for cash scheme. My plan was to build *more* evidence against him. To strengthen the links between him and the characters staging accidents on the road by the Mandela Trading Estate. By leading the witness in the car behind mine, I knew I would be able to sway her memory of events towards the version I wanted her to give. I'd rehearsed the phrasing I would use to convince: speeding, reckless, crash, smash, impact. Words that will colour the way the event is remembered. I'd had it off pat. We would be two more witnesses linking him to the illegal activity of crash for cash. And importantly, no one knew I had any knowledge of Turner, let alone any connection to him...

No one apart from Kathleen and El.

It had all been designed to help them.

My pulse is racing with the shock of what's just happened, my brain jumping from one thought to another as I try to make sense of the series of events. There are so many questions buzzing in my head. What was El doing in that car with Turner? Had Turner really kidnapped her? Threatened to harm her if Kathleen didn't pay up? Last time I'd seen her she could barely walk – how on earth was she able to run down the hard shoulder from Turner's car? And why does she want me to pretend I don't know her?

All I know is that I have to get to the hospital and find El as soon as I can calm myself down.

Once the police have checked my Nissan is roadworthy and I am safe to drive, I'm allowed to leave. I head straight to the hospital. I'm over an hour behind by now. While still in shock from the unexpected turn of events, my priority is to see El.

The hospital is ringed by a new estate, the entrance to the parking so hard to find that I drive past it once and have to loop back round. Luckily, it's pay on exit so I've time later to find out how that all works and can focus on finding A&E.

I need to speak to someone to find out where El is, but inevitably there are queues at the desk in A&E. I stand in line for ten minutes, constantly checking my watch as we inch forward. My thoughts are looping around as my brain searches for answers, when a door bangs over by the vending machine. A man storms through calling for attention, 'My aunt. She needs help now!' Behind him, through the glass in the door, I can see a row of hospital trollies stretching back round the corner and out of sight.

El is probably there, still waiting for an assessment.

I cede my place in the queue to go and check, following the line of trollies along the corridor, passing one patient after the other, their expressions etched with pain or worry. I find El towards the back of the queue, near the doors to the ambulance bay. A cold draft blows in each time they swish open and I pull my jacket tighter around me. El's wearing a thin hospital gown, someone having had the kindness to help her remove her wet muddy clothing, but she must be chilly. She's lying on her side and there's something about the way her curls fall across her face that sparks a memory. Trying not to move too much, no doubt protecting her ribs, she cautiously dips her head, lifting her hand to brush the fallen strand from her eyes.

Long elegant fingers.

I stop in my tracks. My heart beats faster as memories flood my brain.

Fingers I'd watched so many times before: selecting a chocolate from the box, skimming over the hard centres to land on the strawberry cream; delicately holding the stem of a glass, twirling the red wine to check for the 'legs' on that long ago wine tasting course; applying lipstick to her pouting lips then rubbing it off with a tissue as 'too loud'…

It's been thirty-five years but I recognise those hands. My skin responds with goose bumps. My heartbeat quickens.

Can it be?

'Lisa?' I say quietly.

Hearing her name, she looks up at me, her eyes wide, bloodshot and red-rimmed from crying.

'I'm sorry,' she says.

I can't speak. I step closer and stroke her hair back from her face and tears appear in her eyes. 'I am so very sorry,' she says. My heart is pounding and all the questions I wanted to ask fall away, replaced by a surge of emotion.

'Lisa.' That's all I can say. All I need to say.

There's a noise behind me, voices raised.

'Will you please calm down.' The tone is firm, on the edge of snappy, carrying echoes of a long shift.

'It's absurd. Surely there must be a bed for her.' It's Kathleen. The stomp of boots coming down the corridor towards us. 'Don't worry. I'll find her myself.'

Lisa flinches at the sound of Kathleen's voice. 'Don't tell her that you know who I am. I promise I'll explain everything, but not now.'

I take a small step back from the trolley putting an appropriate distance between me and Lisa. My thoughts are pushing over each other: memories demanding attention; one emotion ceding to another; questions, so many questions... I tell myself I must concentrate. Calm my breathing. Stay in the moment. Focus.

'What are you doing here?' Kathleen asks me, her tone milder than the recent shouting would have predicted. 'I got a message to say El was in an accident.' Her eyes flick from me to El, the slight hardness of her face suggesting she's assessing how much I might know. I play dumb. For now, El remains El rather than the Lisa I now know her to be.

'Are you okay?' Kathleen asks El, softening her voice but not managing to hide a flicker of anger. 'Another accident so soon. You're an insurance liability you are.'

'I...I don't think anything's badly broken... this time,' El says. 'Although I might have fractured my ribs.'

'Just as I've got you back on your feet again.' Kathleen shakes her head like a disappointed parent. 'You're a constant worry.' She hails a passing nurse, the speed of his pace suggesting he's already harried enough without Kathleen adding to his load.

'Has she had morphine for the pain? How long until she can be discharged?' Kathleen demands.

The nurse waves a hand in acknowledgement, hurrying on with his previous mission before this interruption.

'For God's sake.' Kathleen addresses his retreating back. She suddenly snaps her attention back to me. 'So, what exactly happened? Does one of you want to fill me in?' Kathleen asks, looking from El to me. I've deliberately kept quiet, waiting and watching, wanting to follow her lead in case I inadvertently provide information that could give away the fact I know El's real identity.

'He was driving too fast. I told him to slow down,' El says. She's shaking; with the horror of the memory, or nerves I can't tell. 'It was... It was...' She stutters to a halt and I decide to take over to help her out. Now is the time to explain my plan – and its unanticipated consequence – to Kathleen.

'I need to explain a few things to you both.'

'Go on,' Kathleen says, her fingertips tapping on the rail along the side of the hospital trolley.

I check no one is near enough to overhear but still lower my voice. 'As you know Turner wanted me to dispute the eyewitness evidence that put him with those two people. You got the witness statements from him for me to look at.'

'Yes. Of course.' Kathleen scowls at me. 'But what's that got to do with El's accident?'

'Well, when I looked at the evidence it was clear they were running a crash for cash operation and Turner was involved.' I pause to see if she's taken this in but there's no visible reaction. 'There were no grounds to find fault with the witness statement. She had definitely seen Turner with those people. She'd given detailed descriptions of the events.' Kathleen is about to interject so I hold my hand up to stop her. 'But given his threats were increasing, I needed to find another way to get him off your back. So, I decided to link him more directly to the crash for cash operation. To make sure the police had the evidence they needed.'

'You... what... ? How?' She frowns confused, turning to El. 'Did you know anything about this?'

El's wide-eyed expression shows this is news to her. 'No. I just happened to be in the car with him when it happened.'

'When *what* happened?'

I summarise my stake out at the wine bar the previous evening; how I followed Turner from the car park that night; briefly outlining the events on the dual carriageway, up to the moment my car bumped his, which is where I stop. I look to El to check whether she is okay, not wanting her to relive the awful final moments of the accident.

I decide it's best not to go into a (literal) blow by blow account. 'You've no need to be afraid anymore. Turner can't hurt you or anyone anymore. He attacked El and fell into the path of a lorry. It was a terrible accident.'

'Where is he?'

El turns her face away on the pillow as I answer.

'He died at the scene.'

Kathleen's face pales and her hand flies to her mouth; tears come to her eyes as she moans, 'No. No. No, no no NO,' the last rising to screaming pitch.

A tired and jaded male nurse rushes over from the reception desk towards us and quickly assesses the situation. 'Please lower your voice. You're disturbing the patients,' he chastises Kathleen. To me he says, 'You can get a coffee in the café, or there are benches in the gardens. I suggest you take your friend out there for a while.' He points to the exit door that leads into the hospital grounds. Kathleen clenches her jaw and shakes herself like a wet dog casting off water. Without looking at either of us, she pulls her shoulders back and strides towards the door letting it slam behind her.

Before I follow her, I quickly take one of my old business cards from my handbag and pass it to El/Lisa saying, 'Here take this. Get in touch with me as soon as you can.'

By the time I get outside, Kathleen is rushing away from the building and I have to jog to catch up with her. I'm a couple of steps behind and can hear her screaming and swearing as she strides along. She ignores the seats in the ornamental gardens and hurries past the car parks, receiving anxious looks from people in the queue at the payment machines who no doubt assume she's mentally unstable, drugged, drunk or all three. A woman pulls her young child towards her; another tightens her grip on her handbag, hooking it under her arm.

Eventually, Kathleen comes to an abrupt stop near the walk-in clinic. 'Kathleen,' I call. She spins round to face me, her face dark with grief and fury, her hands clenched at her sides.

'You bloody stupid fool,' she says, throwing out blame for the tragedy of Turner's death. Maybe thinking I knew El was in the car with him and had taken unnecessary risks in staging an accident.

'It's awful but it was his fault,' I say. 'He attacked El and fell in front of the lorry. It was a terrible accident and he didn't deserve it. But he can't hurt you now.'

'God, you know nothing.' Her voice is scornful. She pulls her cigarette packet from her pocket, fumbling as she removes one, her hands shaking. I watch in silence as she lights the cigarette with trembling fingers. She takes a drag and blows the smoke out in a long slow exhale as she tries to regain self-control.

'You are so fucking gullible,' she says, tears running down her face. 'But then you always were. You never bloody see what's right in front of your fucking eyes.'

'I'm sorry, I don't understand.'

She turns her head away, looking up towards the dark sky above the hospital, her eyes blinking as she battles with her emotions. 'You've just killed my fucking son,' she says, her voice strangely monotone.

'Turner?' I frown, unable to join the dots. 'Turner was your son?' Kathleen doesn't respond. I'm confused. 'But you said you didn't have any more children.'

She sniffs, wipes her nose on the back of her hand.

'Turner was his father's surname.' She pauses, lifts her jaw defiantly and when she speaks again, she emphasises each syllable, 'J. T. Turner... Jed Thomas Turner.'

'Jed?'

'Jed,' is all she says. She wraps her arms tight around herself, rocking back and forth.

'But I thought his surname was Cooper like yours. We looked for him together online.'

She takes another drag on her cigarette, still staring at the sky.

I try again. 'You said you'd lost touch with Jed. Did you know he was using his father's surname?' I don't understand what is going on. 'When did he come back? And why was he threatening you and El?'

'Oh for God's sake.' She turns and stares at me with such contempt that I don't recognise her as the friend I've come to cherish. 'Don't be so bloody stupid. Did all that education teach you nothing? Join the fucking dots.'

I try to get my head round what she's telling me. A flash of the photo of Kit cradling Jed all those years ago comes into my head from nowhere. She's telling me it was Jed who died last night and I wonder what else I don't know. 'You lied about losing contact with Jed?'

'You really shouldn't be so trusting. I'd have thought you'd have learnt that from all those court cases you've dealt with, Doctor Dunstan.'

Her sneering tone makes me cross. 'What else have you been lying about?'

'For fuck's sake. You're trying my patience. This is real life not a playground spat about who lied to who.' She stamps out her cigarette and pushes past me. 'I've got a son to bury. Get out of my way.' She strides back towards the hospital but stops, turning to face me as she spits out her final comment. 'I'm going to get El out of this place. So why don't you fuck off back to your happy little home and we'll fuck off too. Don't come looking for either of us. It's over.'

I watch her slam her way through the doors and wonder if I should go after her to make sure she doesn't take her anger out on El. But I figure I will only make things worse. There are enough hospital staff around that they will corral Kathleen if needs be and El/Lisa is probably in the best place for her right now.

All I can do is try to piece all this together and hope that Lisa gets in touch.

Chapter Thirty-Seven
Explanation

Back at home sitting in the warm safety of my lounge, the monumental events of the past day catch up with me and I start to shake, overcome with all the emotion I bottled up in the moment. The fear, the worries, the guilt, the horror, reach a crescendo. I clutch my head in my hands and rock myself back and forth, tears running down my face as I cry harder than I can ever recall.

I know it's shock, to be expected. But I'm not someone who usually experiences such strong emotions and don't know how to cope. I've no choice but to let go, to allow my body to take its time.

Eventually, slowly, I calm. It's dark now. I sprawl limp in the chair without the energy to get up to turn the lights on. With no motivation to fetch wine, make a cup of tea or take myself up the stairs to bed, I reach for the throw I keep on the sofa and pull it over me, rest my head on the arm of the chair and fall into an exhausted sleep.

Early the next morning I wake with a crick in my neck, but other than that I'm calmer and keen to get a grip on what is going on. It seems everything has been turned upside down in the past twenty-four hours and I've more questions than answers.

I go to put the kettle on but get no further than filling it at the kitchen sink, as I stare unfocused at the garden, lost in thought, trying to piece the events together, to get things straight in my mind.

Assuming Kathleen wasn't lying, Turner, the man who died in the accident, was actually her son Jed; the child I knew – and had loved – when he was a toddler all those years ago. Seeking supporting evidence, I set the kettle down on the draining board and go to the hall cupboard where I'd stashed the photos after my earlier trip down memory lane. I'm in search of the photo of Jed as a toddler. I take it to the kitchen table to study it closely, looking for traces of darkness laying behind that sweet smile, those dimpled cheeks, those watchful eyes. But all I see is baby Jed; it's impossible to see any resemblance between this innocent two-year-old and a man approaching his forties.

El is another matter. She is clearly Lisa. I have no photos to compare, her face obliterated by my jealous hand in those polaroids from thirty-five years ago. But I know. I knew it was her last night, as soon as I saw her properly for the first time. Her hands, the way she moved; those things you don't realise your memory has stored that come rushing back unbidden like an incoming tide. I realise now, why Kathleen kept her out of the way. Why she'd come up with that ruse to hide her in plain sight: making out El had been in a car crash. An excuse to bandage her up, pretending she was concussed and immobile, stuck in that wheelchair or 'resting' in the back room. She didn't want me to find out who El really was.

These two facts could explain why El/Lisa was with Turner/Jed in his car last night: they knew each other. And why she showed no sign of her previous injuries when she ran away from him along the hard shoulder. There was no original accident. The whole story of El accidentally driving into Turner's car was a complete fabrication, the whole thing engineered by Kathleen.

It's all becoming clear.

If Lisa wasn't really injured in a crash for cash car accident with Turner, that means there was no demand for five thousand pounds. No implied threat to burn down the bookshop. It was all an attempt to hook me in, to pressurise me into handing over cash. Then when that failed to convince me to pay up, Turner realised I could be his own, 'get out of jail free' card if he could pressurise me to discredit the witness evidence linking him to the crash for cash case. Something of far more value to him than mere money – *'major repercussions'; 'it wouldn't end well for me.'*

It was all a carefully planned lie. Starting with Kathleen engineering an excuse to just turn up out of the blue. Reminding me of those events thirty-five years ago, forgiving me while making me feel guilty and desperate to atone. Rekindling our friendship, becoming part of my life again. Filling a gap left by the death of Phillip, the end of my career, the lack of a social life. A huge scam from beginning to end. And I fell for it. Like all those others too confident in their belief they could never be tricked; the easiest victims.

I feel such a fool.

But why was Lisa involved? Is she complicit? If so, why did she appear to be under duress last night when she ran from Jed's car? And why is she so frightened of Kathleen, terrified of her finding out that I know her real identity?

My thoughts are interrupted as a text message comes through on my phone. I don't recognise the number and open the message with some trepidation. *Meet me at the Travelodge in Stanton tomorrow evening at 6. Don't call back. Delete this number.* This is either a summons from Kathleen or Lisa reaching out. Whichever it is, I have to go.

I arrive at the Travelodge early and find a corner in the reception-cum-bar-cum-restaurant area where I can watch the room. It's a reminder of that other meeting, only a few months ago, when I sat waiting for Kathleen in that pub restaurant when we first went out for dinner; happy at the beginning of a new friendship. Before she dropped her bombshell memory of that night in our past. Would I have arranged to meet up with her if I had known how things would turn out?

I survey my surroundings, feeling like a character in a

movie as I check for exits, not knowing if I'm expecting Lisa or Kathleen, unsure how the latter might respond. The place is designed for functionality: brightly lit; lifts and loos clearly sign posted; the tables and imitation leather furnishings, easy to clean with wipe down surfaces. All very normal. I'm glad there are people around tonight – a young family eating burgers and chips; three middle-aged men sitting at the bar; a young couple who keep checking their watches, possibly making sure they're not late to meet friends or checking their daily steps on some new-fangled app.

If it's Kathleen who is appearing this evening to challenge or threaten me, she's unlikely to make too much of a scene with an audience like this. But I somehow doubt it's her: she would be more likely to come to my home. And in a belt and braces anticipation of that possibility, I upped my home security yesterday with a quick trip to B&Q and the purchase of security cameras for inside and out. And I actually bothered to set the house alarm last night.

The reception desk is next to the entrance and I keep my attention focused, wanting to see whoever it is before they see me. If it's Kathleen, I may be able to gauge her mood. If it's Lisa...

If it's Lisa I forgive her whatever role she played. There's no blame. I just want to understand.

To understand everything.

It's five minutes to six when the entrance door swings open and Lisa appears. I'm struck by how petite she is, not having been able to see her fully on the roadside or in the hospital. From a distance she could be that twenty-year-old girl again. We're a similar height, around five foot three, but there is no flesh on her and she looks tiny, pale and vulnerable in her loose flowing dress.

When I stand to greet her, I can study her closely for the first time. Her eyes are ringed by dark circles, an inch of white/blonde roots showing at her crown where the brown dye has grown out, a deep frown line between her eyebrows. But it's her.

She nods in greeting and sits down cautiously on the leatherette couch across the table from me. 'Thank you for meeting me,' she says. 'I was worried you wouldn't come.'

I want to say *of course I'd come, how could you ever doubt it*, but instead, guardedly, I ask, 'How are you feeling?'

'My ribs are a bit sore but it's only bruising apparently. Kathleen whisked me out of the hospital before I could have an x-ray but I took myself back to A&E to get it checked yesterday. Their diagnosis was *'you'll live'*.'

'That's good. Did you find somewhere to park? They've got some sort of function going on here tonight judging by the number of cars...' I peter out realising that I'm burbling.

'I got a minicab. I thought I might need a drink.'

'Yes, I'll probably join you.'

We both laugh nervously. 'Listen to us,' I say.

'We are rather dancing round the handbags.'

'We should have subtitles like that scene in Annie Hall.'

'I know the one you mean,' she says. 'Where they go for a drink and they're talking about anything but what they're really thinking.'

'Yes. That one.' I've never had stage fright, but I wonder if this fizzing in my guts is what it feels like. I take a deep breath. 'I'll go first. It's lovely to see you. Strange but lovely.'

'Oh,' she says. 'Amanda. I've so wanted to talk to you... But now I'm here I don't know what to say, where to start.'

'Me neither. How about the beginning?'

'But which beginning?' Lisa stares off into the distance, shaking her head. 'Me recognising your voice in that radio interview, when I told Kathleen I was sure it was 'our Amanda'? ...Or right back to university days when Kit dropped out? Or the disaster that led to Kathleen finding me again five years ago? Where did all this really start, Mand?'

Chapter Thirty-Eight
Recent History

'Let's start with the last few months.' I figure if I can get that straight in my head, I'll be able to close that file temporarily and focus on our past. To be honest, I'm not sure which is more complicated.

'Okay.' She takes a deep breath. 'Yes, that makes sense.'

'You said you recognised my voice on the radio?' I prompt her.

She nods. 'I was sure it was you. The intonation, the way you spoke so confidently. I told Kathleen to come and listen and she got me to Google your name to find a photo. We recognised you straight away. *The Professor*, Kathleen called you. She got herself more and more wound up as she listened to the show. How come you were so successful and she wasn't. Banging on about how you must have loads of money. As soon as the call-in was announced and they asked if listeners had any questions she dialled in.'

Of course, it clicks into place. 'Editing history…' I say.

'Yes. That was her. She hoped it would scare you or she could blame you on air for what had happened to her. But I cut her phone call off before she could say anything else. She was furious with me.'

'I didn't really give the comment much thought. I'd assumed it was something to do with one of the cases I represented, something like that. There was no reason for me to believe it was anything to do with me personally.'

'After that Kathleen became obsessed,' Lisa continues. 'She started researching your career, looking you up on LinkedIn and at the University where you'd worked. She bought your book and read it in one sitting. She even accessed some of your research papers. Her plan was to get close to you somehow. She called herself Devoted Fan Number 1.'

'She came to some of my talks,' I say.

'Yes. She wanted you to notice her, to look out for her. She even wore the same outfit each time she went to one of your book events. She told me she asked for your autograph, looked for ways to be helpful.'

'But what was her plan after that?' I ask, 'What did she actually want?'

'Revenge. She blamed you for everything that happened to her. She believed that leaving University was the start of all her dumb decisions in life.'

'Phew…Give me a moment to take this in.' I lean back against the bench seat to think, brushing aside the internal voice whispering that I've been a naïve fool. If I can just work through the recent events, I'll see the logical pattern of cause and effect and understand what Kathleen's done and, more importantly, why. She was befriending me in order to get close enough to wield the metaphorical knife. Unwilling to let go of her memory of the events thirty-five years ago, she wanted redress. She wanted me to be her victim, to make it her turn to have the power so she could take her vengeance for the decisions I made that day.

'There wasn't really a water leak at the shop was there?' I say. 'There never was a functioning shop.'

Lisa shakes her head. 'It was never a real book shop. Just a front and somewhere for us to live for a while between 'projects'. They made it look deliberately uninviting so no one would come in. But Kathleen had to improvise quickly when you turned up that day.'

'Money laundering. It was a front for money laundering, wasn't it?' I'd come across it on one of my expert witness cases: they call it smurfing, breaking larger amounts of cash into less noticeable transactions and running them through small businesses, like nail bars or shops. 'The money from the crash for cash business.'

'Yes. And more besides.'

I mentally run through the incidents to separate out the order of events. 'So she invented the story of a leak and damaged stock to get my sympathy and suck me in. But when she didn't get the desired response she moved onto your fake accident.'

'I'm really sorry. I swear I didn't know exactly what she planned. She told me she wanted to fake an accident because she thought you'd seen a glimpse of me at the shop and she didn't want you to know who I was. I didn't want to do it. She said she didn't want you to recognise me.' Lisa looks truly contrite and I reach across to place my hand on hers, seeking to reassure her there's no blame. 'I wanted no part in it,' she continues, 'but you don't know what Kathleen's like. How manipulative and cruel she can be.'

I make a mental note to ask Lisa more about what she means by this, but first I need to work out the facts so I can piece together the full story.

'It was soon after she'd told me about the leak that she first asked to borrow money,' I say.

'She asked you for money?' Lisa seems surprised. 'She didn't need it. She and Jed had more cash than they knew where to stash.'

Now everything makes sense to me. 'It wasn't about the money itself, it was about the pleasure she'd get from luring me in one step at a time to her scam,' I say. 'She started small, telling me there was no insurance on the shop. She said she couldn't afford to pay anyone to do it up and, of course, you couldn't help her after the accident. She asked me if I could lend her some money to pay someone.' I snort a laugh, at the memory of me and Kathleen painting the shop together. 'Instead of cash I gave her old tins of paint! She must've been so frustrated.'

'She wasn't telling me anything at that stage. She knew I was angry about what she was doing.'

The raised voices I'd heard in the back room that day: *I just don't think it's right.* 'I know,' I say. 'I heard you arguing with her.' I don't know how much Lisa knows so I continue piecing the events together. 'After that there was the physical threat from the driver you'd supposedly crashed into – Turner as she called him. She had a bruise on her wrist where she said he'd grabbed her.'

'Make up,' Lisa says. 'She'd bought fake blood and stuff off Amazon.'

'All a complete fabrication. But clever on her part – she'd upped the pressure and the amount of money, knowing I'd want to protect you both and I'd feel guilty about not paying up. She guessed I'd eventually agree to try to help Turner with his case.'

'What was it she thought you could do to help him?'

'They wanted me to discredit a witness that linked him to another prosecution... I only agreed to meet him because she said there'd been a threat to burn down the bookshop while you were asleep. She said you were terrified.'

'Oh no, how could she?' Lisa looks aghast. This is all clearly news to her. 'I would've escaped and told you what was going on if I could have.'

'Escaped?'

'They made sure one or other of them was always with me. Or if she went anywhere, she took my phone and locked me in the back room. I was completely dependent on the two of them.'

The boarded-up windows and locked door.

'Oh Lisa. If only I'd known. I'd have gone to the police.'

'There was nothing you could do. She's insane. She could be sweet and caring one minute, then she'd get suspicious and say I was plotting against her and become completely controlling. She could be really frightening.'

'Did she ever hurt you?'

'Not physically, but she was so volatile I never knew what I'd face each day. I thought it was the drugs she'd taken that had messed up her brain. What do you think is wrong with her?'

'You know her better than me and I'm not a psychiatrist. But from all that's happened I guess she'd probably be diagnosed as bi-polar and sociopathic.' I shrug. 'She appears warm and charming but she's manipulative and scheming under the surface and really doesn't care at all about other people.' It hits me: that's why she was befriending Don. There was no budding romance, he was just another person she hoped to scam, another means of extracting money and ultimately getting revenge on me by hurting someone vulnerable that's close to me.

Kathleen had certainly figured out what I wanted – to find friendship and to atone – and she'd scripted the events and played her part to make it happen, manipulating me into the roles she'd designed.

But there was no way I could have known that Turner, the villain she'd created in her story, was actually Jed, her son.

'They were both so evil,' Lisa says, 'I don't know the details but apart from the crash for cash stuff, there was something to do with illegal immigrants. I think they had them working in a nail place and a wine bar somewhere.'

The women I'd seen hustled out of The West Street Wine Bar. Modern day slavery. It all comes together.

Lisa is right. Their behaviour has been evil. But how did they become this way? And how did they get Lisa under their control?

Excerpt from chapter titled 'Vengeful memories'

Reproduced from The Minefield of Memory by Amanda Dunstan

'...he cannot learn to forget but always remains attached to the past: however far and fast he runs, the chain runs with him.' This 1957 quote from the work of the philosopher Friedrich Nietzsche, neatly sums up the experience of someone who carries vengeful memories. No matter what they do, they are tied to the past, carrying their resentment with them.

For some people, the memories of past injustices are like a fire that is constantly stoked, an itch that can't be relieved. By constantly revisiting wrongs that have been done to them, they sustain their feelings of unfair treatment and build on a desire for revenge. The victim of the perceived injustice sees it as 'righting the wrongs of the past'. They cannot forgive and forget. In this way they make themselves the victim of both the initial experience and also of the memory of the event, which remains very much alive in their mind and becomes part of their identity. Their suffering is ongoing. By taking revenge they believe they will psychologically move from perceived victim status to being in control: the previous perpetrator becomes their victim and they believe that everything is back in balance.

Other times, it is not the victim themself who seeks revenge but others. They create a narrative around the event, a group memory, and see it as right and proper that action is taken to avenge the perceived wrong-doing. They may not have directly experienced the event but have created a moral story that this thing needs to be addressed. Typically they share information with others with the same beliefs, and the demands for atonement grow as they create powerful memories and ideas of how they will achieve their revenge.

For these people there is often no closure if a case comes to court. The law is too logical, cold and detached. There is no eye for an eye. Somehow it doesn't feel enough. While they may repress their desire for vengeance, it still continues to colour their lives as they continue to stoke the memory of the perceived injustice.

[Chapter continues]

Chapter Thirty-Nine
Distant History

Around us in the hotel bar-cum-lobby-cum-café, people are still going about their evenings with an air of lightness: they may have bills to pay, impending divorces, ill health to deal with, but tonight they've relaxed into the enjoyment of a drink and a chat, a night away, meeting up with a friend. Looking round the room I feel a twinge of envy: how often in my life have I been able to stay in the moment like that, without my mind straying to pontificate on unlikely problems in the future or analyse the whys and wherefores of the past. But I desperately need to know about our past, however unsettling it may be for me or for Lisa.

I take a deep breath, then ask Lisa to tell me her own experiences of thirty-five years ago, when both she and Kit left college. I need to understand more about all the events that led to this.

'Are you sure you want to talk about it?' Lisa says, frowning. I can see how she got that crease between her brows. A frown seems to come more naturally to her than a smile at the moment.

'Yes. I want to understand. And I want everything to be out in the open between us.'

'Okay.' Lisa takes a deep breath.

'Can you start with what you know about that afternoon? The afternoon I found Kit in her room.'

'Kit told me she'd been beaten up and that you left her alone after you found her battered and unconscious.' Lisa speaks cautiously, her voice so quiet I lean closer to hear. 'She told me you were jealous of how close she was to me... so jealous that you didn't even get help for her. And that you scattered the drugs around her room, to ensure she got in trouble for dealing.' She looks directly at me as she adds, 'I hate to say it, but I believed her, like I believed everything she said back then. She had a hold over me.'

'And now? Do you believe her explanation of that evening now?'

'No. Now I've got more understanding of how things were when we were at university...how manipulative she was to both of us...You would never have been that callous. You were always very moral about everything. Wanting to do the right thing.'

'Well, yes... and no.' I want Lisa to know what I *actually* did that afternoon. How I wasn't the hero of the hour. It's important to me that she knows the truth. No more secrets or lies.

I tell her about me making the 999 call, but then leaving to scurry back to the safety of my room on campus, fearful of being accused of drug taking myself, and the consequences if my parents found out. When I finish my explanation, she nods. 'I get it. A hundred percent. I think I'd probably have done the same thing. You were scared and made a decision you now regret, but fundamentally you were trying to help Kit...We were so very young.'

I feel a wash of relief. Tears prick my eyes as I'm thrown right back to how things used to be between us. No judgement, just empathy and understanding. I swallow hard, not certain if I can trust that my voice won't shake, or I won't burst into tears as I say, 'Thank you. It means so much to hear you say that. More than you can know.'

Lisa stands and takes a step towards me opening her arms to hug me, and there is no tightening of my shoulders in response, no desire to pull away. 'No bear hugs,' she says. 'Remember my ribs!' I lean forward to meet her, let her envelop me in her arms and it feels like coming home.

Lisa steps back to look at me. 'I think we may both need a drink before I tell you my story. All that happened to me after I dropped out of the university. I hate to think what version you may have heard from Kathleen.'

She goes to the bar and I watch her closely trying to take in everything about her, to absorb her essence, as if that could make up for all those decades I've missed.

Returning with two large white wine spritzers, she sets them down on the table and reaches out to take my hand. 'Before I start, I want you to know that there is only one person I blame for all that happened to me, and that's Kit. For a long while I blamed myself for my stupid choices, but I'm over that now. I just need you to know that despite all her lies about you, I never once blamed you.'

As Lisa's story unfolds, I start to perceive those days at college through a different and more nuanced lens. To recognise Kit as the puppet master she was.

'Back then, Kit told us that she only started selling drugs after she lost her job in the café. Because she needed to earn more money. In truth, it was the reason why she was sacked. The manager caught her handing a bag of pills to the bloke that did the fry-ups...You remember him.'

I shake my head, no. 'My memory's really bad.'

'They called him Frank because he had a huge Zappa moustache. I think his real name was Ray. Studied economics. Hung out with Miko.'

Ray. Miko. There's a fizz of familiarity. A man with a ridiculous moustache like a small rodent. Kathleen had talked about them when we were painting the shop. 'Kathleen mentioned them. Something about a pyjama party.' Maybe she was testing what I remembered, how much I knew?

Lisa snorts a short laugh. 'I've got photos of that somewhere. I'll show you someday.'

I grasp the implied promise of a future.

'So she was sacked from the café?' I say.

'Yes. It turned out she had quite a client base there and

when she was sacked she lost her main outlet. That was when she started selling to other students. It was around then she suggested I try some dope...and it felt exciting at first, doing something a bit risky, a bit daring.' Lisa pauses to ensure I'm taking in what she's telling me, measuring my reaction, knowing how much I had disapproved of anything to do with drugs. But as I smile and nod my acknowledgement to show my understanding, it's not a false gesture; I don't feel the need to judge the past. I've come to understand what people mean when they say the past is another country.

Lisa fiddles with the stem of her glass as she continues, averting her eyes. 'She used to give me lessons in how to roll a joint – mine either fell apart or were so fat they looked more like cigars, but she'd just laugh. She made it all seem like fun... And to be honest, smoking it made me relax so I stopped worrying so much, about the course work, about what Kit was doing, about how she was leaving you out and you were starting to drift away.'

So, I hadn't imagined it. Kit had been manoeuvring us apart.

'A couple of months before Kit disappeared, she'd started giving me the occasional tablet. I didn't ask what they were... I assumed she was taking them too. I only found out later that she never did anything stronger that dope. I didn't realise what she was doing...' Lisa looks ashamed at her confession, but she must know I *do* understand.

'She was trying to get you hooked so you were dependent on her,' I say.

'Yes, but I didn't realise. I hero worshipped her. She seemed so grown up and confident about everything. She made everything fun.'

'I thought the same,' I say, wondering how we both managed not to see what was in plain sight: that Kit was one mixed up young woman.

'That afternoon when you saw her at her flat, she was

eventually taken to hospital. She told me there was a huge scene because of the drugs. Then she got thrown out of university –'

'Hang on a minute,' I say. 'That's not what she told me. She said she spent the night in a police cell. Did you actually go to visit her in hospital? Because I didn't. Is there anyone who actually saw her there?'

'No. She wrote to me afterwards and told me what happened.'

I think back to that afternoon, but it's now muddled with the version of events that Kathleen gave me and I no longer know what's true.

'There are so many lies,' I say. 'Kathleen told me she lost everything after she dropped out of university: she got in with a bad crowd and spiralled down into hard drugs. Her mum looked after Jed until she died but Kathleen wasn't fit to take him back. He went into care until he was adopted and she deliberately broke all contact.'

'That's not true!' Lisa shakes her head. She counts off on her fingers as she summarises the lies: 'Kit's mother's still alive, her dad too as far as I know and they all doted on Jed. He was really close to her mum and dad and they adored him – he was their only grandson. In fact, he paid for their villa in Spain. He was never in foster care. If anyone's to blame for how he turned out, it's her.'

'So how do we know what's true and what's not? Was she in hospital or in a police cell that night? Was she even in an accident with a cyclist?' I take a sip of my spritzer. 'I suppose all we can really conclude is that nothing happened the way Kit said it did.'

Lisa has drained her wine glass as we've been speaking and I go to fetch us another. I turn to watch her while I stand at the bar. She has her elbows on the table and has covered her face with her hands, her shoulders hunched. She looks so sad and vulnerable I want to wrap her up and protect her from the world, but I'm sure she must be stronger than she looks to have gone through so much with Kathleen.

When I return with the drinks she lifts her head to look at me and says, 'I've been such a fool.'

I sit next to her. 'We both have,' I say.

Around us, young families continue to come and go throughout the evening, couples ignore each other, laugh or argue, and we continue to fill in the gaps in our history.

It turns out that Kit/Kathleen had used the ultimate deception. The story she'd given me of drug addiction, rejection and poverty was not her experience but Lisa's. Lisa had not decided to leave college due to her poor results then returned to her family home, as I'd recalled. But – by using a combination of threats and promises – Kit had manipulated Lisa into dropping out of college with her. Thanks to Kit, Lisa was pretty dependent on amphetamines by then, and had to take downers to help her get to sleep. All provided by Kit. Consequently she had fallen behind with her studies and was likely to fail the second-year exams.

Kit claimed she was going to take Jed backpacking round Europe, and she proposed that Lisa come with them, reassuring Lisa that she could decide if she wanted to go back to college at the end of the summer if she felt like it. It would be so much fun. And just in case Lisa had second thoughts, Kit had raised the issue of how hard it would be for Lisa to get a regular supply of drugs if she didn't come with her.

Lisa's middle-class parents were horrified when they discovered she had dropped out, even more so when they found she was going travelling with a single parent and her young child. As Lisa described these events to me, I could only imagine the rows I'd have had with my parents in the same situation.

Of course, the trip never happened. It was always "next month", "after the winter", "when we've saved up". Instead they moved into a squat near London with baby Jed. Lisa's addiction grew as Kit fed her habit with MDMA and other pills, and over the years Kit cut Lisa off from all her friends and family, becoming more and more controlling.

'Ten years we lived like that. Ten bloody years before I got away from her.'

'How did you manage to escape?'

Lisa takes a gulp of her spritzer and snorts a wry laugh. 'The irony is that she actually left me. One day she was gone. Just like that! At first, I expected her to come back after a few days, but weeks and months passed. I asked around obviously and someone eventually confessed she'd found a rich older man and she and Jed had moved in with him. More recently I found out that they packed Jed off to boarding school so they could lead the high life together.'

Lisa sits up straight, looks directly at me, her face earnest as she continues. 'I didn't see her for years after that. Thankfully. I got myself clean. It was tough but I swear I've not touched any drugs since. But, by then my family had disowned me, so I was pretty much on my own for years. I made enough to get by, doing odd admin roles for a charity and then setting up a small business, making and upcycling clothes. Things were going okay. Then, about five years ago, Kathleen pops up with a sob story. She'd tracked me down via Facebook where I was selling my clothing range. Apparently, the rich older man had died and not left her a penny. She was homeless.'

Given my recent experiences with Kathleen, I guess what must've happened next. 'You let her move in?'

Lisa nods. 'It grew from there. Small things at first, "Can you store this package?", "Can you drop this car at the motorway service station and bring this other one back?". I genuinely didn't know what they were up to, until I was in too deep and was back under her thumb.'

She looks away, her eyes downcast. 'I was such a fool... I didn't have much, but I loaned her my savings... she kept saying she'd pay me back, but that day never arrived. I couldn't pay the rent and we were about to be thrown out when she came up with a solution. She claimed she'd found somewhere we could both live rent free.'

'The bookshop?'

Lisa snorts a laugh. 'That was the third place and definitely the worst. There was a nail bar and a beautician's before that. All fronts for their money laundering schemes.'

We both lapse into silence, my brain trying to compute this topsy-turvy version of events.

The only people in the bar now are a few business-suited middle-aged men, no doubt relishing their freedom as they enjoy a last drink after their meetings and night on the town. They're ordering room service drinks to be brought to their table, the bar having shut some time ago. I check my watch. It's nearly midnight.

'Where are you going to sleep tonight?'

'I don't know. Kathleen packed up and left this morning with a huge suitcase and her passport. Her mum lives in Spain now so she's probably going there. I've still got the keys, but no way am I going back to that fake bloody bookshop! Too many bad memories. I'd rather sleep on the streets.'

'Come home with me,' I say. 'I have a spare bedroom. It would be good to talk more in the morning.' Realising she may see this as pressure, I add, 'Or maybe we could get a room for you here in the hotel – whatever you prefer, Lisa.'

'Can I come back with you…to your home? I'd like that.'

Chapter Forty
Home

I drive us home slowly, swerving the potholes so as not to jolt Lisa about and hurt her bruised ribs. We're both exhausted, emotionally and physically, but the silence between us is comforting and brings back warm memories of us revising together. Lisa lying on her stomach on the floor, propped up on her elbows, her head resting on her hands as she studied the pages of a textbook. Me sitting on the bed, legs crossed and a pillow over my lap to rest my revision notes on. Happy just working in the same space.

It's nearly one in the morning by the time we get back, so I don't offer coffee but park Lisa in the armchair in the spare bedroom while I go to fetch fresh sheets, pyjamas and towels from the airing cupboard. By the time I return Lisa has her head lowered, her face hidden in her hands as if she's crying.

I drop the armload I'm carrying onto the bed. 'Are you okay? Are your ribs hurting? I have aspirin and Panadol if that will help.' I squat down next to her to see her face and there are tears in her eyes. 'What's wrong?' I ask.

'I can't believe I'm here,' she says, 'I can't believe you're here...*we're* here.'

I take her hand. 'We're here,' I say. 'We're both here.'

The one good thing that's come of this mess.

The next morning, I get up early having been awake most of the night, my nerves jangled, my emotions a rainbow of colour, and my brain running in a cat's cradle of loops trying to untangle everything.

Not knowing what Lisa likes, I lay the table with everything I can find in the fridge that might be suitable for breakfast: a carton of Greek yogurt, a loaf of brown bread, a tub of Flora, a jar of honey, a block of cheese. Luckily the eggs are in date, so I get out the frying pan in case Lisa fancies fried eggs, then a saucepan so I'm ready if she opts for scrambled or boiled. I put coffee in the filter and tea leaves in the pot, not knowing which she prefers. Then I sit down to wait, but bounce up again five minutes later to fetch an assortment of cutlery. Five minutes after that it's bowls and plates.

I'm just searching in the cupboard for some napkins when I hear Lisa's bedroom door open. I put the kettle on.

'I don't know if –' I say, as Lisa says, 'I haven't –'

We both stop, laughing nervously, like a couple on a first date both reaching for the salt at the same time. 'You first,' I say.

'I haven't slept so well in years. It's like...' She pauses, flexes her fingers, shakes her wrists. 'It's like I can feel *me* coming back. You know, like when you've fallen asleep on your arm and it loses feeling, then the blood starts to flow again?' She lifts her arms and puts both hands to her forehead, tipping her head back as she runs her fingers through her hair. 'It's like everything's starting to feel *real* again.' She laughs and spins in a circle. 'You are real, aren't you? Tell me I'm not dreaming!'

'I'm real,' I say. 'This isn't a dream.'

'Can we make a pact?' she says.

I nod, happy to go along with anything she suggests.

She holds her right hand towards me, her little finger crocked ready for me to link

fingers with her, just like we used to do all those years ago – *'Promise you'll come to the disco with me'*; *'Promise you'll help me with my report'*; *'Promise...Promise...Promise.'*

Without knowing what she's about to ask, I link my finger with hers in our mock ritual and we look into each other's eyes.

'Whatever else happens, whatever form our...' She pauses

a beat, searching for the right word, 'friendship…takes, let's promise not to lose each other again.'

As I watch our joined fingers confirm our vow, the kettle calls us back to the everyday world by spluttering water onto the counter.

'I overfilled it,' I say. I lift it off the base as Lisa grabs a dishcloth from the sink to mop it up, a synchronised domestic dance like one of those kitchen adverts. And just as portrayed by those advert couples, I feel immensely happy.

Later that morning we drive to the bookshop for one last time, to collect Lisa's belongings. As we get nearer the street, she shrinks into her seat hunching down and wrapping her arms around her chest, her hands in tight fists. I stop the car and turn towards her.

'Favourite things?' I say. She gives a faint smile, remembering our ritual when we were at university, whenever one of us was feeling low or worrying unnecessarily. 'No cheating. No rain drops, no roses or whiskers on kittens.'

'I suppose you're ruling out brown paper packaging too?'

'Hmph.'

She wrinkles her nose, thinking. 'Pink and white nougat all sticky in the wrapper.'

'That's a new one,' I say. 'The crack of ice when you pour gin on it.'

'Running through fresh cut grass, barefoot.'

'Buddleia covered in butterflies.'

'The smell of old books.'

'Ah, that's a good one,' I say.

'I know. I stole it from you.' She says, 'I remember it was always somewhere on your list.'

She remembers…

She is smiling now. 'It's a beautiful day,' she says, looking out of the windscreen at the clear blue sky.

'Are you ready to carry on to the shop? We could go out somewhere afterwards if you like.'

She nods. 'Thank you... for this... for everything.'

Later, we go to a pub for lunch. It's nothing special – a bog-standard ploughman's served with tired lettuce and tired service – but I still tip the waitress more than she deserves. This day is the start of something.

Later still, we take a detour to Don's on our way home. I need to explain recent events face-to-face.

He lives down a cul-de-sac of ten semi-detached houses; a combination of hanging baskets, children's play things, ramps and grab rails. Cars line the access road, half on the pavements, and I wonder how they negotiate the parking. In all these years I've never asked him about his neighbours.

With Lisa at my side, I push the doorbell and the first bars of a catchy tune ring out. It takes me a moment to realise it's Abba. That must be new. There's an old railway sign posted in the middle of the front lawn – 'KEEP OFF THE GRASS by order of the Station Manager'; a ship-in-a-bottle on the windowsill of the front room, its full sails taking it nowhere; a faded neighbourhood watch sticker, its peeling edges warning would-be thieves that there's little of value inside. I've not been here since Phillip died, before lockdown; not for years. Apart from the doorbell, nothing's changed. There's a nibble of guilt in my chest. I dial up the natural smile on my face a notch.

'Amanda!' Don says, as he throws the door wide, his eyes flitting from one to the other of us, a broad grin on his face. His shirt is missing a button, but he's had his hair cut. 'Come in, come in. What a lovely surprise on a beautiful afternoon. Sunshine forecast all day.'

I'm about to cut him off, anticipating that he's going to launch into the minutiae of the weather forecast, but I stop myself: he looks so genuinely happy that I swear I will make more effort with him in future.

'Don, meet my friend Lisa. Lisa, this is Don.'

'You will stay for tea? Or squash? We can sit in the garden. I've got a sunshade in the shed.'

Fifteen minutes later we're set up in the back garden, perched on the motley selection of chairs Don retrieves on several journeys to the house. The fabric of the promised sunshade having perished, we're under the shade of a willow tree, (planted by the previous owners apparently, now too big for the space). No sooner are the three of us finally seated than Don leaps up from his kitchen stool, knocking it backwards into a rose bush. 'Tea! I made the tea and I've not poured it!'

Lisa smiles and rights the stool. 'Let me help.'

I watch the two of them walk the short distance up the garden path to the house. Lisa asks a question about a tree peony, the flowers now fading, and Don stops in his tracks to answer. I register my cynical thought that he can't walk and talk at the same time, then consciously bat it away: you see what you want to see. He points out something about the plants nearby, his explanation too quiet for me to hear, but Lisa laughs and they both turn to step into the house.

Over tea and an assortment of odd biscuits I give the cover story that Lisa and I have agreed to explain Kathleen's absence. She's been called back to Spain to look after her mother and intends to retire there permanently.

'What a kind woman she is. Giving up her shop and leaving all her friends to be at her mother's side like that,' Don says. 'So thoughtful.'

There's no need to disturb his map of the world with the horror of recent events. We discover that Kathleen's exit stage left at this point is fortuitous for Don: he'd agreed to lend her some money to buy a second-hand car. He was going to drive her round some dealers later this week.

We talk about plants and the weather, the resignation of the manager at the local Labour club (something to do with petty cash), the number of bees this summer (with an aside from Don to show us the holes made by carpenter bees in the side of his shed). Nothing yet everything. I don't register time passing, until a glance at my watch tells me we've been sitting there chatting with Don for a couple of hours.

'Oh, before you go!' Don says, 'I nearly forgot. I so wanted to tell you. My neighbour's son. You remember, Tommy? You were going to help with his case until all that stuff with McCollins blew up.'

The lad who was accused of theft by an eyewitness. 'Ah, yes. How's his case going?'

'Well, ironically, as well as the advice you provided, it seems all that fuss with McCollins helped! Everyone was talking about your book and the problems with eyewitness testimony, and what with all that hoo-ha the company looked into it again. They found CCTV showing the two supposed witnesses thieving supplies on several other occasions – it was them all along! Can you believe it?'

'Sadly, I can,' I say. 'What's happened to Tommy?'

'They offered him his job back but he refused. He's decided to go to university instead. He wants to study law!'

Don knew how much this would mean to me. He's a kind-hearted man. Spontaneously I reach out and touch his forearm and we both look down at my hand, surprised.

'I nearly forgot,' I say. An idea has come to me: it's time to start a new regime. 'It's the last Sunday of the month this weekend and I usually have a roast dinner. I'm thinking of cooking lamb. Will you join me and Lisa?'

He nods like one of those lucky Chinese cats, his eyes crinkling with happiness to be invited. My smile back is genuine.

Chapter Forty-One
Six Months Later

A letter arrives giving me the date and time of the inquest for Jed Thomas Turner. Lisa's letter turns up a few days later, having been redirected from the (now empty) bookshop by the Post Office.

The events of that awful night seem so long ago. So much has changed...

Along with the letter, there's a document that outlines my role as witness and a copy of my own statements as a reminder of what I said. I feel numb, unmoved, not the sense of closure I expected now the final chapter is about to finish.

On the morning of the inquest I dress in my old court garb. Flat shoes, a dark skirt and jacket, crisply ironed blouse. I am in role. I can do this.

The inquest is to be held in one of those old traditional courts where there are few facilities. Not like the modern ones which have comfortable waiting areas and coffee machines. I arrive early – force of habit – and perch on the upright wooden bench watching others come and go. It feels familiar and yet also strange to be here, in a court again. However, today I'm not the expert but an eyewitness to the events of the night when Jed Thomas Turner died.

I watch for Lisa's arrival and she suppresses her smile when she spots me. We both briefly nod to each other in acknowledgement, as we'd agreed. We'd arrived separately. There's no need to complicate the case with our entwined back stories, or our current lives. Today we are merely two separate witnesses to the tragic events of that evening six months ago. She sits at the other end of the bench and fiddles with the strap of her handbag, unused to this environment. We've run through her testimony together enough times for her to have her story straight, but she's still anxious and jumps when the young woman who was driving the silver-grey Vauxhall comes over to say hello to us both.

'I've never been inside a court before,' the woman says. 'It's a bit nerve wracking, isn't it?'

Lisa smiles her agreement.

'Don't worry. It's quite straightforward. You'll be told what to do and when,' I say, seeking to reassure both her and Lisa.

Like a lot of the courts I attended in a professional capacity, when we enter the court room it's panelled with dated antique pine colour wood, reminding me of my mother's furniture. The world evolves but some things never seem to change, and I guess we can decide which camp we are in.

As the session starts, the atmosphere changes; everyone is suddenly silent and extra attentive.

The Coroner outlines the purpose of the inquest: 'We are here to identify who the deceased is, and when, where and how they died. The aim is to find out what happened that night.'

There are not many people in attendance: the witnesses and a scattering of people observing. The Coroner announces that there is no family present. Thankfully Kathleen has completely disappeared, no doubt on the run, fearful of possible arrest if the police have discovered her connection to Turner's wider criminal activities.

The Coroner calls on the pathologist to give the cause of death. She outlines the medical results of Turner having been hit by the lorry: skull fractures, burst blood vessels in the body and brain, traumatic tears in the soft tissues. Death was thankfully instantaneous.

The first witness is the lorry driver. His name sounds Polish and he speaks with a slight accent as he confirms his job – he is a long-haul driver for a European company, or at least he was; he hasn't returned to work since that night. He repeats his name and takes the oath. In answer to the Coroner's questions he describes events as he recalls them: his journey that night, the road conditions and speed limit, the rain and visibility, his twenty years lorry driving and clean driving license; how he slowed down when he saw people on the verge but the man suddenly toppled backwards into the path of his vehicle. Too late for him to stop.

I feel sorry for the lorry driver. None of this was his fault, just wrong place wrong time. I'll talk to Lisa about setting up a Go Fund Me page for him.

Lisa is next to be called. She gives her job as shop assistant, which is true. She's taken on a part-time role in the local charity shop. She describes her relationship to Jed quite simply, 'He was the son of a woman I met years ago at university and I had recently got to know him through his mother.' Lisa explains that her car had broken down and he had offered her a lift. 'He was driving like a maniac, swerving in and out of lanes. I was terrified and asked him to slow down but he just laughed.'

When they ask how he came to fall into the path of the lorry, Lisa is visibly shaken. The court usher fetches her a glass of water and the Coroner asks her to continue when she is ready.

'When the Nissan bumped into the back of our car I leapt out and ran back to check the other drivers were okay,' she says. 'He – Jed Turner – got out and was shouting at the driver of the car that hit us. He was really angry because he thought his BMW had been damaged. I was worried he might get violent because he was so furious. I got between them to try to calm him down, but he was so angry he pushed me out of the way...' She describes a confusion of shouts and shoving until Turner stumbled backwards over the tyre debris on the verge. She doesn't look at me as she leaves the stand but hooks her hair behind her ear, the signal we'd previously agreed. A sign to me that she's okay.

I am called next. I straighten my back and slow my breathing as I walk to the stand.

'State your name and profession for the court.'

'Amanda Dunstan. Retired university lecturer.'

The Usher hands me the oath. 'Please repeat your name and read the oath.'

'Amanda Dunstan. I do solemnly, sincerely and truly declare and affirm that the evidence I shall give shall be the truth the whole truth and nothing but the truth.'

1988
THAT AFTERNOON IN JUNE

Kit's lying on the floor, her eyes closed, but at least her head is no longer spinning. Her cheek throbs where the bloke had punched her, her forehead still bleeding, but thankfully the kid has stopped crying. The child is nuzzled against her side, the slurping noises telling her he's sucking his thumb. She could do with a drink but doesn't want to risk him kicking off again if she tries to get up.

Everything aches and she doesn't really have the energy.

It's so hot.

The child goes silent as he falls asleep and she finds herself drifting into a welcome, drowsy, limbo state.

She doesn't know how much later it is when she hears someone enter the room. She doesn't bother to open her eyes to see who it is. If it's him who's tracked her down, she's probably in for another kicking and there's not much she can do.

'What the fuck?' A voice above her.

She groans. She doesn't need to open her eyes to know it's Miko. Her friend from the café where she worked until recently.

'What's happened to you?' he asks. 'What the hell is going on?'

'Too many questions,' she mumbles, still not opening her eyes.

'Who did this?'

'I walked into a door.'

'Don't be stupid.' He squats down next to her and Jed wakes, startled, immediately resuming where he'd left off with the crying and bawling. 'Look at me,' Miko says.

She rolls over onto her good side, the side that didn't get kicked after she'd been thrown to the ground, landing hard on the pavement.

'Who was it?' Miko asks.

'Flick,' she says. A name they both know well. The local drug dealer who claims this side of town as his own. His patch.

'He found out you're dealing?'

'No, he was just bitterly disappointed when I told him I couldn't come to the barn dance with him this weekend. What do you think?' She flops back down again, dizzy with the effort of lifting her head and the racket Jed's making. It was her backchat that had got her punched.

'What's he want?' Miko asks.

She keeps her eyes closed as she answers. 'The money he thinks I've made, plus interest.'

Miko lets out a long low whistle. 'That's not good news. How much?'

'Five hundred,' she says. 'By the end of the day.'

'Christ. This is serious.'

'No shit Sherlock.'

'Have you got any cash in the house? Any drugs you could offer him in exchange?'

Kit waves her hand towards the cupboards. 'Take a look.'

She can hear him banging about opening drawers and cupboards, pulling out kitchen pans, knocking books off the shelf on the off chance there's something hidden inside them.

'There's nothing here. There's nothing here!' Miko sounds panicked. She opens her eyes to see what he's up to.

He comes over and squats beside her. 'You're in deep shit,' he says, raising both clenched hands to his forehead. 'What on earth are you going to do?'

She doesn't respond. Wishes he would go away so she can think.

He gets up and starts pacing the three or four steps between the TV and the door.

'How are you going to get the money?'

'I'll get it. I'll get it.'

'Bloody hell. This is a fucking mess. I warned you.'

'I'll get it.' She leans up on her good elbow to look at him. 'I know where I can get the money but I just need a few days.'

'Why would he trust you?' Miko says. 'He'll want something to prove you're going to pay up.'

Jed is plucking at her in that persistent needy way he has, trying to climb on her lap. It gives her an idea. She pushes him towards Miko. 'Take the kid then. Tell him he can hold onto the brat until I pay up. I'll get the cash in a couple of days.'

'Don't be so fucking stupid.' Miko looks at her with contempt. 'I'll go and reason with him. He may take my word that you'll pay up. But you owe me big time.'

He rushes to the door, turning to shout that he'll be back later just as she flicks him a V sign. As he leaves there's a movement outside the window and she spots Amanda just before she ducks out of sight. So there's been a spy there all along.

How much did she see and hear? Who will she tell?

Kit eases herself to her feet, holding onto the wall for support and makes her way to the hallway, shutting the door to her flat behind her to stop Jed crawling out. By the time she gets to the front of the house Amanda's no longer there. Kit spots her scurrying down the road in the direction of the bus stop. Kit follows to check where she's going. Turning the corner, not expecting to catch Amanda up, Kit sees her standing by the phone box. She watches as Amanda opens the heavy red door, picks up the phone receiver, then just as quickly puts it back again. Amanda stands there for a minute but doesn't pick up the phone again. She leaves the box, then crosses the road towards the bus stop. The route back to college. Kit watches until she gets on the bus.

Back in her studio flat, Kit leans in the doorway contemplating the scene before her. The half-opened cupboards, their contents scattered; the plastic medicine bottles with one or two tablets in each; small plastic bags ready to be filled with dope and the scales she uses for weighing out marijuana to sell, all strewn across the floor; her son asleep now, huddled at an uncomfortable angle having climbed into his pushchair on his own.

She loves Jed in her fashion, would never do anything intentionally to harm him, but she doesn't always like having him around. The child cramps her style. But the cash that flows into her bank account each month from his father is a huge asset. He's a married man with a reputation to protect. Kit had pointed out to him that this monthly payment was cheaper than a divorce settlement if his wife was ever to find out. Kit chooses not to see it as a bribe for keeping quiet: after all *most* of the money goes on Jed and she keeps her additional requests to a minimum. She's not asked for anything extra since the deposit for the bedsit and a top up on the monthly allowance, but she's starting to think a car would be handy, a second hand mini, something like that... He's getting off lightly given she's lumbered with a kid she didn't plan for.

And now she's in a lot of shit. Flick will no doubt be back later and who knows what Amanda is bleating out to someone at the college even now.

Amanda.

Kit hates her. She hides it well, but she hates her. Hates her prissiness, her stupid ironed jeans, her middle-class accent, her dumb smiling face, her stoic lack of reaction, her stupid growing-out perm, her virtuous virginity.

To be honest, this wasn't the reaction she would have expected from Amanda... but interesting nevertheless...

Kit would've expected her to panic, seeing her lying beaten up on the floor. She'd have expected her to rush in wanting to help, hurry to fetch water, try to sit her up to help her drink, gently wipe her forehead, maybe call for help from the neighbour upstairs. All the Mother Theresa things you'd predict she would do given her holier than thou image. But no…

The more she thinks about it the angrier Kit gets. Amanda should never have left her there alone, on the floor bleeding, with the threat of a dealer turning up later for round two of her beating. What was Amanda thinking?

Jealousy, Kit surmises. Jealous that I've got her buddy Lisa under my thumb. Well, if she wants to play games I'll show her what I can do.

She scrawls a note for Lisa on the back of the brief for the essay which is due very soon. This university experience isn't all it's cracked up to be. Another year to go and she's already bored.

Hey Loverly Lisa, she writes. *Something's happened (can't tell you in a letter). I'm in hospital. I just wanted you to let you know, because you're such a worry bag. My mum came to pick up Jed from Mrs P upstairs. She's going to look after him for a while until I'm back on my feet. I brought my work with me to hospital but I don't feel up to it. I can't wait to see you when I'm out of here and feeling better. I've got a <u>really</u> fun plan for us both. I'll write and let you know where you can find me. Lots of love Kit xxx PS Always remember – as Madonna says Open Your Heart!! PPS Don't mention this letter to <u>anyone</u>. Our secret. Love ya! xx*

She stuffs it into an envelope, scribbles the address and adds a stamp.

She grabs a rucksack and starts filling it with odds and ends from around the flat: her battered copy of *Looking for Mr Goodbar*, some underwear and a change of t-shirt, the emergency cash she'd hidden behind the mirror, a few supplies for Jed.

She doesn't need much, after all she has a ready stream of income she can tap into to buy replacements. Jed has his uses. She hangs the bag on the back of his pushchair.

'Come on, brat,' she whispers to the sleeping child. 'Time to move on to our next big adventure.'

ACKNOWLEDGMENTS

While I have a professional background in psychology and psychotherapy, I am not an academic and couldn't claim to be an expert in the field of memory. Consequently, I needed to refresh and update my own memory of theories and research in this area.

I am grateful to the authors of the following books for their insights into the role of an expert witness:

· *Psychology, Law and Eyewitness Testimony*, by Peter B. Ainsworth, Wiley 1998

· *Psychology and Law*, by Andreas Kapardis, Cambridge 2003

· *Witness for the Defense*, by Dr Elizabth Loftus and Katherine Ketcham, St Martin's Press 1991

· *Victims of Memory*, by Mark Pendergrast, Haper Collins 1998

And for reminders on the workings of memory, amongst others: *The Memory Illusion*, by Dr Julia Shaw (2016), The Centre for Investigative Reporting's 'Reveal' podcast and the BBC's 'All in the Mind'; various publications and articles from the British Psychological Society; numerous Netflix documentaries about miscarriages of justice and the treasure trove that resides in TED Talks and YouTube.

My thanks to:

· My Faber Academy writing friends, for their constructive feedback, beta reading and moral support: Shivanthi Sathanandan, Di Wilson, Anna Davidson, Tamara Henriques, Stella Barnes and Elizabeth Price.

- Whicdhemein One for providing the cover image
- Ruth Loten and Jane Langan at Castle Priory Press, for being the role model of what publishing should always be like.
- My friends, Ken Hummerstone and Carolyn Simon for their backing and encouragement in all my creative endeavours; Jolea Green for helping me stay calm; Stacey Theedom for helping me look professional.
- My partner, Martin, for his unending support through the ups and downs of a writer's life.
- And to everyone who read and reviewed my first two novels, *Her Little Secret* and *The Accident*. It means a lot.

ABOUT THE AUTHOR

Julia Stone is a business psychologist and psychotherapist by profession. She attended Faber Academy in 2017 and in 2018 won the *Blue Pencil First Novel Award*. She is a member of the Society of Authors and co-leads the East Anglia chapter of the Crime Writers Association.

www.JuliaStoneWriter.com
linktr.ee/JuliaStone

Other psychological suspense novels by Julia Stone

Her Little Secret

Psychotherapist Cristina knows all about boundaries and keeps her clients at a professional distance. Enter new client, Leon, following the death of his married lover, Michelle. Cristina soon discovers that Leon has an ulterior motive for wanting therapy: Michelle had been one of her clients and he is desperate to find out the secrets of the woman he loved. Torn by her conscience and curiosity Cristina is about to discover the truth is beyond anything she could have imagined...

The Accident

An unidentified woman falls from a bridge onto Janice's car. The police say it's misadventure, an accident. But Janice feels like fate has thrown them together and sets out to discover more about this stranger's life. But when Janice lies about her own identity, she becomes entangled in the lives of the woman's family and friends. What will she discover about the dead girl? Will Janice be uncovered as a fraud?